By the same author

THE LATIMER MERCY

BELLRINGER STREET

THE BOOK OF THE DEAD

THE DYING OF THE LIGHT

SLEEPING IN THE BLOOD

THE LAZARUS TREE

HAND OF STRANGE CHILDREN

SIGNIFICAN

THE

SIGNIFICANT OTHERS

Robert Richardson

VICTOR GOLLANCZ

LONDON

First published in Great Britain 1995
by Victor Gollancz
An imprint of the Cassell Group
Wellington House, 125 Strand, London WC2R 0BB

A catalogue record for this book is
available from the British Library

ISBN 0 575 06181 2

Typeset by CentraCet Ltd, Cambridge
Printed in Great Britain by
St Edmundsbury Press Ltd, Bury St Edmunds, Suffolk

In memory of Trevor Murray Jones,
one of my significant others

Author's Note

One question that the night lawyers may want answering is: Do any of the journalists in this book exist and could they be identified? After a career of more than thirty years, it would be absurd to pretend I have totally forgotten everyone I've met while working at various times on twelve newspapers, four magazines and two press agencies. However, these characters are either fictitious, amalgams of personalities, or types found throughout the profession. If anyone tries to make connections with actual people that is their affair, not mine.

Most of the newspapers mentioned are referred to by their real names because it seems pointless to invent titles (which never sound right in any event). The practices attributed to any specific paper are, I would suggest, not unlikely.

BOOK ONE

Cornwall and London

Resonant in the hollow of its mahogany case, metallic pulses ticked out of the grandfather clock, echoing off white-painted plastered stone walls. It was the only sound inside the cottage, but occasional noises invaded through the sun-brightened open window of the room at the back; sobs of gliding gulls, distant bassoon groan of a cow, a tractor on a cart track clattering and fading as it passed. Behind them all was the ceaseless rustle of surging waves washing smooth rocks at the toes of the cliffs.

Then there was another sound, a cat troubled, miaow fretful, seeking reassurance. It padded across the hall's flagged floor into the front room, leaping on to the arm of a tapestry settee by the window, seeking a human presence. Empty landscape climbed from the sea across hedged fields to open moorland with weather-pitted bones of grey granite bursting through the skin of coarse grass. The cat growled softly as it jumped down and returned to the silent back room, entering cautiously to see if something wrong had corrected itself.

The woman lay on the rug in front of the black Cornish range, eyes closed, one leg hooked beneath the other. She was dying as the blackening stain grew out of the side of her head, oozing through fibres of soft green carpet like ink dropped into water. The cat raised its tail, rubbing against a wooden chair leg for comfort, before crossing the room, quivering with a coaxing purr. It sniffed the blood then placed a persuading white-tipped paw gently on her face. When there was no response, it abruptly began to wash, then sat, patient and confident. Eventually there would be milk and fish, a ready lap or the luxury of sleeping on the sun-warmed deep window sill. Later there would be the freedom to leave, to hunt shrews or fieldmice and bring one back as a gift, or to return to the farm where it lived and come again the next day. Being ignored was outside its experience and it felt a feline resentment at not receiving due attention. Washing again, it jerked in alarm as the fax machine on the desk spewed out another message, adding to the pile in the tray.

'Are you there? Mildly urgent we talk. New York have managed to balls up the tour and we need to sort it this end. Call me soonest. Emma.'

Acid primrose eyes warily watched the paper slide out, twitching at the shrill beep when the message finished; then there was silence again. The cat stretched, trotted to a small dropleaf table, tensed, then jumped to the open window, stiffening as a blackbird landed on the lawn and began pecking the grass, but it was too far away to stalk. It balanced on the ledge before dropping, a fluid stream of black fur, on to the narrow gravel path, twisted to rapidly lick its flank, then scampered away through a gap in the fence. Inside the cottage, the telephone rang, stopping as the answering machine engaged.

'Hi. This is Katrina Darcy's country retreat. Sorry, but I'm either out, asleep or too busy to answer. Leave a message after the tone, and I'll get back to you.' There was a pause until the tone had sounded. 'Katrina, it's Miranda again at . . . quarter to six on Friday. For God's sake, ring me if you pick up this call. I've turned the system upside down, but I can't find this week's copy anywhere. Just get in touch. We're starting to panic here.'

Inquisitive and daring, the blackbird fluttered on to the window frame where the cat had been sitting minutes earlier. Nervous head constantly darting in all directions, its song filled the room before it hopped round and flew away. Pacing to the clock's immutable tattoo, the silence of creeping death returned.

'Keep it quiet!' Steve Hamilton glared at a reporter laughing too loudly over a joke, then shouted into the news desk telephone again. 'What? For fuck's sake, where are you calling from? It's a piss-awful line . . . Yes, the copy's come through on Tandy, but it's garbled . . . What? Sod the pics, we've got them . . . OK, OK.

Try sending again, then call me back. And find somewhere your bloody phone works from.'

He crashed the receiver down and ran both hands through brush-stiff copper-coloured hair in frustration. It was nearly six o'clock on Friday evening and five of the *Sunday Register*'s early pages were behind schedule.

'Hell's teeth! We'll have a three-thousand-word hole on twelve at this rate. Mike! What have you got on?'

'Profile.'

'Christ, that page should have gone an hour ago. Store it and let the subs sort it out.'

Clatter and activity gave the editorial floor what Hamilton cynically called an air of creative incompetence in conditions of controlled chaos. Desks were crowded together, so that apart from one central aisle it was impossible to take more than about six paces in a straight line. Untidiness amplified the atmosphere; window ledges and filing cabinets piled with reference books and forgotten official reports; overflowing wastepaper baskets; notice boards bearing out-of-date memos, appeals for inexpensive flats, invitations to film screenings, a car for sale; potted plants surviving despite the fact that they were scarcely ever watered. Smudged with coffee spills, grey cord carpet tiles were littered with discarded daily papers, and a fading poster for a 1992 press freedom rally remained taped to the wall between two of the high sash windows. One side of the room was blocked off by steel-framed contemporary office units, functional convenience crudely grafted on to original nineteenth-century proportions standing like decaying ruins amid computer technology.

As Hamilton snatched up a pack of cigarettes and began to light one, the woman sitting opposite glared at him.

'We voted for a smoking ban in here.'

'I voted against,' he snapped.

'That makes no difference.'

'It does to me.'

'Haven't you seen the leaflet on passive smoking?'

'Seen it, binned it, didn't read it.' He deliberately blew smoke at her. 'Die.'

11

She stood up, waving a hand in front of her face. 'I'm going to complain to the union, Steve.'

Ignoring her, Hamilton turned back to his screen, impatiently scrolling through another story before storing it.

'OK, Mark, you've got the basement for nine. Miles over, but it cuts like cheese. There's a literal on line twenty-six and check the spelling of MacGregor.' He spun his chair round to speak to the news desk secretary. 'When's Emily filing?'

'Seven o'clock . . . and she says the sister talked.'

'Thank God we've got some bloody professionals in this place.' He glanced up at the muted television suspended above his head, then used the remote control to increase the sound, inadvertently raising it so much that the music for the BBC news blasted across the office.

'Sorry!' he bellowed and turned it down, then listened to the headlines. 'Bollocks! They've got the pollution story. Drop it, Alan. Every bugger'll have it tomorrow.'

'Have they got quotes from Greenpeace?'

'Bound to have. Watch it anyway. I'm going to conference.'

Hamilton picked up a metal clipboard, brief summaries of potential stories originally printed out in organized lines now scribbled over, crossed out, added to, labelled with question marks and comments in mangled shorthand only he could read: 'great pics', 'Alistair reworking', 'crap', 'left hand lead?', 'Jenny ringing contact Sat a.m.', 'PA rewrite', 'must below fold', 'dull but virtuous', 'good follow-up', 'killed by lawyer – bastard'. Pausing to extinguish his cigarette, he glanced over the shoulder of a reporter playing patience on his screen.

'Has that MP of yours called yet?'

'Should be any time now.'

'Good. Three hundred words in the news queue by six-thirty. Black seven on red eight.'

Hamilton was the last to enter the editor's office, a sanctuary of relative quiet and order; eight floors below, a Thames riverboat hooted amid the rumble of homegoing evening traffic. He closed the door and sat between the picture and sports editors at the long oval table. The conference was being taken by Malcolm

Kendall, the managing editor, because Charlie Taylor had reluctantly accepted his wife's insistence that the *Register* could survive for two weeks without him and a family holiday was an inescapable part of his private life.

'Right,' Kendall announced. 'The bad news is that the *Observer*'s outbid us for the Bennett autobiography, the good news is that Trevor Marshall is joining us from the *Independent*. Don't ask how much. In the meantime we have the minor problem of filling edition number six thousand eight hundred and twenty four . . . Steve?'

Hamilton glanced at his clipboard. 'Front no problem. Exclusive about the education changes and a great read by Claire on the French village vendetta which we can turn inside. Gerald's done an off-beat anchor piece on the bishop who's produced Christ's astrology chart, and there's a knock-out colour pic of the PM playing chess with a six-year-old genius. Brian swears no one else got it. Has to be worth four columns. Inside, take your pick of disaster areas. Emily's filing in an hour, which will fill the Nineties Britain slot, but apart from that . . .'

There was a slight creak, a whirr, a mechanical tension released as soft chimes marked the quarter-hour, the notes gliding out of the hall and filling every silent room they reached, fainter and fading before leaving echoes only imagination could have detected. The late afternoon sun had slipped lower, casting a lemon streak that lay across the woman's head, gleaming in the trickle of blood that had nearly ceased to flow. The phone rang again and a man's voice spoke to the answering machine; the accent was deep Cornish.

'Katrina? It's Ted. You gone back to London? If you haven't, I got some crab in Newlyn today half price. If you want a couple give me a call and I'll bring them over tomorrow morning. All right? Madge'll take a message if I've gone out. 'Bye, then. Take care.'

The woman's chest rose and fell more deeply, almost as if she was struggling to regain consciousness, but then settled again,

13

breath now so shallow that it was barely perceptible in sound or movement.

'Hang on, Steve. There's something we've got to talk about.'

Half out of his chair, Hamilton sat down again. The conference finished, his immediate concerns were filling space and he was in no mood for discussions about anything else. Without being asked, Miranda Webb, the features editor, remained as well, and he prepared himself for the standard argument about which of them should occupy the no man's land of page fourteen. The news flow was so bad that he was prepared to surrender it and claim it back the following week. Kendall waited until the others had left and the door was closed again.

'It's Katrina,' he said. 'We can't find her.'

'What do you mean?' Hamilton's interest was limited; far removed from the coalface of home news, Katrina Darcy wrote a weekly column and the occasional special when she felt like it. He had no authority over her; in fact no one did except the editor. She was the best-paid writer on the *Register*, opinionated, precious, likely to draw blood if she spotted that a comma had been deleted from her copy. Hamilton regarded her as overrated, but the *Mail on Sunday* had offered her £120,000 a year plus unlimited expenses and a chauffeured Daimler to join them. The *Register* could never have matched that sort of deal and how they had persuaded her to stay was an office mystery surrounded by wild rumours.

'She didn't arrive this morning to write her column,' Webb explained.

'What is this?' Hamilton demanded. 'I've not got time to sort out a bloody guest columnist.'

'I've already dealt with that,' Webb said sharply. 'I run the features department.'

Among the staff, Hamilton and Webb were mockingly called the Love Birds. He had left school at sixteen and clawed his way up from weekly papers; she had read Classics and English at Somerville, joining the *Register* after less than a year on *Time Out*. Each despised what they perceived as the other's ignorance.

14

'Keep your fights out of here.' Kendall's reprimand was flecked with impatience. 'The point is, Steve, where is she? There's no reply at her flat and we just get the answerphone in Cornwall. We haven't found anyone who's seen or heard from her since Monday.'

Hamilton shrugged. 'She's probably decided she'd like another holiday.'

'No way.' Webb glared at him. 'If Katrina's taking time off she lets me know and writes her column in advance.'

Sensing that her anger was matched by Kendall's mood, Hamilton felt it best to co-operate. 'What about Anthony Delamere? He knows her better than anyone.'

'He was one of the first we tried,' Kendall told him. 'He's in Birmingham for a piece on those Balti House Asian restaurants, but I managed to catch him just before he set off to come back. He hasn't seen or heard from her either – and this is worrying him as well.'

'You've obviously been to her flat.'

'I went a couple of hours ago,' Webb appeared to have registered Hamilton's change of attitude. 'The porter saw her on Monday afternoon, but her car wasn't in the parking bay on Tuesday morning. He didn't see her go out, but he has to leave his office to do security checks of the building so he could have missed her. He called her flat on the internal phone while I was there, but there was no reply. He's got a key, but said he can only use it if the police order him to.'

'Call the police, then. She might be ill.'

'Her car's not there, Steve,' Kendall reminded him. 'So presumably she went somewhere in it.'

'What about her boyfriend?' Hamilton suggested. 'Some guy on the *Sunday Times*, isn't it?' He resisted the pejorative of toy boy.

'She split with Ray months ago,' Webb said impatiently. 'As far as I know, she's not seeing anyone at the moment.'

'Makes a change.' That was irresistible, and Webb flared back at him.

'I'm not even answering that.'

15

'Leave it out, both of you,' Kendall warned. 'And keep your opinions to yourself, Steve. I know you think Katrina's a prima donna, but she's as much a professional as you are. Miranda's sorted out filling the space, so that isn't the problem. Finding her is.'

Hamilton shrugged. 'If you've filled the slot, why not just wait until she turns up?'

'Because I don't like the fact we can't find her. All right?'

'OK, but what about her family? She's got a daughter ... Stephanie, isn't it?'

'Yes,' Webb confirmed. 'But she doesn't live at home any more and I don't know where she is. Katrina's mother's in Manchester, but she hardly ever goes there. Anyway, we don't want to worry her.'

'Publishers, then ... or Channel Four?'

'For Christ's sake, Steve, we've checked with them,' Webb snapped. 'I know someone at Drabble and Farrant and they're not expecting another manuscript from her until the New Year. And in case you hadn't noticed, *Spiked Copy* is off the air at the moment.'

'Look, Steve,' Kendall said. 'Miranda and I have been on this half the afternoon. Katrina missed an appointment with her hairdresser and didn't turn up for a lunch date at Joe Allen's on Wednesday. No phone calls, no explanations. Now we're pressing panic buttons.'

Hamilton looked at him. 'What are you thinking?'

'That something's happened to her. Possibly serious.'

'So where do I come in?'

'I want you to send someone down to Cornwall and check out the cottage. She might be there but unable to answer for some reason. As you say, she could be ill.'

'If that's what you want,' Hamilton agreed. 'But the nearest stringer we've got's in Exeter. It must be nearly a hundred miles away.'

'Nobody nearer?'

'I can't think of anyone. We don't get much news from that

part of the world. Plymouth's nearer. I could try a freelance there.'

Kendall nodded. 'Get on to it. The line is that we think she's down there but her phone's out of order and we need to contact her urgently.'

'So why don't we fax her?'

'Who knows that she's got a fax machine at the cottage? Just keep it businesslike. If some agency gets hold of the idea that Katrina Darcy's disappeared they'll be calling every bloody tabloid.'

'OK.' Hamilton hesitated. 'And what else do we do?'

'What do you mean?' Webb demanded.

'Like Malcolm says, if she's disappeared without an explanation, it could be a story.'

'But we don't have to publish it.'

Hamilton shrugged. 'Try that line on Charlie. Great career move.'

'Concentrate on finding her, Steve,' Kendall told him. 'We've got no reason to think there's a story here at the moment.'

'But if there is?' Hamilton repeated. 'If someone tipped us off that Katherine Whitehorn or Lynda Lee-Potter had mysteriously vanished, I'd put people on to it. And if it was Bernard Levin . . .'

Webb flared into anger. 'Don't you ever think of anything but bloody news angles?'

'No. It's what I'm paid for.' Hamilton turned to Kendall. 'Have you told Charlie about this?'

'There's no need at the moment.' Kendall sounded dismissive.

'You're in charge. But he'll go apeshit if it turns out there is a story and we're not leading the pack on it.'

'Just get on to that freelance, Steve. And keep this to yourself.'

Monday Evening

I can't decide whether I want to write a confession, an apology or a cry for help. What is certain is that I must write; my analyst says I use words to protect myself from emotions because words are what I can control. So however frightening and terrible this is, once I've written it down, perhaps I'll be able to . . . Written *what* down? Not just the agonizing events of the past week, because for them to be understandable I need to say what happened before that . . . and before that, right back to . . . To explain completely, it has to be almost my life story.

God knows how many people I've met, names I knew for a period because we worked together or our paths casually crossed; others who left traces that became occasionally recalled memories; and that handful who were critical. It's the same for everyone. Who taught you, loved you, hurt you, betrayed you so deeply that they shaped you, subtly but indelibly? Had I met others on my personal Dante's Bridge, I would have been different, not what I am now. There are two interpretations of now, public and private. First, Katrina Darcy, successful trash novelist, presenter of *Spiked Copy* on Channel Four; nicknamed Katrina Bossy by *Private Eye* after someone told them that my *Sunday Register* column cannot be cut or altered. The private now is a 46-year-old woman in her Cornish bolthole, trying to come to terms with what's happened to her, with what she's done.

My photograph album here is a vivid catalyst; I've rediscovered a lot of pain, happiness and confusion in snapshots going back thirty years. Some of the later ones remain in their envelopes, but most of the mounted ones have brief notes beneath them – a date, the name, sometimes a location, triggering recollections that become more detailed as I look at them. They could be used for an illustrated history of my life, material for a double-page spread with extended captions that a creative sub-editor would headline 'Significant Others'. But I need to give them a much fuller text.

I've just remembered what Joe Mellor, who was chief reporter on the weekly paper where I began, once said to me. I was his newest junior, all of six weeks in the business, when I walked up to his desk with my write-ups of a pile of wedding forms; he was reading the lunchtime edition of the *Manchester Evening Chronicle*.

'What's new?' I asked brightly, determined to show I was keen.

'Nothing,' he grunted. 'It's just happened to different people.'

I've spent the rest of my career discovering how true that is; unbelievably, it's now happened to me.

And what did Joe always growl when I was stuck on how to tackle a story? 'Just start at the beginning, go to the end, and meet the sodding deadline before the pub shuts.'

All right, it's eleven-thirty on Monday evening and I'll begin first thing tomorrow, with a Friday deadline. If Joe was still alive he'd bollock me for overwriting – he said the history of the world could be told in five paragraphs with the last one optional – but there's a lot I want to put on the record before my absence turns from an irritation into an emergency; not a newspaper crisis, but – shock, horror, drama – a murder hunt. Then it will be a salutary experience to be on the receiving end of the nastier brand of journalism, and a few scores will be settled. But before they start churning out the lies and distortions – I'm not bleating about that; I've done it myself often enough – I'm going to tell it. I've got the Macintosh PowerBook, life support systems in vodka, tonic and Silk Cut, and copy to write; I've been here a few million times.

Point, par. Standfirst ends, more follows – as I'd say if I was dictating this to the copytakers.

JUDITH

She's sitting beneath a beech tree, cream summer frock patterned by leaf and branch shadows, looking away from the camera. ('Take a picture of me, not at me,' she said.) Her training created an instinctive pose, right hand resting on the grey and green woollen rug, holding the copy of Gerard Manley Hopkins from which she read aloud that afternoon. If it was sepia, the image could be Edwardian, smooth chestnut hair parted in the centre and pulled back to the nape of her neck then falling as if she has unfastened the bun, no make-up. Her face is reflective and slightly distant. If someone tried to analyse her character what would they say? The book suggests culture, the simple yoked, long-sleeved dress perhaps modesty, the composed features control and intelligence. They would probably think her younger than she was; she was twenty-five, and we had met two years earlier, when I was sixteen.

Several years ago I was at a press awards evening where they had an impressionist as the cabaret and he did some of the media celebrities in the audience; when he came to me, exaggerating gestures and mannerisms, everybody laughed, but all I could hear was how he was picking up the tiny flaws that remain in the way I speak. The voice you hear on radio or television, near enough received pronunciation and BBC-speak to appear perfect, is not how I sounded at first. I was born in Bramhall, just outside Stockport on the edge of Manchester; then it was all short vowels and audible gs at the end of participles. But Bramhall, snobbish and well-heeled, was in Cheshire and felt itself superior to the North of England of music hall, Blackpool and black puddings. There was a Cheshire voice, with a sheen of refinement, but it was still distinctly provincial. Judith taught me to speak differently, and in doing so disturbed my roots; on the very rare occasions I go back there they regard me as a southerner, a stranger.

This is on record in various articles, but I ought to spell it out again with added comments. I was the daughter of an industrial chemist and a part-time nurse, a banal, middle-class background. Home was a kitsch mock-Georgian house, just detached – next door was less than six feet away – with a declining mortgage in a suburban development of closes, avenues, roads and crescents (never streets, which had working-class connotations) with a parade of shops, park, schools and its own neighbourhood cinema. My childhood was comfortable and unremarkable. I wasn't outstandingly gifted at anything, my parents weren't eccentric or creative. My younger brother, whom I now hardly ever see, became an insurance salesman and a Rotarian in Lytham St Anne's. What I've never told any interviewer is that he and I shared a fundamental problem; throughout their lives my parents were devoted to each other, and the children of lovers are orphans. Don't misunderstand me, we were loved and cared for, but as we grew older we became subconsciously aware that when we grew up and left home they would be perfectly happy and complete alone together again. The advantage was that we had a great deal of freedom to go our own way; what we lacked was a dimension of family closeness.

They never expressed any particular ambition for me, but, being so happy, they would have assumed I would want the same as they enjoyed. Some sort of career for a while, then a good marriage and a home like the folks who live on the hill (one of their favourite songs). I can best sum up what actually happened by quoting what Paul McCartney once said: 'Inside every famous person is a little person who just got very good at their job.' Somewhere beneath this slick metropolitan personality are the remains of a slightly lonely girl with limited horizons who changed beyond all recognition; and Judith started the process.

We met in 1963, when she joined the staff of Elizabeth Harmer School in Stockport as the new drama teacher just as I entered the sixth form. The school was private – my parents were

21

snobs – and drama was an optional extra which my father agreed to pay for when I asked him; like anything else, acting would have been an acceptable job from their point of view if I'd shown any talent for it. In fact I did, and perhaps it's significant that I ended up earning my living as another kind of liar. It was Judith's first job, and while at twenty-three she was younger than most of the staff, to a teenager she was a grown-up. She was not very tall, but she was slender and graceful as a dancer, with expressive hands and a curious slight croak in her voice. She came from Surrey and had been to RADA before teacher training college. Seeing the Beatles in their one Manchester concert at the Odeon cinema in Ardwick had been the high point of my sixties experience; everything else seemed to happen in London, and as far as I was concerned Surrey was London, so she carried with her the glitter of a sophisticated unknown.

New young teachers were always the focus of playground gossip. Were they married? If not, did they have a boyfriend? Most importantly, had they *done it*? It may have been the liberated sixties, but we were children of the fifties, still conditioned by our parents' conventional behaviour patterns; much of our boasting was wish-fulfilment rather than reality. (One girl swore she'd lost her virginity, but none of us really believed her until she abruptly left and was later seen pushing a pram through Stockport market.) While we speculated, we discovered that Miss Hurst – I ought to call her that at first – behaved differently from the rest of the staff, treating us like the adults we pretended we were; she actually wanted to know us as people. In turn, we acted differently towards her.

'Have you got a boyfriend, miss?' one girl asked her one day. Having dared her to do it, the rest of us giggled in embarrassment; to have put such a question to any other teacher would have been almost scandalous.

'Yes, I have, Susan. But he lives in London.'

'Are you going to marry him?'

'I don't know. I might.' She looked at Susan, amused eyes challenging her to continue. 'Go on . . . Ask me.'

'Ask what, miss?'

22

'Ask me if I've been to bed with him. That's what you're wondering, isn't it?'

God, it was an age of innocence; we could hardly bring ourselves to look at her. Sex education classes still used rabbits. A teacher being so frank, so perceptive, was incredible and slightly disorientating. We were accustomed to being patronized by grown-ups, not disturbingly understood.

'Anyway, if I have, it's my business,' she added. 'OK? Come on, let's do some work.'

It wasn't just her attitude to us that made her different; unlike most of the staff, who concentrated on making sure the exam results justified the fees, she constantly pushed us beyond our limitations. There were sessions when we had to imagine ourselves as inanimate objects – a standard lamp, a lemon, a hole in a wall – and say what it felt like, Shakespearean readings in which we had to base characters on unlikely people – Romeo and Juliet as Edward and Mrs Simpson, Ophelia as Cilla Black, Puck as David Frost. It was incomprehensible at first, but then we started to understand and enjoy it. One day she told us all to take off our shoes and socks then sit crosslegged scattered across the floor of the drama room, as far apart from each other as possible.

'Tactile senses,' she announced when we had settled. 'Close your eyes and keep them closed. Now turn round five times as quickly as you can.' We all did so. 'Not quite sure where you are, are you? You're all blind, no peeping. When I say go, I want you to move around the floor until you bump into someone. Because we're an odd number, I'm going do it as well. When you've made contact, don't look, but feel the other person very carefully. Touch their feet and hands, feel their faces, stroke their hair. No giggling. Just concentrate. In a few minutes you'll hear this alarm ring on my desk. When it does, keep your eyes closed and each call out who you think you're with. We'll do it in roll call order, so Sylvia will begin, and I'll go last. Right, start moving.'

Overcoming the urge to peep, I cautiously crawled forward, one hand exploring the floor in front of me until I touched what felt like a calf. Another hand took hold of mine, then whoever it

23

was moved so that I could tell she was kneeling in front of me. As I knelt, I found I was sniffing, trying to identify a smell (not that I was aware of any particular smell from anyone). I could hear others still shuffling and there were occasional giggles. I raised my hands and found an unseen face; at the same time, fingers touched my cheeks and began to trace the shape of my mouth and lips. My mind was absorbed with trying to identify contours of features, texture of hair. It wasn't Angela because her hair was severely short . . . Daphne? No, her lips were very thin . . . It might be Marjorie . . . or Jennifer . . . ? The other hands slid down my sides, over my hips and thighs and down to my feet, stroking softly, then quickly moved back up to my head. All the giggling had stopped and it was very quiet, almost as though this other person and I were alone in the room. I took hold of the hands; Elizabeth bit her nails, so it . . . Gently but firmly my hands were raised and brushed against breasts, so fleetingly that it could have been accidental, then our fingers unclasped again and returned to faces. I heard a soft hiss of breath and smelt mint toothpaste as my ears were pinched and my closed eyelids caressed . . . The alarm clock cheeped and there was a short pause before Sylvia called out.

'I think it's Wendy.'

'I'm with Bernice.'

'Katrina,' came a wrong guess from the far side of the room.

The names went on until it was my turn; I had no idea and also had to guess. 'I'm not sure . . . Frances?'

Finally Miss Hurst's voice, firm and confident, spoke straight in front of me. 'One of you was certainly wrong. This is Katrina. All right, you can look now.'

Amid the others' laughter of recognition and surprise, our eyes met and she looked at me, amused and slightly quizzical, before standing up and walking away.

'Good,' she said briskly. 'Now who got it right? Well done some of you. Can you see how it helps? The more you can relate to another actor as a person, the better you'll be able to work together. You've got to know all about them, including exactly what they look like. OK. Now back to *Richard III*. Let's see how you play the scene where he courts Anne over King Henry's coffin. Sarah and Marjorie first, with Sarah as Richard. From "Lady, you know no rules of charity".'

As the lesson continued, I realized that when I had closed my eyes Miss Hurst had been standing by her desk and there had been at least six girls between her and me. Did I think anything? No. I was very young. It just struck me as odd.

At the end of the Easter term came the school play, with the sixth form drama group taking the leads and Miss Hurst producing. She chose Shaw's *Saint Joan*, which was unexpected for a girls' school, because while it offered a classic female role every other part was male. We all thought that Bernice (who went on to become an actress) would play the lead, but when we auditioned in front of Miss Hurst and the senior English teacher, reading from Joan's 'Where would you all have been now if I had heeded that sort of truth?' speech, she froze for some reason and I was given the part.

Once the play was cast, Miss Hurst became almost obsessed. It would be her first production for the school, a public showcase for her abilities, and she rehearsed us relentlessly. She coaxed, bullied, shouted, spent hours discussing motivation, analysing the text and organizing movements. There were no allowances for our youth and inexperience, just her utter determination that everything had to be right.

'What are the rest of you doing?' she yelled in the middle of one of the final evening rehearsals. 'You're just standing there! For God's sake, how many times do I have to tell you? You act in the pauses!'

'But we've got nothing to say,' someone complained.

'Of course you have! All of you have got marvellous things to say – but you're not saying them. Now, come on! You're a bunch of total bastards tricking Joan into recanting everything she believes in before you burn her at the stake. So don't just stand there like a queue at the bloody supermarket! Start again from ... from "You wrestle in vain with the devil for her soul".'

25

Within minutes she leapt to her feet again. 'No! Katrina, you're not . . . Come here.'

She dragged me to the side of the drama room and slapped my hand against a radiator, fiercely holding it down with her own. I winced at the heat and tried to pull away, but she pressed my skin harder on the metal. Her voice was rigid with impatience.

'Just feel that! It hurts, doesn't it? How long could you stand it before you started to scream with agony and begged me to stop? What you're facing is a million times worse. They're threatening to burn you alive and it's scaring the shit out of you! The audience has got to *smell* that fear!'

We had never seen her like this; it shocked us, but that evening it began to work. I watched for the tiny nods she made when she was satisfied. Finally she stood up and actually clapped.

'Good. Well done. We're getting there. Thank you, thank you, thank you. Right, three more rehearsals after school, then it's dress rehearsal on the afternoon of the fourteenth. Just remember everything we've done. All right, off you go.' She dropped her text on to a chair. 'Katrina, can you hang on for a few minutes . . . ? Are you being picked up or anything?'

'No. I catch the bus.'

'OK. It won't take long.'

After the others had left, she took me down to the school hall and stood me at one side of the stage.

'Now this is just between you and me. I'm going to stand in the corridor out there . . .' she pointed to the far end of the hall '. . . and I'm closing the doors. I want you to scream so that I can hear you. Not just hear you, but loud enough to make me jump. When we actually do this thing, you're going to shriek like a banshee at the end of scene six when they're burning you off-stage. The rest of the cast won't be expecting it, so it will shock them as much as the audience. We'll play it down in rehearsal and hit them with maximum volume on the first night.'

She walked away and the heavy doors closed behind her, then I heard her voice faintly calling me to start. It took twenty minutes and I was becoming hoarse before she was satisfied.

'Hold that one,' she called as she reappeared. 'It'll be easier during the performance because you'll have built up to it. We'll practise again tomorrow . . . Oh, what time's your bus?'

I glanced at my watch. 'The last one's in . . . It's all right. I'll call my parents and one of them will come and collect me.'

'Oh, no.' She sounded dismayed. 'I'm sorry, Katrina. I shouldn't have kept you so long. Where do you live?'

'Bramhall.'

'No problem, then. I'll drop you off. I live at Heaton Mersey.'

'But it's out of your way.'

'That doesn't matter. Get your things and meet me in the car park. I'll tell Mr Grangewood we've finished and he can lock up.'

She had a battered Ford Prefect – 'Two-tone. Yellow and rust,' she joked – with an exhaust that sounded as if it was about to blow and a sticker from the 1961 Edinburgh Festival in the rear window. She drove the way she taught, pushing and demanding, jumping a set of traffic lights with a savage thrust of acceleration, chatting all the time. She asked about my family, what I planned to do when I left school, how I enjoyed being in the play, what music I liked. When we reached home, she looked admiringly at the house.

'Much better than a one-bedroom flat with dodgy heating.'

'Would you like to come in?' I asked. 'My parents would probably like to thank you for—'

'No thanks, Katrina. I'm bushed. I'll see you tomorrow. Hang on, that handle's awkward.' She leant across me and fumbled with the passenger door. 'Stop playing up, you sod.'

Her free hand was resting on my right thigh and her fingers squeezed slightly, then there was a click and the door edged open.

'Off you go.' Both hands went back to the steering wheel.

'Goodnight, Miss Hurst,' I said as I got out.

'Goodnight.' The engine roared as she revved and what she said next was so muffled that I might have imagined it. 'And it's Judith.'

I watched her drive away. I don't think I had a crush on her at that stage, and if I did it wasn't sexual; after all, she had a boyfriend. But she had dug into my personality and helped me

27

to explore my stage character. It was all part of the production, but we had moved from a teacher–pupil relationship into a person-to-person one; something like friendship was emerging.

The following night, we practised the scream again and this time I was more confident.

'Terrific!' She sounded delighted as she came back into the hall. 'You'll blow their minds with that. Come on, let's get you home.' There was no suggestion of the bus, even though there was plenty of time for me to catch it.

That evening she told me how she had wanted to be an actress but had realized she was not good enough to be a star and would have hated small-part jobbing work. She asked if I had a boyfriend and said there must be something wrong with the local boys when I told her I hadn't.

Saint Joan was a great success, packed out every night with loyal parents, of course, but we also knew it was much better than any play the school had ever put on. On the first night, my unexpected scream shattered everyone and afterwards in the classroom we used as a communal dressing room Miss Hurst produced an enormous box of chocolates for us and said we had been magic. The play ran for five nights, and after each perform-ance, except the second which my parents attended, Miss Hurst ran me home. After the final performance on the Saturday, we held a party, played records and drank Coke. Miss Hurst, who had been fizzing and hyperactive all week, looked tired when we finished, as though the pressure inside her had gone and left her deflated. She drove more slowly than usual and when we reached my house she laid her head back on her seat and sighed.

'God, I feel absolutely dead, but it's been worth it. Thank you, Katrina. You were tremendous.'

'Thank you for all your help. I wouldn't have been able to—'

I stopped as she took hold of my hand. She was still gazing at the roof of the car and there was a silence before she said anything.

'I had a friend at RADA who looked rather like you. She was called Chris. I was very fond of her.'

I sat very still, agonizingly uncertain. She turned to look at me. 'Am I shocking you?'

I'd noticed her eyes before, autumn brown with swimming traces of dark green; they looked tender and slightly apprehensive in the half-light. I think I knew then that I loved her.

'No,' I replied in a very small voice.

'That's all right, then.' She released my hand and looked away. 'Anyway, I think you can probably open that door yourself by now.'

She was offering me a way out, but I remained where I was, staring at the road straight ahead to where a lamp-post cast electric lemon light in the darkness. In the silence a neighbour drove past and turned into his drive, then I stiffened slightly and closed my eyes as I heard her move. She kissed my lips very gently, with no sense of demanding desire.

'Goodnight, Katrina,' she said softly. 'You'd better go in now. It's late. I'll see you at school on Monday.'

I heard the clock in the hall strike three before I fell asleep that night.

On Monday Miss Hurst gave us back our drama notebooks, which she had marked over the weekend; inside mine was a sheet of blue notepaper with her address written on it. It could have been left there accidentally, but I hurriedly tucked it in my blazer pocket. I secretly looked at it a lot that week, and each time the moment when we had last been in the car together came back more insistently. I was not sure what to do, but the following Saturday I told my parents I was spending the afternoon with another girl to do some homework and cycled to Heaton Mersey. The address was a flat on the first floor of a three-storey Victorian house. There were five bells by the front door, and one had a strip of card with 'J. M. Hurst' typed on it in the little plastic box. I rang and waited, then heard a voice calling.

'Hello? Who is it?'

I moved out of the deep porch and looked up. She was leaning out of a top-floor window straight above me, hair in an apricot towel wound into a turban. For a moment, neither of us spoke.

'Hang on. I'll let you in.' She disappeared, then through the

29

mottled glass of the front door I saw her appear in the hall. She was wearing jeans and a beige canvas shirt with symbolic trees embroidered on the pocket, its sleeves turned back on her forearms. Her feet were bare. She indicated the towel. 'Just drying it.'

'I didn't know if you'd be in.'

'Well, I am.' She did not ask me what I was doing there. 'You can leave your bike in the hall.'

I followed her upstairs and along a landing to a door leading into a short passage that opened out into a sitting room with an old-fashioned picture rail running round the walls and a high sash window that looked out across a patch of open land to a disused railway line. A thirties settee clashed with a modern shell-shaped easy chair; half of one wall had been fitted with shelves crammed with books; a portable typewriter stood on an oak dining table, surrounded by scattered papers. The paintwork was dark brown and the walls papered in pale cream with a Regency stripe; the curtains were a rich brocade and I noticed an old foot-driven Singer sewing machine in one corner.

'Cup of tea?'

'Sorry? Oh. Yes, please. Thank you.'

She went into the kitchen off the living room and I looked at her pictures. Framed prints of Westminster Abbey, Jane Austen's house and Alnwick Castle; a poster for an exhibition at the Tate Gallery showing Dali's *The Persistence of Memory*; another a billboard for Ellen Terry in a production of *The Merry Wives of Windsor* years and years before; a third of an Aubrey Beardsley; a photograph of a group of young people striking silly dramatic poses on the steps of the Old Vic. I was trying to identify her when she called to me.

'Sugar?'

'No, thank you.'

She came back into the sitting room holding two mugs, one with a black italic J stamped on it. 'Here you are. Hang on while I finish this.'

She went through another door and I heard the hum of an electric drier as I looked at her books, classics, poetry, a few

30

crime novels, theatrical biographies, plays and Eastern philosophy. I was flicking through *The Catcher in the Rye*, which I hadn't read, when I heard the drier stop.

'Katrina.' Just my name; not a summons, but a simple invitation. She had not tried to make any conversation since my arrival, and I had been unable to think of anything to say.

I put my mug on one of the bookshelves and walked towards the bedroom door, tense with nervousness but accepting that I was there because I chose to be. The curtains were drawn, translucent ox-blood material turning April sunshine deep pink, and she was sitting on the three-quarter bed, staring down as she traced the diamond pattern of stitches on the sand-coloured quilt; her shoulder-length hair was dried but still unbrushed. I stood uncertainly just inside the doorway.

'The boyfriend doesn't exist, of course,' she said quietly. 'Did you realize that?'

'I didn't think about it.'

'Yes, you did. And you still came here. Why?'

'Because I wanted to. I can't explain it any more than that.'

She thought for a moment. 'That's understandable.' The catch in her voice was more pronounced than usual, and she cleared her throat. 'As always, the Greeks had a word for it. They called it sapphism. It's been happening for a very long time ... but it will only happen now if it's what you really want.'

Beyond turning back, I dumbly nodded then found my voice. 'Yes ... Judith.' My eyes blurred, and I trembled as she stood up.

Now her kisses had appetite, those eloquent fingers increasingly eager. But she knew my inexperience and guided me carefully, delicate caresses, encouragement and permission, unimaginable warmths and sensations of little pains that made me cry out hesitant protests as her lips fluttered across my face, murmuring hurried assurances. Only when I was ready came the panting demands, the insistence of inflamed flesh as our bodies urgently sought some abstraction of unity. When it was over I lay with my eyes closed, content, grateful, quietly weeping at the first skilfully aided achievement of physical love.

31

'Oh, my pretty vestal.' Her hand traced my profile, catching a tear and smoothing it away across my cheek. 'Have I corrupted you?'

'No. Don't say that. I love you.'

'And I love you. Say my name again.'

'Judith ... Judith ...' I began to shake with sobs. 'Judith ... Judith.'

'Enough.' Fingers firmly stopped my quivering mouth. 'Come back to earth.' She swung her legs on to the floor and put on a white towelling robe that was lying on a chair beside the bed. 'More tea, I think. No. Wine.'

Leaning against the pine headboard, cuddled together and drinking Hock from cheap tumblers, was as warm and satisfying as naked arousal had been. Judith did not make love to me again that afternoon, although I felt she wanted to.·We dressed and went back to the living room, now chatting as incipient equals with her showing me more photographs of herself as a student, telling me about her past, making sly remarks about other teachers. When I reluctantly said I should go, she came downstairs and kissed me again in the empty hall.

'Goodbye, Katrina.' She ruffled my hair affectionately. 'If you want to, visit me again. I'd like that.'

Private elocution lessons were the perfect excuse to spend each Friday evening with her. She had a strict rule that the first hour had to be spent on what my father was paying her to do, making me repeat 'Good luck' twenty times if I ever slipped and it sounded nearer 'look'; recording my reading passages of prose then playing it back so that I cringed as she shook her head in despair; hammering into me how to pronounce 'sugar' and 'one' ('It rhymes with "won" not "gone", stupid'). Then she would grin at me and hold out her hand. She was a wonderful, funny mimic; bodies intertwined in bed, she would press her mouth against my ear and growl 'Yer ma hinny, nae one else's' in thick Geordie and we would giggle helplessly and roll about in a mock fight until our eyes met, then our lips trembled and made hungry contact again. But sex was only part of it. She introduced me to

32

writers I didn't know, suggested I changed my lipstick, let me try on her clothes and said I should wear soft browns more often, taught me how to stand and walk gracefully. She changed me into somebody else.

I spent one whole weekend with her when my parents were attending a conference on behalf of my father's company and my brother had gone to stay with friends in Wales. On the Saturday we drove to Chester, where we wandered round the Roman walls and bought vegetarian food that we cooked together in the evening. Sunday was a beautiful day, and we decided to go to Alderley Edge, the dramatic escarpment overlooking the Cheshire plain. We had a pub lunch in the Wizard, then walked through the trees on the Edge until we found somewhere to ourselves and I showed off by identifying wildflowers; Judith was hopeless at botany. She had a copy of Gerard Manley Hopkins with her, but quoted 'Pied Beauty' and 'As Kingfishers Catch Fire, Dragonflies Draw Flame' without having to look at it. I took her photograph and picked a sprig of meadowsweet, which she promised to press in the book. I suddenly wanted her very much, but she resisted when I pulled her towards me.

'Anything but the woods,' she murmured. 'There are people around.'

'It's important,' I said.

'It's lust, you little vixen,' she teased.

I shook my head. 'No it's not. We've gone past that.'

If I'd been honest with myself I would have recognized it had to end; what hurt me was the casual brutality of it. Perhaps she was protecting her own feelings. She went away to tour Europe with a group of acting friends for virtually all the summer holidays, and I spent weeks wishing I could be sharing what she was doing, envying whoever was in her company. When we met again in September she was a stranger. She said there was no need for more elocution lessons, she'd taught me all I needed to know and I just had to keep practising. After one drama class, I stayed behind and asked when I could visit her.

'Not here.' She sounded impatient. 'Show some bloody discretion.'

'But I want to see you.'

She didn't look at me as she continued putting papers in her briefcase. 'All right. Sunday afternoon.' She snapped the case shut and walked out of the room. I convinced myself she was not feeling well or in a bad mood over something. On the Sunday I invented an imaginary game of tennis as an excuse to go out, which meant I arrived at Heaton Mersey in my tracksuit, carrying a racket.

'I don't play,' she said as she opened the door. 'Remember?'

'It was just to give me a reason for going out.' Her coldness frightened me.

'You'd better come in, anyway. We have to talk.' She turned and walked into the sitting room, leaving me to follow her. When I entered, she was lighting a cigarette.

'I didn't know you smoked.'

'I never have when you've been here. You don't like it.'

'But I'm here now.'

'Yep . . . Sit down.'

I shook my head. 'Don't tell me what to do.'

'All right, stand up. It makes no difference.' She drew on the cigarette. 'I've spent a lot of time thinking about this, and the best thing is to simply get it over with. I'm leaving at half-term.'

'But you always said you were happy here.'

'I have been, but I've been offered a job in London.'

She had her arms folded across her chest and it suddenly struck me that the cigarette was like some stage prop; she was putting on an act.

'And what else is in London?' I demanded.

'What do you mean?'

'I mean who else is in London?'

Her lips twisted and she sighed slightly. 'I could tell you there was nobody . . . but I don't think you'd believe me. I really was hoping that while I was away you'd find a boyfriend.'

'A *boyfriend*?' I gestured towards the bedroom. 'After everything that's happened in there?'

'Yes.' She shook her head. 'Katrina, you're not a lesbian. Believe me, I know. When I started teaching you, there were no boyfriends – God knows why not – but your body was pumping sex hormones through you. You're very attractive and I fancied you. No, that sounds dreadful, but . . . Jesus, why doesn't life supply film scripts so we can do scenes like this in a few meaningful sentences and a fade-out?'

I blinked away painful tears. 'Just tell me who it is. I think I deserve that.'

'It's not going to help, but . . .' She hesitated. 'All right. It's Chris. I've told you about her.'

'The one you knew at RADA?'

'That's right. She was in the group I went away with, and . . . Come on, you don't need diagrams.'

'And that's it? You two went to bed again on holiday and now I'm just the stupid schoolgirl who let you seduce her?' I was beginning to feel very angry.

'You're not a schoolgirl, Katrina. You've grown up a lot in the time I've known you . . . and getting hurt is part of growing up.'

'But you're not hurting.'

'Yes I am, but not in the same way.'

'Liar.'

For the first time, she looked sympathetic. 'No, but you'll think that. I'm sorry, darling. Really. I knew right from the start this was going to end. We were never going to pick out the furniture. I just hoped that it wouldn't be as shitty as this.'

'And this is it? You just break my heart and walk out?'

'Don't be so melodramatic. I've not broken your heart, I've hurt your feelings. It happens in relationships.'

I looked down. 'I loved you.'

'I know you did. And I loved you – in a way I always will. Katrina, believe me, we can love lots of people.'

'And hate them?'

'Yes, that as well. They often overlap.' She stubbed out the cigarette. 'Come on, there's no point in dragging this out, but I've got something to give you.' She picked up a small box that was on the bookcase. 'You'll probably want to throw this away at

35

first, but please wait a couple of weeks to see if you feel differently.'

It was a narrow silver bracelet with a pattern of vine leaves engraved on the surface.

'It's Victorian,' she said. 'It's not worth a fortune, but it's to say thank you for a very good year. I want you to have it. Please.'

I accepted, and I kept it; after a while, I started to wear it. Judith was the first person I loved, and her betrayal hurt me so deeply that I never allowed anyone – not even my husband – to come that close to me again until . . . No, that comes much later, and stories like this should be told as they happened. Anyway, even if I could have somehow miraculously seen so many years ahead, I would never have believed it; I'm finding it very hard to believe it now.

London and Cornwall

Hacking into the *Register*'s internal message system was endemic among certain members of staff, usually to pick up confidential information or some embarrassment to pass on to *Private Eye* or another paper's diary page. After one of the subs had read a message from Webb to Kendall, he casually announced he was going to the canteen. On his way, he used the payphone next to the drinks machine in the basement.

'News desk, please. Richard? Alex McIntyre. Could have a good one for you. Katrina Darcy's disappeared.'

'What do you mean?'

'She hasn't been seen for a week and isn't here today. She always comes in on Friday to write her column. They're starting to panic.'

'What do they think?'

'They don't know what to think. They've apparently checked out everywhere, but no show.'

'Interesting. Where does she live?'

'Stanmore Mansions.'

'Where's that?'

'Somewhere off Bayswater Road. Block of upmarket flats. It's high-profile security, so you may have trouble getting in.'

'We'll worry about that. But she was definitely expected in today?'

'Her page one puff's in the system waiting for the cross-ref copy. As far as I can make out, someone else is filling the space.'

'Rumours?'

'There aren't any. They're trying to keep it quiet.'

'Are they? OK, we'll look into it. Is Charlie Taylor in?'

'No, he's on holiday. Kendall's editing.'

37

'I'll call him. Thanks, Alex. Cheque in the post if it stands up.'

Richard Harvey rang off and turned to the *Sunday Times* deputy news editor.

'Is Ray Morgan still knocking off Katrina Darcy?'

'Not since his wife found out. Why?'

'Just had a tip. Where is Ray?'

'Somewhere between here and Sevenoaks. He left about twenty minutes ago. What's the tip?'

'The *Register* seems to have lost her.'

'She's left them? Christ. Who for?'

'Not lost like that. She's gone awol. Try Ray's mobile before he gets home and see if he's got any suggestions. Meanwhile . . .' Harvey picked up the phone again, 'let's find out what Mr Kendall has to say.'

In the cottage, the phone rang again, but the answerphone tape was now full. On the word-processor screen the cursor rested on the final letter of one incomplete sentence: *My darling Stephanie, I'm posting this before I return to London. They are going to print a great many lies about me, and . . .*

An alarm clock next to the word-processor on the oak table began to cheep, a reminder to turn on the television for *Channel Four News*; the irresistible journalistic instinct to know what's happened. Silently, the automatic oven switched itself on to bake mackerel.

Kendall was discussing a pull-out supplement on private schools with the *Register*'s advertising manager when the call was put through.

'Mr Kendall? Richard Harvey, *Sunday Times*. Have you got a minute?'

'What about?'

'Katrina Darcy.'

'Hang on.' Kendall pressed the mute button. 'Personal call, Nigel. See me later. Close the door.' Left alone, he hesitated a few moments before connecting Harvey again.

'Sorry about that, I had someone on another line. What about Katrina?'

'We've heard she's disappeared.'

Kendall laughed. 'Who told you that?'

'Reliable source.'

'From inside this office?'

'It might have been.'

'Then I suggest you check back with them.'

'You mean she's not disappeared?'

'That's right.'

'So her column will be appearing on Sunday?'

'No.' Caught unprepared, Kendall made a snap decision. 'She's been taken ill. That's all.'

'Too ill to even phone her copy in?'

'Her doctor says she needs complete rest.'

'And that's the official position?'

'There's no need for an official position.'

'But we can quote you.'

'Look, Richard, I don't know what someone's been telling you, but they're trying to make a story out of nothing. Katrina called in this morning to say her doctor has ordered her to rest.'

'So she was well enough to ring you but not to fax her copy?'

Kendall grimaced, annoyed at leaving a gap for a journalist to exploit. 'She's got a phone by her bed.'

'And she rang you only this morning. It was sudden, then? What's the matter with her?'

'I don't discuss my staff's personal lives.'

'Fair enough. But there's no panic.'

'Of course not. Don't make the *ST* look silly over this, Richard. These things happen. All right?'

'You're telling us not to run a story.'

'I'm telling you there's no story to run.'

'Can you let me know where we can contact her?'

'No, I can't.'

'Then could you call her and have her ring me?'

'What the hell for?'

'So we know she's all right.'

39

'She is all right.' Kendall's voice hardened. 'And if your people start pestering her, I'll talk to Dave Godshaw about it.'

'Would you like to speak to him now?' Harvey asked mildly. 'I can put you through.'

'There's no need at the moment. And there won't be if you'll just accept the facts.'

'Which are that Katrina Darcy is ill.'

'Correct. Is that it?'

'Unless we hear anything else.'

'You won't. Cheers, Richard.'

Harvey looked intrigued as Kendall hung up; that so experienced a journalist had threatened to complain to someone as senior as Godshaw had been inexplicably inept, virtually an open admission that Katrina Darcy was missing and the *Register* wanted to keep it quiet.

'Did you get hold of Ray?' he asked.

'Yeah, but he hasn't seen her for months. Apparently, she just wound it up.'

'So who's she been seeing since? Ms Darcy likes to be escorted.'

'Ray doesn't know, and I've not heard of anyone. Have you?'

'No, but we'll ask around. Have Penny check out Darcy's neighbours. Here's the address, but she may have trouble getting in. And tell picture desk to dig out everything they've got of her.'

'You want to go big on this?'

Harvey tapped his shorthand notes. 'I do now. Kendall's lying.'

TOM

This is the one wedding photograph I kept. We did everything by the social conventions of my upbringing, me in white satin and a cascading veil, Tom in a morning suit hired from Moss Bros, tails and a grey top hat which he didn't know what to do with. My bridesmaids were in pink, we had the traditional marriage service and photographer with a tripod. The picture was my mother's favourite, the one she had framed for the sideboard, a close-up of us outside the church, gazing into each other's eyes. We both look adoring, and I was very happy. I was twenty years old and naively believed I had found the only love I would want.

Having become so successful, it's strange that journalism was actually a chance career; my first job was in a bank as a trainee cashier. After Judith, all I wanted was to leave school and I took the first thing that came up. My major responsibility was checking that the postage balanced at the end of each day and one night I had to stay behind with two senior people while they hunted for some missing amount (it was only about five shillings, but their attitude was that I was in danger of undermining Britain's entire banking system). My boredom was beginning to show, but I didn't have any other ambitions. Most of my friends had gone on to college and none of the others had found jobs that appealed to me in the slightest. Then my father mentioned that one of his golfing partners was the managing director of the group that owned the *Stockport Courier*. It was a profession I'd never thought of, but once I did, it seemed attractive ... It was as casual as that, although I met other people who'd drifted into the business almost by accident. It's all university intake these days, but then you could join a local weekly with no more than a handful of O-levels, as long as one of them was English. It was

41

the standard training ground; some of the biggest names on what we still call Fleet Street have covered a lot of parish councils.

The *Courier* was a classic old-fashioned broadsheet, chronicles of very small beer; police, fire and ambulance pars, magistrates' court cases, WI and Mothers' Union reports, people living in fear near dangerous road junctions, weddings, reviews of amateur dramatic societies which always had to mention the ladies who made the tea, school exam results, silly season stories about giant sunflowers. Deaths were important – one of my first jobs was standing in the rain outside a church collecting names of mourners at an alderman's funeral. One thing I rapidly learnt was that news value came a bad second to discretion. When I unearthed a story about a JP's wife running off with a scout leader, it was spiked; the JP had the town's Ford franchise sewn up and we had the advertising exclusively. We're not talking super, soaraway *Sun*. The staff was divided between dead-end seniors who'd lost what ambitions they'd ever had and underpaid juniors. The editor was a Methodist lay preacher with a passion for fly-fishing; a remarkable number of competitions seemed to occur on press day.

In some ways it was like being at university, a group of us learning the job, including an erratically attended day release college course, where I missed most of the law lectures because there was a cinema across the road and several of us went to the matinées. I didn't experience any emotion even mildly like falling in love, but there was a series of boyfriends, including Duncan Walsh (or was it Welsh?) who introduced me to heterosexuality on the single bed in his grubby bedsit. Inexperienced and smelling of beer, he left me with the feeling that I really might be a lesbian. I began to think differently with Alan Forrester, deputy head of display advertising, mid-thirties and married. He chatted me up at someone's leaving do, bought me enough vodkas and tonic to dissolve my resistance – which wasn't all that great – and bonked me in the back of his company Triumph Herald. After that, usually when I should have been calling on local contacts and he should have been selling advertising space, we used the flat of an obliging friend. Three months later he mentioned that his wife

42

was pregnant, which saved me the trouble of finishing with him. He'd served his purpose; I'd got the sex thing sorted out.

Stockport's great advantage was that it was next to Manchester, in those days the most important newspaper city outside London. All the nationals had separate editorial and printing operations there – the *Mirror* and *Telegraph* in Withy Grove, *Daily Mail* on Deansgate, *Guardian* in Cross Street, the *Express* in a copy of Fleet Street's black greenhouse – and we often met their reporters. I began to do unofficial lineage to supplement appalling pay and very limited scope to fiddle my expenses, tipping them off if the *Courier* had broken the habits of a lifetime and dug up a half decent story (the JP's wife and the scout leader earned me thirty pounds, good money in those days, from the *Mirror*). I decided to try for one of the nationals – I wasn't particular which one – and the break came when an *Express* reporter took me to the old Press Club in Albert Square after we'd been covering an evening media launch at Granada TV. I was the wide-eyed innocent, trying to be blasé but secretly impressed at meeting journalists who worked for real newspapers. I must have made a fool of myself, but most of the members were middle-aged men who would forgive an attractive young girl anything. Someone invited me to play snooker, probably so that he could look up my mini skirt as I leant over the table.

Shortly after midnight and the third edition deadlines, more people arrived and I was introduced to Tom Darcy. He was in his early thirties, long brown hair and floral shirt – flower power was in – and was an assistant editor on the *Daily Mail* back bench; I'd been drinking since seven o'clock – and was very green – which is probably why I told him it was a classy job.

'I used to think that,' he said. 'When you get down to it, it's about as exciting as working in a bank.'

'No it's not,' I told him. 'I've done that. And don't be cynical. You're on a national, not a local rag.'

'I started the way you did. *Accrington Observer*.'

'But you got out. I've written to every Northern editor, but they don't want to know.'

There was more to the conversation than that – he certainly

started chatting me up, directing standard approving glances at my fashionably pert 34As – and I must have impressed him with something, because he introduced me to Neville Jarvis, the *Mail*'s news editor.

'Katrina Smith. Works on the *Courier* in Stockport. Remember that mother who lost two kids in a fire a few weeks ago? We used some copy from her on it.'

Neville nodded. 'Good quotes. We had them exclusively, didn't we?'

'That's what you asked for.'

'Katrina's looking for a job,' Tom added. 'Any chances?'

'How long have you been with the *Courier*?' Neville asked.

'Nearly three years.' An accurate twelve months and a bit was not going to impress him.

'Indentured?'

'Yes, but no one takes any notice of them.'

'How's your shorthand?'

'Hundred words a minute.' As long as they spoke in very simple words. He was no more going to check that than he was going to confirm how long I'd really been on the *Courier*. Neville turned away for a moment as someone came up and spoke to him; I could have killed them. Then he spoke to me again.

'Come and see me Monday. Eleven o'clock.' Then he was gone, leaving a rather startled trainee reporter behind.

'Thank you,' I told Tom. 'That was great. Let me get you a drink.'

In less than twenty minutes my career had achieved lift-off and I had met my future husband. When Tom ran me home that night I granted him a quick snog in the car and agreed to go out with him the following week. Before that I saw Neville and he offered me a job – lowest of the low, but still the *Daily Mail* – and, by the time I joined, Tom and I had slept together. I moved into a flat in Fallowfield, and he arrived every night after work; he proposed to me and I accepted in bed, which I later realized said a lot about our relationship, but I genuinely believed I was in love with him. After that, trapped in the expectations and norms of my upbringing, it was the traditional white wedding,

44

emotional women, fussy bridesmaids, self-conscious father, silver paper horseshoe, bad jokes from the best man and a report in the *Courier*. We spent our honeymoon in Scotland, and I accepted what I'd chosen. What did he look like? He had a very long head accentuated by a sharp chin, and his nose was nipped in at the nostrils; in profile he looked ascetic, full face you saw eyes that were rarely warm and glittered when he was emotional. He had the wicked handsomeness of a tall leprechaun.

We mortgaged ourselves into suburban Didsbury and it was DIY home decorating, weekly trips to the supermarket, dinner with neighbours who talked about their children (with hints from the women about when were we going to start), and a garden we both worked in. It was a mundane but perfectly acceptable life, occasional worries about money, entertaining our parents, flickers of arguments, buying more furniture, me buying the odd meal, me, defeated by the central heating, finding ourselves a cat. I remained at the *Mail*, competent but unspectacular, and Tom became deputy night editor.

Things changed in 1971 when he was offered the chief sub's job in London. We talked it over, agreed it was good move, and I stayed in Manchester until we found an affordable 1930s semi-detached in Barnet. The *Mail* had nothing for me, so I accepted an offer from the *Barnet Press*, back to the weeklies, but I'd reached the stage where all I really wanted was to become a mother. I wrote in my diary about the 'exquisite agony' of giving birth, a romantic illusion that was shattered by nine hours of labour before Stephanie was born in 1974. But she was gorgeous and Tom had always said he wanted a daughter first. My life became limited, but as far as I was concerned being a wife and mother while my husband was the breadwinner was the natural order of things. Not that I became the total *hausfrau*. Tom and I went to the theatre and I accompanied him to various functions, I had my own circle of friends and kept in touch with journalism by writing a weekly column for one of the smaller women's magazines and an advice column for another. I made a special effort not to let my looks go.

*

45

New patterns creep into marriage so slowly that you don't realize how much has changed. Juggling motherhood, housework, my small but essential social life and writing, my relationship with Tom was running on auto-pilot and I wasn't paying enough attention. He was an adequate father, reading to Stephanie, running her to the nursery each morning and keeping her occupied if I was busy, but there were whole areas of his life I neither thought about nor had time to take an interest in. The marriage ceased in many ways to be a bond between us; it rested on shared responsibilities. None of this, I must point out, occurred to me at the time. I was like any other wife maintaining her own identity while my husband got on with his career. The shit hit the fan in 1977, the evening that Stephanie fell downstairs, cutting her head on the corner of the bookcase in the hall. Terrified by her screams and trying to staunch the blood, I went into maternal protective mode, holding a towel against her temple with one hand as I rang Janet, a ward sister at the local hospital who lived across the road, with the other.

'On my way,' she said, and was at the front door almost before I'd struggled to unlatch it. 'Let me see. At least she's conscious. Come on, hospital. My car's outside.'

'Thanks ... Can you grab my bag? It's in the ...' Stephanie suddenly went limp. 'Don't go to sleep! Call an ambulance!'

'The car'll be quicker.' Janet led me out, my child's blood warm against my hand through the fabric of the towel. As we drove away, I was keening softly over her, begging her to live, frantic in the parent's ultimate nightmare. Janet kept up a quiet commentary of reassurance, interrupted by impatience, as she broke speed limits.

'It's all right ... Hold her more upright ... We'll be there in a minute ... Get out of the way, you stupid bastard!... Can you feel her pulse? ... Good ... One of mine did this once and was demanding Smarties twenty minutes later ... Accident and emergency's this way ... Come on.'

The worst horrors of all raced through my mind. Janet heartbroken, the sympathetic doctor, the gentle staff, the unthinkable grief, the little body, the tiny coffin, my mother

46

wailing ... My imagination saw Stephanie moments after she'd
been born, the first time she stood up in her playpen, the clumsy,
endearing clown's face she'd painted at nursery and I'd stuck on
to the kitchen cupboard; her pleading 'Mummy make it better'
when she had grazed her knee. I allowed her to be taken from
me, then I was alone in a room with a cup of tea, waiting for ever
until Janet's voice reached me from another dimension.

'She's fine. No concussion, but we're taking X-rays just in
case. She needs a couple of stitches and we'll keep her in
overnight. She'll be as bright as a button in the morning.'

'Jesus Johnson.' Relief was almost as painful as terror had
been. 'I must stay with her.'

'That's no problem, but what about Tom?'

'Is there a phone I can use?'

'In the office, and I'll pop back and collect some things if you
tell me were to look.'

'Thanks.' I gave her my house key. 'Red toothbrush, nightdress
from the top right-hand drawer in the chest in the bedroom ...
spare knickers are in there as well ... any towel from the
bathroom ... I've got make-up ... I think that's it.'

'If I think of anything else, I'll grab it.' As we'd been speaking,
we'd been walking through to her office. 'There's the phone.
Back shortly.'

I sat for a moment to compose myself, then couldn't remember
Tom's direct line number and had to check in my diary. As I
dialled, I glanced at the clock on the wall; just about first edition
deadline. The phone was answered almost instantly, but I didn't
recognize the voice.

'Hello, can I speak to Tom Darcy? It's his wife.'

'Tom? He's not in tonight.'

'Pardon? He's on late shift. He left home at five o'clock.'

'Oh ... Hang on, I haven't seen him, but perhaps he's on the
stone.' I could hear the chatter of voices as I waited. 'I'm sorry,
he's not here. Are you sure he was due in?'

'Positive. He said he'd be back around three.' Still in shock, I
felt a chill run through me. 'If you hear from him, would you tell

him his daughter's had an accident and I'm at the hospital with her . . . Who is this, incidentally?'

'Peter Matlock.' He was the copytaster, and I knew him only vaguely from a Christmas party.

'Sorry, I didn't recognize your voice.'

'It's OK.' He was starting to sound uneasy. 'Look, I might have got it round my neck . . . Tom might be in later . . . I'll—'

'Just give him the message if he turns up.'

I hung up, trying to cope with shrieking suspicions and instant fury, but it all had to be pushed down when they told me Stephanie was about to leave X-ray. I held her hand as the trolley took her to the ward; she was bewildered but wide awake, a crêpe bandage around her head. I promised I wasn't going away and sat by her bedside as she began to drift into sleep. When Janet came back, she was carrying a teddy bear and a stuffed rabbit as well as my things.

'Had to guess which were her favourites,' she whispered. 'These two seemed to have pride of place on the pillow.'

'Bless you.' I tucked them under the bedclothes. 'She's nearly away.'

'Did you reach Tom?'

'I left a message . . . Where can I sleep?'

'I'll show you. The nurse'll call you if she wakes up.'

For more than an hour I had been the hysterical mother surrounded by care and concern. Now I was the suspicious wife alone in a vacant side-ward. I tried to think it through. Was Tom off that night, but had an appointment somewhere? No, I'd have remembered that. Anyway, Tuesday had been his night off that week, and this was Friday. Correction, he'd told me he was off on Tuesday, then had to go in at the last minute because someone was ill. They'd rung him while I was out. Of course they had . . . I didn't sleep.

In the morning, as I sat with Stephanie waiting for a doctor to confirm I could take her home, Tom walked into the ward.

'Hello, Daddy. I hurt my head.'

'I know. Is it better now?'

I kept hold of her hand as he leant across the bed and kissed

48

her. Then he looked at me uncertainly. 'Janet told me what happened.'

'That was kind of her. I tried to tell you last night.'

'Yeah . . . I was . . . I wasn't there.'

'So I gathered.'

'Teddy's here as well. He ought to have a bandage.'

'You can give him one when we get you home.' He turned to me again. 'The Sister says they're letting her out.'

'If the doctor clears it. She's due any time.'

'Good.'

For the next few minutes we ignored each other as Tom chatted to Stephanie about things they could see in the ward, then the doctor arrived and we waited in the corridor. He stared out of the window.

'Sorry about last night.'

'I thought she was dying.'

'But over-dramatic, wasn't it? She only bumped her head.'

'How would you know? You weren't there. Where were you?'

'At a party.'

'Really? Whose?'

'Chap I know from the *Telegraph*.'

'Why did you say you were going to work?'

'Because you wouldn't have liked me going out on my night off.'

'You could have taken me with you.'

'It was a stag night. I'm sorry it was when this happened. OK?'

'What time did you get home?'

'About the usual time. I didn't know where the hell you were. It was too late to ring anyone and I was worried.'

I held up my hand. 'Worry I know. In spades.'

'You could have asked Janet to put a note through the door.'

I smiled sarcastically. 'Why didn't I think of that? Perhaps it was because I'd been nearly driven out of my mind! All right?'

'There's no need to make a war out of it. It was one of those things.'

'Yes, I expect it was.' For a few moments we stood in silence,

49

three yards and several light years between us. 'Who on the *Telegraph?*'

'You don't know him.'

The reply was too neat and came too quickly. 'What's his name?' I demanded sharply.

'What does that matter?'

'To me, a lot.'

'He's just a guy I know at the pub.'

'Who else was there? Anyone I do know?'

'For Christ's sake, what is this? We've got Stephanie to worry about and . . .' He turned at the sound of the ward door opening behind us. 'Is she all right, Doctor?'

'She's fine, but keep an eye on her. If she starts feeling sleepy bring her back immediately. Otherwise just make an appointment with outpatients so we can take the stitches out.' She smiled reassuringly. 'Nasty shock for you both, but kids bounce back.'

Tom was walking back into the ward before the doctor finished speaking and he deliberately used Stephanie as a barrier to hide behind. When we got home he played the conscientious parent, ringing the nursery to explain what had happened, going across to Janet's to let her know, suggesting to Stephanie that they could set up a tent in the garden which they could pretend was a hospital. He couldn't have been more blatant if he'd just come straight out and told me the truth. I put a stop to it after lunch when I said she must have a sleep.

'I'll sit with her, just in case.'

'No,' I said. 'Stay down here and practise a few more lies.'

Having settled her, I needed time to think. I remained upstairs, cleaning a stain off the side of the bath, rearranging the airing cupboard, changing the covers on our bedside tables. I was crying, in a sort of quiet, functional way. Downstairs I walked right past him and dropped an armful of washing on the kitchen floor.

'There's no one to interrupt now, so we can have this out,' I said as I loaded the machine. 'I don't believe this party crap. I think you were in bed with someone last night. Were you?'

For a moment I thought he was going to deny it, but he saw

50

the look in my face. 'Yes. But it's not important. Nothing permanent.'

'Oh, that makes me feel so much better.' I straightened up and selected the wash cycle. 'Who is she?'

'You've never met her. She works for a PR company.'

'How long's it been going on?'

'Does that matter?'

'Probably not,' I agreed. 'But I gather you're not about to leave me for her.'

'No . . . She's married as well.'

'Children?'

'No. She doesn't want them.'

I picked up a pair of tights I'd missed. 'Is she younger than me?'

'Why do you want to know that?'

'I just do. Indulge me.'

'All right . . . She's twenty-two.'

'Of course she is. You're having your mid-life crisis a bit early. Or don't I satisfy you any more?'

'Our sex life has always been all right.'

I laughed bitterly. '"All right" just about sums up a competent fuck every week or so.'

'You've never complained.'

'Oh, dear. Touchy about our virility, are we? God, you're pitiful.'

I'd never realized – or allowed myself to accept – how essentially weak he was. Big man on campus in the office, but broken reed at home. Instead of arguing back, he started pleading.

'Look, I'm sorry. I don't want to lose you.'

'Of course you don't. I'm an inexpensive washerwoman, cleaner, nursemaid, mother, cook and home-help you screw occasionally. Birthdays I get presents and we go on holiday together. You, meanwhile, get out of the house nearly every day, enjoy regular drinks with the boys and have found a willing shagging block. So who's shovelling all the shit in this marriage?'

He looked apprehensive. 'So what do you want to do?'

51

'Cutting your balls off seems a good idea at the moment, but . . .' I glared at him. 'I'm ten days bloody late!'

'What? Why didn't you tell me?'

'Because it's happened before, but it's been no longer than a week. I hope your girlfriend's been taking precautions, because otherwise you might have got two of us pregnant at the same time.'

'If you're right, when's it due?'

'I don't know. I'll have to take the tests. Eight months?'

'So we can't split up, can we?' He sounded relieved.

Had it been now, I could have left him, but this was long before the Child Support Agency. A court would have granted me no more than Tom could afford, and if he remarried, his wife – and possibly more children – would take precedence. That's how it worked then. I had hardly any money of my own and did not want to bring up two children on the breadline.

'No . . . but I have terms. This weekend we buy single beds and I'll find a reason to call you every night you're supposed to be at the office. Christ help you if you're not there again.'

'OK.' He looked abashed. 'I deserve that. I'm sorry, Katrina. I'll tell her it's over. I love you.'

'Tell me about it.'

That night and that day would have changed any woman. Being cheated on I could come to terms with – I knew plenty of wives who'd had to accommodate a passing adultery – but what I resented most was that my lifestyle depended almost totally on my husband. I had a little girl to look after and another baby on the way; I was trapped and hated myself for having allowed it to happen.

Anyway, we hammered out some sort of truce. I changed my mind about the single beds, and even allowed him to make love to me again as the bump grew. If anything, he was over-anxious to please at first, although the flowers were nothing more than the rubbish they sell at Tube stations as peace offerings from guilty men. That wore off after a few weeks, but he was always there when I rang the office, and eventually I stopped. He got a rise, and we bought a second car. By the time I was wobbling like a barrage balloon we had at least papered over the cracks, and he was at home just after Christmas when the contractions started and he drove me to the hospital. Benjamin was born at half past three on the morning of 29 December and died within six hours; his little heart had pieces missing. Whatever sorrow I've ever known since, I always relate it to that. I'd become convinced that another child would complete our family, that Tom's affair would fade into forgetfulness and we'd find another form of happiness. Hope can be a wicked delusion.

When I was allowed home I stripped all the new paper off the walls in what would have been Benjamin's nursery and gave the off to a charity shop. The doctors had assured me I could have more children – they even seemed to think I should – but I was not prepared to risk that pain again. I walked a lot in the park with Stephanie, who showed an awareness I'd never have thought possible in so small a child. Women friends rallied round, and Tom behaved in a way that made me feel grateful towards him, although I resisted love-making again. Spring, which I thought might have cheered me up, was unexpectedly depressing (I learnt later that it's a high point for suicides in Britain). Images of new life constantly reminded me of a life cut off at the start, and people being cheerful at better weather licked raw wounds.

Then, early in April, Phil Underwood, a sub on the *Mail*'s foreign desk, unexpectedly arrived at the house one afternoon. He and his wife lived in Hadley Wood, not far from us, and we'd been to dinner at each other's homes. When I opened the door, my hands were blotched with flour from baking.

'Hello, Phil. I hope you haven't come to see Tom. He's on earlies this week, covering for Andy.'

'I know he is.'

'Oh . . . Come in.'

As I led him down the hall and through to the kitchen, I felt pleased to see him. We'd only met a few times, but I liked him, easy-going, good with Stephanie, very complimentary about my cooking. Any thoughts about hidden agendas behind casual visits when husbands were known to be at work never entered my mind.

'Drink?' I suggested. 'There's wine in the pantry. Sorry, my hands are a mess. How's Patricia?'

'All right.' He sounded dismissive as he opened the door and bent down to reach for the bottle.

'Glasses in the top cupboard. Sorry, I really must get this finished.' I plunged back into the dough. 'Put it where you can find a space. Thanks. Lovely day. How's that garden of yours?'

'It's fine.'

'You still haven't let us have those cuttings you promised and I've got a space for them ... Pass that bowl, will you? And we've got some geraniums I need to split. Any use?' I was conscious of making small talk and getting minimal responses. He stared into his wine as I tried to think of something else to say. He and Patricia had no children, so there was no mutual conversation there. I could ask about how things were at the *Mail* ... where had they been on holiday ... ?

'You don't know why I'm here, do you?'

I picked up the flour-shaker. 'I assume to see Tom.'

'I told you I knew he was at work. That's why I'm here.'

'Oh.' Mystified, I put the shaker down. The thought suddenly occurred that he might ... No, his behaviour was all wrong if he was planning a pass. 'What is it?'

He looked uncomfortable. 'You don't know?'

'Know what?'

He took a rather large mouthful of wine. 'Sorry, Katrina, there's no way of leading up to this ... Tom and Patricia are having an affair.'

'Oh.' Even now I can't analyse my immediate reaction. It was some combination of dismay, fear, instant hatred ... The one thing I didn't feel was disbelief. I blinked rapidly and left flour on my face as I urgently wiped away tears I didn't want him to see. 'Could you pass me the rolling pin? Top drawer. I forgot to get it out, I ... For God's sake don't come near me!'

He stopped in mid-stride. 'I thought you knew.'

'Why should I?' I gulped and sniffed, wiping my face again. 'I don't get out, I don't know what's happening . . . How long have you known?'

'Patricia admitted it six months ago. She said you didn't know at the time and I felt it best to try to leave you out of it because of Stephanie while we tried to sort it out. I'm afraid that makes me sound pious.'

'No, it was considerate . . . Six months ago. When I was pregnant.'

'That was another reason I didn't want to say anything.'

'So why are you doing it now?' I became conscious of my hands and began to pull sticky fragments of pastry off them.

'You haven't got time for the full story,' Phil said. 'After I found out, I told Patricia she had to end it with Tom so we could try to sort out our mess. She said she would, but she didn't. I began to feel bad because I was cheating you as well in a way by not saying anything. We've had endless rows and last night I said I'd had enough.'

'They were together last night?'

'Yes. Patricia told me it was over, but I didn't believe her. I left the office deliberately early and saw him driving away from the house.'

'He said he was at the rugby club. He's been there a lot lately.'

'Useful excuse.' Phil commented. 'Anyway, I've just played hell with Patricia and told her I'd see you on the way to the lawyer's.'

'Are you going to name Tom?'

'No. What's the point? It won't make me feel any better to do any more damage to your marriage.'

I managed a thin smile. 'You're sounding rather noble, Phil.'

'I know. It's not like me, but we can act differently in extreme circumstances. I'll spare you the details because they make me look a prat, but I've ballsed up my marriage. I'm sorry it's spilt over.'

'It's not your fault. But what made you think I knew?'

'Patricia said she met you in the High Street a few weeks ago and – I don't know – there was something about the way you spoke to her that made her think you did.'

55

'I was probably just feeling tired. Had I known, I'd have hit her.' I held my glass out. 'Can you pour me another one, please?'

'You're taking this very calmly,' he remarked

'Only on the surface. Look, Phil, I need to think about this. Come and see me again – you know when Tom is at the— hell, you have to work with him! I hadn't thought of that.'

'That's no problem now, I moved desks. Anyway, I'm leaving the *Mail* next month and joining the *Mirror*.' He finished his wine. 'However, I'll go and talk to the lawyer. No kids and no desire to save it, it needn't be too heavy.'

I closed the front door behind him, rested my forehead on the wood for a moment, then turned to find a movable object. Satisfyingly, the nearest thing was a Staffordshire figure on the hall table that had belonged to Tom's parents. As it shattered against the wall, I screamed 'You fucking bastard!', then raced upstairs, dragged all his suits and shirts out of the wardrobe then went into the garden and threw them on the compost heap. I wanted to set fire to them, but there wasn't any petrol to start it with.

Having burnt off the worst of my rage, I went back inside to go through my address book. I needed somewhere I could take Stephanie. Now. There were at least three options and I chose Amanda, who'd been one of my bridesmaids – and had, interestingly, never liked Tom. She'd married a farmer in Bedfordshire, little more than two hours' drive away, and they had a large house to which I had a standing invitation. When I rang her, she took it in her level-headed stride.

'He's a bigger shit than I thought. Of course you can come here. Long as you want . . . You're OK to drive?'

'I'll take care.' I checked my watch. 'Stephanie comes out of nursery in an hour. I'll just pack essentials and come back for the rest later. We should be there between six and seven. Thank you.'

'I'll tell Roy to slaughter the fatted calf.'

I momentarily thought about leaving a note, but then decided letting Tom panic would be better. Stephanie was surprised but excited, and talked about the animals as we drove up the A1.

When I pulled into the yard, she scrambled out and ran off to where Amanda's children were feeding the chickens. Amanda appeared at the door and I could see she had a glass in her hand.

'For medicinal purposes,' she said as I reached her. 'Scotch and water. Good for the heart.'

She'd become fatter, contented, rustic. Her hands were a disaster area and her hair looked as if she hadn't paid it the slightest attention since she had pulled it into a hasty ponytail that morning. But she was as warm and comforting as a deep bed.

'I told you so, and I'm now telling you I told you so. I'm allowed that. Now come and perch on the Aga while I finish cooking and tell me what you're going to do with the rest of your life.'

In certain circumstances, the one thing a woman needs is the right sort of another woman.

It crossed my mind that night – my rather woozy mind by the time Amanda and Roy had refilled my glass several times - that Tom might contact the police, but I was too indifferent and hostile to ring him. In fact, Patricia called him at the office after Phil got back, so he could work out why I wasn't at home and just had to sweat it out. We stayed in Bedfordshire for more than a week, Amanda supplementing my hastily packed wardrobe with clothes she swore she'd get back to the right size for one day. I went for long walks across the fields while Stephanie played around the farm under Amanda's mother hen eye. I became curiously aware of myself, that I felt no need to cry, that I could detach myself and look back at so many things that had happened, critical of my own failures, my own complicity in becoming less than what I was entitled to be. I'd been a good mother, a stupid wife and a flaky individual. Either I stopped that right now or disappeared into the hole I'd helped to dig. I articulated emerging thoughts to Amanda and she nodded in a 'You're getting there, dummy' sort of way.

I timed our return for when I knew Tom would be at work, and took great satisfaction in seeing the frozen meal packets filling the waste bin. I was amazed at how untidy a house could become in such a short time, but it made me feel better to recognize that he obviously couldn't manage without a woman trailing around in his wake. When I went to bed – I changed the sheets – I put a note reading, 'We're back. You're in the spare room' on the door before locking it. Around three o'clock I heard him trying the handle, but rolled over and went back to sleep.

There was no sign of him in the morning as I got Stephanie ready, but he was up by the time I returned from the nursery run with some overdue shopping. He hadn't shaved and was wearing a shirt that needed washing.

'Good morning,' I said cheerfully. 'You look like shit.' I dumped three carrier bags on the table. 'But, of course, you are one.'

'Where've you been?'

'Away. With people I like. Talking, thinking a lot. Remembering what it's like to be something called happy.'

He grunted. 'OK, get it over with. I'm not going to make a fight of it.'

'Too right,' I told him. 'And getting it over with is going to take a bit of time. First thing is, I want you out of here.'

'What do you mean? This is my home.'

'You don't have a home, Tom. You have this house and you've had me as the doormat wife to look after it for you. Not any more. Go and shack up with Patricia or whatever other bit you've got lined up on the side. I'll find a lawyer to sort out the maintenance.'

'What about Stephanie?'

'If you want access, I'll go along with anything reasonable. I don't want you as a bloody husband, but you are still her father. She'll see through you eventually.'

He picked at a loose cotton on his cuff. 'I've had things to think about as well.'

'I bet you have, but don't waste my time.'

'There's something you don't know.'

I began unloading the shopping to emphasize my indifference.

Suddenly he was as transparent as glass, inadequate, selfish, amoral, some perverse distortion of the man I thought I'd married.

'I've been given the push at the *Mail*. There's a new guy come in and . . . Come on, you know what happens.'

'My heart bleeds.'

'For Christ's sake, I've been with them twenty years!'

'It's the ten you've been with me that I'm sorry about. Anyway, you can find a new job and somewhere else to live at the same time. Sorry if it gets in the way of your screwing around.'

'You can't just throw me out.' I caught the note of uncertain aggression.

'I probably can. I've been talking to a lawyer friend of Amanda's – that's where I was, incidentally. He said a court would almost certainly favour me keeping the house for Stephanie's sake. Try to think with something other than your prick for a change. It'll be easier all round if you just get out.'

Oh, he argued, protested, did the I-know-I-don't-deserve-anything-better-but routine, tried moral blackmail, but he only made himself more contemptible. He was an irritation, getting in the way of plans I now had. Finally, I simply said I was taking Stephanie to visit my parents and I expected him to be gone by the time I came back. I instructed a solicitor to write him a letter spelling out my terms and that if he didn't accept them I'd see him in court. It finally dawned on him that he was dealing with a different person, which was the whole point. If I'd had a reasonably normal marriage to even a husband who eventually became a habit, I'd probably still be with him, looking forward to the grandchildren and a cruise on the *QEII* when we retired. For all the grief he caused me, Tom changed me and I changed my life.

London and Cornwall

Following Hamilton into the editor's office, Miranda Webb felt instantly uncomfortable. Kendall's angry 'Get in here!' on her internal phone seconds earlier had startled her; normally he never raised his voice. Now she could see he was furious, the whiplash rage that only very rarely erupted out of his passive control.

'Shut the door!' he snapped. 'The sodding *ST* are asking about Katrina.'

'What?' Webb sounded appalled. 'How do they know?'

'Someone must have told them,' Hamilton said drily. 'It's called a tip-off.'

'But only the three of us know.'

'Well, it wasn't me and it certainly wasn't Malcolm . . . which leaves you.'

'Butt out, Steve! I've not told anyone.'

'But someone knows, which means . . .' Hamilton paused, then shook his head. 'No. Not even you could have been so dumb as to send a message about this.'

'Only the one to . . .' Webb realized as she saw Hamilton's eyes narrow, then turned to Kendall. 'Only the one to you.'

'Oh, well done.' Hamilton sounded resigned.

'When did you send it?' Kendall's voice matched the contempt of Hamilton's look.

'About an hour ago. Jackie was in here with you and I didn't want to . . . Haven't you read it?'

'I haven't looked at my screen for . . .' Kendall turned to his terminal; the warning TO AVOID LOG OFF PRESS A KEY was flashing in the header field. He hit one at random and MESSAGE PENDING appeared. There were five of them, the third from Webb:

Channel Four don't know where Katrina might be and I can't find anyone who's seen her since last Friday. I've left another message on the answerphone at the cottage, but this is getting serious. Have you had any luck?

'Jesus Christ!' Academically, he deleted it. 'And someone hacked in.'

'Who?' Webb was conscious of the question's futility the moment she asked it.

'Take your pick. And they'll have done it so we can't trace them. Not that it makes any difference. For fuck's sake, Miranda! I sometimes think the message system in this place has got more readers than the bloody paper.'

'Reads better most of the time,' Hamilton murmured.

Webb scratched her ear, an instinctive childhood reaction to criticism that remained in the thirty-year-old woman who resented being in the wrong to the degree that she would rarely admit it. She was not going to apologize with Hamilton in the room.

'So what do we do?'

'I tried putting the *ST* off by saying Katrina's ill, but they're not buying it. You get out there and think damage limitation. Steve and I'll handle this from now on.'

Webb was about to argue; as features editor Katrina Darcy's absence was her business. But Kendall and Hamilton were already ignoring her. Embarrassed and angry, she walked out.

'Who've you sent to the cottage, Steve?'

'Freelance in Plymouth. He reckons at least an hour and a half to Penzance, then he's got to find the place. I've given him the address, but it may take him a while.'

'Let me know as soon as you hear anything.' Kendall sat back in his chair. 'So who's going to be on to us next?'

'We've got two ex-Wapping people here for starters,' Hamilton reminded him. 'So expect the *Sun* and the *Screws of the World*. And wait till the *Mail* gets hold of it. They've never forgiven her for turning them down.'

'Are they going to be that interested?'

'You know they are. She's not just another journalist. She's got her own TV show and writes sexy books. It's manna from

61

heaven in August.' Hamilton hesitated. 'And how many people know about you and Katrina?'

Kendall shook his head. 'They can't rake that up.'

'You mean you don't want them to – but they probably will. Virtually everybody knows about it in this office. It was one of the first things I was told when I arrived.'

Kendall sighed. 'Jesus. It ended years ago.'

'But you're both still here, and now she's a star.'

'That's because she's bloody good. It's nothing to do with anything else.'

'Try telling that to the *Screws*.'

Kendall gazed through the window at the Houses of Parliament down river on the opposite bank of the Thames, reluctantly accepting the inevitable. Katrina Darcy disappearing had news value and the imperative of getting the details into print would mean that private relationships would not remain private. He remembered how grateful Carol had been – how grateful he had been – when he had denied everything so convincingly that she had believed him. In some ways, she would hate him more for having lied than for being unfaithful; admission could heal, untruth festered. Of course, Katrina had been the one who had made the first move . . . No, that was betrayal by self-deception.

'And how do you want me to handle this?' Hamilton added.

'We don't know what the story is.'

'Yes, we do. She's vanished. We just don't know how strong it is. Whatever the others do, Charlie'll want our version to be better. We'll have to start working on it now.' He waited while Kendall remained silent.

'All right,' he said finally. 'But nothing about me and Katrina is to appear in this paper. That's absolute, Steve, so don't give me a fight.'

'And if the others use it?'

'I'll worry about that . . . and you handle our piece yourself. Catchline it something obscure and work in a queue called Eagle – then forget I've told you about it. The name's changed every week anyway and even the hackers haven't found it yet. I'll read

62

it while you're writing and if I come up with anything I'll let you know.'

'OK.' Hamilton's agreement was equivocal. 'Is there anything you haven't told me? Off the record?'

Kendall shook his head. 'No. I don't know where she is or why the hell she isn't here.'

'Then why are you so worried?'

'No comment.' Kendall grinned sourly. 'And don't quote me on that.'

Hamilton turned to leave. 'Oh, I want to go through her desk. I might find something that helps.'

'Like what? She always locks the drawers anyway.'

'They're not difficult to force.'

'I'm not happy about that, Steve.'

'I thought you wanted to find her.'

Kendall stared at him. 'All right, but I'll do it. I'll check if security have spare keys. If I find anything relevant I'll tell you.'

'How will you know what's relevant?'

'I'll decide that.'

Wearing full evening dress, the *Sunday Times* executive editor was putting on a maroon velvet bow tie when Harvey entered his office.

'Make it quick, Richard.'

'We may have a good Katrina Darcy piece. She hasn't turned up at the *Register* and no one can find her.'

'There could be a reason.'

'Yes, but I've spoken to Malcolm Kendall. He tried to cover it by saying she's ill, but our contact read a message the features editor sent him. They're wetting their pants.'

The tie appeared satisfactory. 'So what are we doing?'

'Geoff called Ray Morgan. He and Darcy had a thing going a while back.'

'So I heard. What does he say?'

'Nothing. Hasn't seen her for months.'

'Any problems over the break-up?'

Harvey shrugged dismissively. 'It was only recreational screwing and the novelty wore off. Katrina Darcy's not going to start falling in love with run-of-the-mill reporters.'

'Particularly when they're a lot younger than she is. What else?'

'Penny's at Darcy's flat to do some door-stepping and we're ringing round anyone who knows her.'

'That'll take a while. What do you think's happened?'

'No idea. But when I was on the *Register* I was told that she'd never missed a deadline, not even when she had gastric fever and a temperature of a hundred and two. She can be a pain in the brain, but she's a good operator.'

'Anybody else on to it?'

'If they're not now, they soon will be.'

'True. All right, let me know what you've got in the morning. If Kendall's still being evasive, I'll talk to him. He won't try bullshitting me. Could be a good piece if it stands up.'

'Where's the dinner?'

'Carlton Club with the Home Secretary, chairman of the party and dear Jeffrey, with a fat exclusive for dessert.' He gave his appearance a final check on the wall mirror. 'They want to keep us onside.'

Buzzing frenziedly, a bluebottle passed through the open window and zig-zagged about the room, locating the source of blood that scented the warm evening air. It landed on the carpet and sucked the fibres for a moment before crawling across the dark stain until it reached the woman's cheek where the meal was fresh, then drank in the silence as she died.

Tuesday Evening

It's strange how tiny details and obscure names I thought I'd forgotten come back. If I could remember every one of them, the cast of *The Katrina Darcy Story* would run into the low thousands, most of them bit players. How many envy me, the way people convince themselves that someone else's life is more exciting, complete and happier than their own? Quite a lot, probably, because I have the brittle charisma of being famous. Media success is like showbusiness; living their humdrum lives, people think that Fame makes those who possess it different. Russell Harty used to recall being recognized by two women while he was shopping and hearing one of them say, 'Fancy him buying underpants,' as though television chat show hosts live in some exotic, rarefied world where reality doesn't intrude.

Anyway, one day's hard writing has covered first passion and failed marriage, despite time wasted gazing out of the window; it's been clear enough to see the Lizard, now dissolved in the shimmer of sunset. I bought the cottage – actually two knocked together and modernized – with the advance for *The Leopardess*. It's the genuine article, grey granite and slate, original black Cornish range (for decoration only; the heating is slimline radiators), plastered walls and exposed varnished floorboards. I chose Cornwall because this was childhood holiday country and it still holds a sense of innocence I would never find in London. Now I'm going to the pub for fish pie and a pint (what would they think in Bibendum?)

It's turned eleven o'clock and it's too late for any television news, but there's nothing on Ceefax or Oracle; it's unlikely anyone would have discovered anything so soon anyway. I didn't turn on

65

the answerphone, but there's already a fax from Miranda: 'No reply at the flat. Are you in Cornwall? Call me.' She won't start to panic until Friday.

I've become an honorary local in the Miner's Hammer (generous donations to the lifeboat fund and the pub crawl for handicapped children helped). Maggie Trevarthick told me about her grandchildren again; Ted had been on his weekly fishing trip and promised to bring some mackerel to the cottage tomorrow; Judy behind the bar showed off her engagement ring; Sid's still not finished that conservatory – which everyone calls his lean-to – for Betty; dear Stan died three months ago, keeling over from a final heart attack after a good last evening with them all, ceasing almost upon the midnight, please God with no pain. I've never appreciated their undemanding friendship as much as I did tonight. Puffed up by bylines, regular columns, on first-name terms with the great and the good, journalists delude themselves that they're important; in the saloon bar of the Hammer I'm just a person they accept and like.

I have no monopoly on tragedy, of course. There was a reporter I knew as a trainee, ambitious, great company, level-headed; I last met him at his wedding, by which time he was climbing the ladder on a provincial evening. Their Christmas card a few years later was a photograph of them with flaxen-haired sons and the message 'Call in if you're ever up here. Pauline and I often talk about you.' Then I was told they'd found his body floating in the Humber. And about a year ago I was reading the PA tapes when I spotted a name I remembered from the *Mail* in Manchester. He'd been an innocent, the type you wanted to mother, obsessed with football; he made it to sports editor on one of the nationals, which must have been his dream. Now he was being jailed for his part in a massive insurance fraud. Or Sara, who had a flat opposite us in Barnet, as sparkling as she was gorgeous, daughter of a history don and engaged to a solicitor. We lost touch for years, then I learnt that she'd died, riddled with heroin and God knows what else, in Johannesburg. When I knew them they were undamaged, golden lads and girls. How did life twist and corrode them, hurt them with its truths

66

as painfully as its lies? While so many others made peace treaties with treacheries, what broke them? What broke me? Perhaps that's what I'm trying to work out.

It's deeply quiet, only the soft sound of the sea, and outside I know it's totally dark; the nearest house is quarter of a mile away. I've been crying. Not violently, but tears that flow easily and unprompted from the eyes and the heart. It's a comforting misery, a tender bleeding that brings relief.

ANTHONY

He's standing by the Serpentine, leaning on a stick, incredibly elegant in powder-blue shirt and grey slacks, straw Panama tilted just so. The operation which arrested the cancer has left him looking agonizingly frail, but that wonderful enthusiasm for life is still there. It was the day he told me he'd cancelled the order for a designer shroud trimmed with Honiton lace. I'd cried more at the thought of losing him than I would have done over the actual death of almost anyone else I know. The doctors warned him that the cancer could return one day, but as far as I'm concerned that's not allowed.

Still tender at the edges – skin-shedding is a traumatic process – I began to tackle the realities of new attitudes. Tom had landed a job on *The Times* and agreed to pay what I demanded for Stephanie's support; he had found a flat somewhere in Deptford, not the ideal place for my daughter to spend weekends, but it was only once a month. I furnished the main bedroom as a self-contained flat and found a lodger, carefully selecting a girl from the police college at Hendon, which seemed safe; her rent paid for a child-minder and I was free to polish some rusty journalism. Actually, I'd always been better at it than my role as wife and mother had allowed me to be, and it was the only talent I had. Finding ingenious ways to deal with school holidays and Stephanie's mercifully rare childhood illnesses, I made the phone calls, wrote the letters and chased up lost contacts.

Work was thin at first, but I got some freelance shifts with the Press Association and a couple of small agencies, one of which I walked out of after the boss started speculating how much of my bra contained the genuine product. Cracks like that passed for wit in his brain, and he obviously thought that separated women were as obsessed with sex as he was. There was the occasional late shift as holiday cover on nationals that summer (Stephanie slept overnight with supportive friends), which got my foot in the door again, but money was hideously tight. I wrote features and submitted them everywhere, achieving a strike rate of about one in ten, and only determination kept me going. I'd let myself down too often.

Then, one evening in August, while waiting to be given something to do on the *Daily Telegraph*, I spotted a small run-on ad among the displays in *UK Press Gazette*: 'Civilized journalist seeks researcher for book on vaguely interesting subject (details on application). Ridiculously good pay by starvation standards. Based south of the Thames, so not for transpontine snobs.' The phrasing amused me, and there was a telephone number.

'Toby Lawrence.'

'I'm sorry it's late, but I'm calling about the job in *UKPG*. For the researcher.'

'Oh, you want Anthony. Hang on.'

There was a short silence, then one of the loveliest male voices I've ever heard came on.

'Good evening. Anthony Delamere. How nice of you to call. You're interested in the job? Tell me about yourself.'

'Oh.' He caught me unprepared. 'Well, I'm a journalist – Fleet Street – and I've worked for . . .' I waffled on, decorating where necessary, until he interrupted.

'And what are you doing at the moment?'

'Freelancing. I'm calling from the *Telegraph*.'

'Your secret is safe with me. Are you free tomorrow? Good. All you have to do is find six Cromer Road, Clapham. Will eleven o'clock be all right?'

'Fine. Thank you.'

'Thank you. I'm so sorry, I didn't write your name down.'

'Katrina Darcy.'

'Katrina? Not quite the shrew, then. I look forward to putting a face to the voice. *A demain.*'

*

Cromer Road was just off the Common, two rows of solid Edwardiana with token front gardens but long narrow stretches at the back. Number six had a massed rose bush garden and the bell was a large brass acorn on a wire; I pulled it and heard a muffled chime. Moments later the door was opened by a man of about thirty, black haired and wide shouldered, wearing shorts and a National Theatre T-shirt with splodges of paint as though he had wiped brushes on it.

'Katrina Darcy?'

'Yes. Anthony Delamere?'

'No. Toby Lawrence. I answered the phone when you rang. Anthony's in the garden.'

As I followed him along the hall, I saw that the front room was an artist's studio, bare floorboards and white walls, two easels, table covered with paints, brushes and assorted bottles, blown-up photographs pinned on a large corkboard as if for studying while someone was working. We went through the kitchen and I retained an impression of stripped Victorian pine, orange Le Creuset, bunches of garlic, old-fashioned cast iron scales, posters of France and Italy and dozens of cookery books as Toby led me down four steps into the garden. Beyond a paved patio, wooden fences sandwiched a long lawn hemmed with flower beds ending in a small greenhouse and a vegetable plot. Halfway down, Anthony was sitting on a deck chair beneath a sun umbrella, reading an advance proof of an Iris Murdoch novel, a drink decorated with sprigs of mint on the table beside him. He was wearing a straw-coloured Sea Island cotton shirt, lightweight linen trousers and cream canvas shoes; all of them looked brand new.

'How very punctual you are,' he said as we reached him and he stood up. 'I approve of that. Coffee?'

'Thank you.'

'Can you, Toby? Or would it shatter the muse?'

'I've nearly finished. Fifteen minutes.'

Anthony smiled and offered me the chair beside his as Toby returned to the house. He had an ability, which I was to see so often over the years, of making even a complete stranger feel as

70

though they were the most important person in the world to him. And it wasn't an act; he genuinely delighted in meeting people and could find something that amused or interested him in virtually anyone. As he told me, he collected human beings.

He was thirty-eight when we first met, a slight, bantamweight figure, although his bare forearms were moulded with muscle; I discovered later that only professionals could beat him at squash. His hair was burnt orange, short and parted just off centre and his skin had a natural sandy tint, as though he was permanently tanned. His lips were thin and his nose finely pointed; his face reminded me of a Renaissance legate, perceptive, subtle and much more intelligent than his masters. And that voice ... I could have listened enchanted as he read *Yellow Pages*.

'Now I know something about you, but I rather think that the name Anthony Delamere doesn't mean much to you, does it?' he said.

I shook my head. 'I'm afraid not.'

'No apologies, you're in a considerable majority. I write for the *Sunday Register*, which uses long words and therefore doesn't attract a mass audience.'

'I've read the *Register*, but I don't think I've seen anything you've written. I'm sorry.'

'Well, unless you're into art or food and drink – and latterly, God save the mark, Style with a capital S, whatever that means – you won't have done. I'm given extravagantly designed spreads in the colour section, which are a bit off-putting if the subject doesn't interest you.'

'Oh ... I think I've seen some of them.'

'Don't be obsequious. It doesn't become you. You're a reporter and probably think that features are self-indulgent trash – which a great many of them are. However, the job. I've been commissioned to write a tome on provincial British cookery, all tripe and onions or Scotch pancakes. It's going to be one of those dire coffee table books for Christmas so it's got deadlines last week, but the money they're paying me is irrefusably excessive. What I need is someone to go to the British Library or wherever, copy out forgotten recipes and beg, borrow or steal ancient illustrations. Then I'll pour the gilded prose over it. I'm sorry I can't make it sound exciting, but the money's quite good.'

'How good?'

'A thousand pounds for the month. Half in advance and the rest when you've delivered everything. You should still have time to do other work as well.'

Five hundred pounds was very tempting at that moment; the gas board's patience was running out. 'Fine, if you're sure I can do it. I'm a very basic cook.'

'You won't have to cook anything. I'm the one who'll test drive them and hope I survive the experience. Your job is to ferret out the information for me.'

'If you think I can do it . . .'

For the first time, I saw him make the idiosyncratic gesture and comment that became so familiar; both hands made three rapid circles in the air, then stopped with the fingers spread upwards.

'Of course. And it will be so.' He smiled. 'Please accept.'

It was impossible not to be charmed by him. 'All right. Thank you. When do I start?'

'What's your availability? I'm sorry, that's theatre jargon. As soon as you can.'

'I've got a couple of shifts at the Press Association on Friday and Saturday, but I'm clear after that.'

'Monday, then. I'll give you an official letter to show the library you're *bona fide* before you go . . . and, of course, your cheque.' I was sitting with my back to the house and he suddenly glanced past me. 'You haven't been cutting corners, have you, Toby? This is suspiciously less than fifteen minutes.'

'It's fine.' Toby arrived with fresh coffee, fine, gold-rimmed china mugs with anemones printed on them, cream, multi-coloured sugar crystals, a glass dish of artificial sweeteners and bourbon biscuits.

'Good, you're joining us,' Anthony said, then turned to me again. 'Toby designs theatrical sets and has been slaving away for an operatic version of *Titus Groan* at . . . Where is it? Somewhere disastrous.'

'Watford Palace,' Toby said.

'I shan't be going. It's north of Hampstead, and I don't know what shade of woad is fashionable this year. Where are you from, Katrina? Originally.'

'Bramhall. It's near Manchester.'

He looked appalled. '*Quel embarras!* I withdraw the woad comment unreservedly.'

'No, you don't,' Toby said. 'You were incredibly rude about Welwyn Garden City when you met me.'

'That's different.' He turned back to me. 'I first heard of that place on the side of a breakfast cereal packet made by the Welgar Shredded Wheat Company. For years I thought it was in Wales. It was all tied up with Welco ice cream, which I remembered from holidays in Prestatyn. It wasn't my idea, I had an aunt who lived there. Anyway, Welco was short for Welsh coast, and in my childish mind Welgar and Welco . . .'

I'm making it sound as though all he did was talk about himself, which is so wrong. There were to be nights in my life when Anthony was the only light in them; I've never known anyone who loved his friends so much and asked so little from them in return.

The work was ideal, research during the day and typing up my notes at home in the evening after I'd put Stephanie to bed. Over the month, I met Anthony about half a dozen times when I delivered batches of recipes. Each time he went through them scrupulously, wanting to know precise sources, occasionally irritated and sending me back to check when I was not sure. Once he instantly spotted where I'd made an error in copying out the ingredients, even though he'd never heard of the dish, and for the first time I experienced that savage lash of impatience with anything less than meticulous care; I didn't make any mistakes after that. But he congratulated me as well, pleased when I presented him with something bizarre or found a print of Elizabethan cooks stuffing peacocks. And there was always more than politeness to our conversations; I learnt very little about him, but he extracted a great deal of information about me.

73

'It must be difficult having a job and looking after your daughter,' he said one day.

'Oh, I'm one of London's legion of coping women.' I grinned sourly. 'Wives consider us risky guests at dinner parties – not that I have the energy for them. There are too many others out there hunting the elusive unattached man.'

'And are you in the hunt?'

'Not really. I thought I'd miss the sex, but that doesn't matter. I'd just like to be hugged regularly and not always have to pour my own gin and tonic in the evening. But that's the price of being independent. My choice.'

'Well, we've nearly finished – and you will be invited to dinner. Here. Just the three of us to celebrate – unless you'd like to bring Stephanie. She can snuggle down in the spare room until you go home.'

'Thank you, but it's all right about Stephanie. She's starting to enjoy sleeping at friends' houses.'

'Very resilient, children,' he said. 'And she must get something from you as well. Let's say in a couple of weeks. I can't promise hugs, but Toby will pour your drink.'

The meal was some of the dishes I had found, but each subtly enhanced with herbs, wine or exotic fruits. He apologetically served elderberry wine as an aperitif, Somerset cider drawn from a barrel with the main course and sloe gin with the coffee.

'I know it's repulsive, but wine of the country, wine of the country,' he told us. 'Just be grateful I've not chosen something meant to be accompanied by what I understand is called New-castle Brown.'

Afterwards we sat on the patio in late September twilight and Toby played his oboe while Anthony sang Cole Porter, Gershwin and Jerome Kern ballads in his sweet baritone. They were lovely, civilized men. As I was leaving, Anthony walked with me to my car and asked what I was going to do next.

'I'm not sure,' I told him. 'There's a chance of some shifts on the *Mirror* working holiday cover, but that's about it.'

'Oh, we can't have that,' he said. 'I'll be in the *Register* on

74

Thursday. Come for lunch and I'll introduce you to the news editor.'

'The *Register*?' A staff job, even a contract, with one of the nationals was the permanent fantasy. 'Do you mean it?'

'I wouldn't have said so if I didn't. There's a vacancy, nothing special, but you could handle it.'

'Thank you, but what are they like about women with small children?'

'I wouldn't know personally, but the news editor's in a similar position, so she ought to be sympathetic.'

'She?' A woman in such a job was almost unheard of in those days.

'Didn't you know that? The *Register* is very avant-garde. We even regard the *Guardian* as a touch suspect on the feminist front.'

I laughed. 'All right. Thank you, but do you really think I'm good enough or are you just being nice to me?'

'I'm being nice to you. I'm like that,' he said. 'And I don't *think* you're good enough, I know you are.'

I felt more surprised than complimented. Anthony wasn't flattering me because there was obviously no point, and all I'd shown I could do was some run-of-the-mill research.

'What makes you say that?' I asked.

'Instinct,' he replied. 'It can't be explained, but you'll have it one day. You'll know that certain people are going to make it. It'll help you to spot the ones who are out to get you.'

'And I'm like that?'

'Don't play the innocent, Katrina.' He hesitated. 'I can speak frankly, mmm?'

'Of course.'

'Very well. Whether you realize it or not, you've got a streak in you that's as hard as nails. The legacy of your marriage, I rather think. You know what you want and nobody's going to stop you getting it.'

'God, you make me sound like a bitch.'

'Your word, not mine. But it's a business where bitches succeed.'

75

For a moment I just looked at him in the glow of the streetlamp; there had been no regret in his voice, just quiet statements of fact.

'And what do I want?' I asked.

'Total independence – the best for Stephanie, of course – respect, envy, perhaps even a touch of fear. You want to be . . . a name.'

'Aren't you worried that if they give me a job I might be out to get you?' I asked.

Now he laughed. 'Oh, I'm triple ring-fenced. Anyway, even the hardest bitches need to keep some people on their side.' He kissed my cheek. 'I'll see you on Thursday, about twelve-thirty. Ask for me at reception. Drive carefully.'

As I drove home I was partly elated, partly shaken. Had what happened with Tom really hardened me so much? I had regarded it as a case of essential survival, an almost animal determination to protect my child. But I realized that simple survival had become insufficient, too close to slipping back to dependence on another husband one day. I wanted total in-your-face freedom, so that all the decisions in my life rested with me. I'd been slapped very hard and felt revulsion at what I'd allowed myself to become. I'd have recognized it myself eventually, but Anthony had short-circuited the process – and his confidence in my abilities was a tremendous accelerator. It crossed my mind that it was a pity I would only ever be able to have him as a friend, but he was to prove more precious – and frequently more bitingly honest – as that than any of my lovers.

London

Lying to the press is stupid; telling them more of the truth than is unavoidable is unwise. Reporters try to coax out half-admissions that become embarrassing quotes, expose contradictions, move away from an angle as though they've lost interest then switch back to it without warning. Having spent his career mastering one half of the game, Malcolm Kendall was playing it in reverse with a *Daily Mail* reporter as the *Express* waited on another line.

'I can't tell you anything, because we don't know. She was expected in today but she didn't arrive. That's the situation.'

'And you're worried?'

'Of course we are. Wouldn't you be if it was one of your people?'

'I expect so. What are you doing?'

'Trying to find her. What do you think we're doing?'

'Where've you tried?'

'Everywhere we can think of.'

'Have you been in touch with the police?'

'Not at this stage. They can't do anything more than we're doing, and we've got no reason to think there isn't some explanation.'

'Can you think of one?'

'Such as what?'

'I don't know . . . Family problems?'

'That's possible. She's got a private life like anyone else. Perhaps there's been an emergency.'

Kendall had half expected the pause; earlier questions about Katrina's private life had stopped, but he knew they would start again and he was saving time by offering an obvious opening to see if the *Mail* had anything beyond rumour to go on.

'This private life, Mr Kendall. Are you involved in that?'

'What do you mean?'

'You and Miss Darcy have known each other a long time.'

'We've worked together for a long time.' He emphasized the verb.

'And that's all there is to it?'

'What else could there be?'

The probing stopped. 'Mr Kendall, we've been offered some photographs by a freelance. He says they're of you and Miss Darcy together at a hotel during a Liberal party conference.'

Kendall relaxed; if that was all they had, it could be handled. 'So? As far as I remember, she was doing a feature on political wives and I try to attend all the party conferences.'

'Yes, but these pictures are said to be – I haven't actually seen them yet – but you appear to be . . . very friendly.' A nicely coded word, open to any interpretation someone wanted to put on it.

It must have been one evening in the bar of the hotel where most of the press were staying; Kendall had vague recollections of flash bulbs. That happened so much no one took any notice. What had the *Mail* got? He and Katrina laughing together, perhaps even touching? It would have been meaningless, but a subtly worded caption could suggest something more: *Party time: Katrina Darcy and her boss discussing political affairs at an Eastbourne hotel.*

'If they're some that I've seen, we were part of a crowd. Your lawyer's not going to be happy if you try cropping everyone else out to back up insinuations that won't stand up.' He could have added 'in court', but it was never wise to threaten to sue.

Another fractional pause suggested the *Mail* were fishing.

'Mr Kendall, I must ask you this. Are you and Miss Darcy lovers?'

'No, we are not.' A simple denial that had the advantage of being strictly true to a question that gave him a reason for refusing to talk further. 'Now I've told you the position and I've got another caller holding. Right?'

'You'll let us know if you find her?'

'Naturally.' Kendall rang off, then beckoned through the window of his office to the news desk secretary.

'Take the call on line eight,' he told her. 'It's the *Express*. All we're confirming is that Katrina is missing, we don't know where she is and we're trying to find her. Apart from that, it's no comment. That goes for anyone else who calls. Tell them that if anything significant happens, I'll release a statement to the Press Association.'

'I've just had a woman from *Today* on, saying she's a personal friend.'

'Does she know where Katrina might be?'

'No. She wanted to know what we knew. I said I couldn't tell her anything.'

'And that's what you say to all of them.'

Hamilton knew that handing over the news desk to his deputy would heighten interest in the office, but it was academic; the story would become as sensational as people wished to make it. He asked the library for any personal cuttings they had on Katrina Darcy, then rang her literary agent, who had not been answering when Webb had called earlier.

'Emma Sullivan.'

'Hi, Steve Hamilton at the *Register*. Do you know where Katrina is?'

'No. Why?'

'She's not turned up today. When did you last see her?'

'About ten days ago, and I've been trying to reach her. There's been a hitch over her American tour. I thought you might be her returning my call.'

'Where've you tried?'

'Usual places. The flat, Cornwall. I rang the office earlier, but someone told me she wasn't in. What's going on?'

'We don't know. She's just disappeared Did you get the impression anything was wrong when you saw her?'

'Far from it. We had lunch in Chinatown and she was telling me . . .' Sullivan paused. 'It was personal, Steve.'

'Could it explain her not turning up?'

'Possibly, but I haven't told you this. All right?'

'Agreed.' Hamilton wrote a question mark on his pad. 'Go on.'

'Do you know about Leonard Drummond?'

'The writer? What about him?'

'He and Katrina've got a thing going.'

'Since when?'

'Long story. She told me she'd had an affair with Leonard ages ago, then they split up. But now they're back together and it's serious. She said he was leaving his wife and they were planning to get married.'

'Married?' It was a line Hamilton would never have expected. 'Who else knows about this?'

'Only Anthony – she tells him everything, of course. Anyway, she mentioned that Leonard was going away about now. Where the hell was it? Wales, I think. She might have gone with him.'

'But she'd have said she was taking time off, not just vanished,' Hamilton argued.

'I know, but it's a big thing with her and Leonard, Steve. She said it was the most important thing in her life.'

'If it's more important than her column, it must be gigantic.' Hamilton still sounded disbelieving. 'Whereabouts in Wales?'

'I can't remember. Sorry.'

'Might his publishers know?'

'Probably, but there'll be no one around this time on a Friday,' Sullivan pointed out. 'And the only other person I can think of asking is his wife. There's a tricky one for you.'

'Where does he live?'

'Harrow. I remember that. He's probably in *Who's Who* or *People of Today*.'

'I'll check. OK, thanks. In the meantime, can you ask around and call me if you come up with anything?'

'Of course. Usual number?'

'No, use this direct line.' Hamilton gave her the extension. 'If I'm not about, ask for Malcolm Kendall. Don't talk to anyone else. This has already been leaked to the *Sunday Times*.'

'Are they doing a piece on it?'

'Is Pavarotti fat? Everybody else will be on to it next. That's why I'm working on a piece for us. We don't know what's happened, but this isn't like her. She could be ill.'

'Bloody ill.' Sullivan was becoming alarmed. 'Have you been to the flat?'

'Security won't let anyone in.'

'What about Stephanie?'

'We can't find her either. We're not sure if she's living with Katrina now. Do you know?'

'I think Katrina told me she'd moved in with a friend in Islington, but I don't know who it is. There are people I could ring on that, but . . . Steve, you're getting me worried now. What about the cottage? No, I've tried there. I just got the answerphone.'

'So did we. We've sent a freelance from Plymouth to check it out. If she has been taken ill, she could have collapsed or something.'

'Oh, Christ. Does he know where it is?'

'I gave him the address.'

'That's not much use, it's seriously remote. Katrina's let me and my boyfriend use it and it took us for ever to find it the first night. Can you contact him?'

'I can try his mobile.'

'Got a pen? Of course you have. When he gets to Penzance he wants the A30 to Land's End and tell him to watch for signs for St Buryan. He goes straight through the village, and after about five miles he'll reach a sharp right bend and a pub called the Miner's Hammer. He wants the lane on his left. He goes through two farmyards – literally – and just after the second there's a tiny turning. We're talking cart track. About a hundred yards further on he'll come to a five-barred gate. It looks like two cottages, but they've been converted into one.'

'Got it.' Hamilton had been writing as rapidly as she spoke. 'Keep in touch.' He called the freelance with the directions, then walked through to Kendall's office.

'Emma Sullivan thinks she might be in Wales,' he said.

'Why the hell should she be there?' Kendall demanded.

'Because Leonard Drummond is.'

Hamilton realized Kendall was as amazed as he had been; Katrina Darcy was known to have a personal resistance to marriage.

'It still doesn't make sense,' Kendall said when he'd finished. 'She wouldn't have just . . . Is Emma certain about this?'

'That's what Katrina told her. You didn't know?'

'She's never mentioned it to me. And Emma doesn't know where in Wales?'

'No, but presumably his wife does. I'm going to call her and say we want him to write a piece for us. When she says he's away, I'll ask for a number where we can contact him.'

'If her husband's leaving her for Katrina, she won't want to talk to us at the moment,' Kendall pointed out.

'I'll have to risk that.'

MALCOLM

The first picture of him is in the news room, taken when I was finishing off a film. He's standing next to Dennis Bruce, who was then editor of the 'Register', and they're both looking at the camera in surprise; I must have called one of their names and took it as they turned. Tie pulled down an inch from unfastened top button, shirt sleeves rolled back to mid-forearm, the inevitable cigarette in one hand, he only needs a green eyeshade to be the caricature journalist. The second is of him sitting in the garden at Barnet. It was a very hot evening, and he's drinking from a can of beer and wearing only a pair of shorts. I took the picture without him expecting it, and he was cross because he said it would show how his hair was thinning at the back. Perhaps it was me who made him vain.

National newspapers make Cuba's economy look as solid as the World Bank; the *Sunday Register* is 137 years old and the last time it staggered into profit they were still insisting that the *Titanic* couldn't sink. For years it was kept alive by wealthy Liberals and not until the sixties was it forced to recognize that the twentieth century was not just a passing humour. Facing bankruptcy and the prospect of being taken over by the Thomson organization – and becoming a token reference temporarily incorporated into the masthead of the *Sunday Times* before burial – it sold its soul to Sir Jack Hepplewhite, a very distant descendant of the furniture maker, whose fortune was based on 'the greatest chain of butchers' shops in t'history of Yorkshire'. He had married the daughter of a Labour peer and it was said that the *Register* docilely following his father-in-law's party line secured Harold Wilson's wafer-thin general election victory in 1964.

Strapped for cash, Hepplewhite sold it in 1970, which turned out to be a remarkably stupid move. Years earlier, for no other reason than that the husband of the chairman's cousin worked for Shell, the paper had made itself a laughing stock by investing in the quixotic belief that there could be retrievable oil under the North Sea; they say that God looks after drunks, little children and journalists, probably because he can't differentiate between them. Its new fortunes enabled it to buy the Sandringham Court group, publishers of specialist glossy magazines which in the eighties were so profitable they could have afforded to print them on banknotes. It is now also a middle-rank player in European cable and satellite television, has bought up three highly successful provincial newspaper groups and owns a national concessionary chain serving pub lunches, causing *Private Eye* to nickname it the *Sunday Roast*. Register plc profits would be very comfortable if it wasn't for the expensive flagship of the Sunday paper.

Its home is Gladstone House, a listed Victorian pile on the outside, totally gutted inside to make it almost practical. From the beginning it felt superior to the grubs of Fleet Street, refusing even to live with them, setting up instead on the south bank of the Thames just up river from Westminster Bridge, from where it could see both the Houses of Parliament and Lambeth Palace; it can now also see the exclusive block of flats where Jeffrey Archer lives.

All this is adjacent to my story, but the *Register* is inextricably bound up in my life; becoming one of its senior columnists has helped to make me famous, even though Anthony was always putting me down.

'Think of the most celebrated names you can imagine,' he would tell me. 'The superstar bylines, great photographers, legendary editors. One day they die and the waters close over them and it's as if they had never been. Newspapers survive, journalists perish.'

He was right, of course; he invariably was.

*

84

Dennis Bruce, who was editor when I joined, was spectacularly useless, a relic of the days when it was considered a job for gentlemen who knew which knife to use and had at least an uncle in *Debrett*. He had surrounded himself with an Oxbridge/ Athenaeum Praetorian guard whose careers depended on his patronage; all of them had wondrous titles, swish company cars and ill-defined responsibilities in inverse proportion to their inflated salaries. But he was an impeccable judge; he never hired anyone whose competence could have threatened him. Whenever money got tight, he imposed a non-replacement policy which only applied to reporters and subs; our usual condition was two chiefs for every Indian. Dennis smiled at everyone who passed him in the building on the grounds that they might be members of his staff, once famously asking a reporter who had been with the paper more than three years how he was settling in. He wrote the first leader each week after discussing it with the chairman of the Conservative Party. (Over the years, the *Register* has supported everyone except the Monster Raving Loonies.)

God knows how Dennis had managed it, but below the sycophantic executives playing at journalism there was genuine talent in the office. Cathy Trent, the news editor, had been one of the best reporters on the *Daily Express* and had a cynical prejudice against university graduates.

'At least you learnt this job properly on a local weekly,' she said when she interviewed me. 'I've got berks here who could write me an essay on the influence of Chaucer but who'd have missed the news angle on the Great Train Robbery.'

'Why do you hire them?' I asked.

She pulled a face. 'Upstairs have introduced a bloody graduate intake policy. They think it adds tone.'

'I didn't go to university.'

'No, thank God. But Anthony says you're a good operator. Are you?'

'I want to be . . . and you know about my daughter?'

'Oh, yes. How old is she?'

'Nearly six.'

85

'The awkward age,' Cathy grinned. 'Although a friend of mine says it lasts until they're twenty and leave home. It needn't be a problem. There's a strong NUJ Chapel here that looks after women members and the management almost passes for intelligent in some areas. They put up with my two, who have an inbuilt genius for falling ill at the worst possible moments. Anyway, fill in the forms and let me know when you can start.'

'Thank you.'

'Thank me with the copy you turn in ... and we'll exchange notes on ways to stay sane.'

Conscious that I was unlikely to get another break like that, I really tried, being carefully polite to everyone, even the subs, biting my lip when Cathy bawled me out – which she felt obliged to do to everyone from time to time *pour encourager les autres*. Dennis metaphorically patted me on the head when someone told him I'd dug out an angle the *Sunday Telegraph* had missed. I also – and this is as good a time as any to confess – missed a cracking story, and mercifully nobody ever found out. It started when Toby told me he'd persuaded Anthony to venture out of town for a day and they'd been to St Paul's Walden in Hertfordshire, the village where the Queen Mother's family had a country home.

'There's an odd thing about that place,' he remarked. 'They always talk about it being where she grew up, or her childhood home, but they never actually say she was born there.'

'Was she?' I asked.

'Everybody assumes so, but why don't they make a big thing of it?'

'You ought to check it out,' Anthony said casually, but he was obviously bored by the subject.

Vaguely interested, I did check as far as ringing the registrar of births in Hitchin, who told me they still had her birth certificate, signed by her father, Lord Glamis, saying his daughter had been born in St Paul's Walden; I could have a copy if I wanted. And that, damn it, is where I let it drop, stupidly never bothering to ask why no one in the village boasted that it was her birthplace. It was 1980 before somebody chased it properly; the Queen Mother had been born in London, and Glamis committed perjury when he signed the certificate, although nobody could understand why. The *Sunday Times* ran it as an anchor piece on the front and everybody followed it up. I kept very quiet; they say that the copytaster on the *Daily Mirror* spiked the Reuter snap on the start of the Hungarian revolution and ended up running a chicken farm.

And apart from that, I was working my little cotton socks off, scouring everywhere I could for ideas; obscure magazines were a marvellous source – journalism cannibalizes other journalism much of the time – and all it needed was to add some human interest angle to dry facts. You'd be amazed at what a dearth of water beetles in Wiltshire can be transformed into with a little ingenuity and a minor botanist who speaks in naturally good quotes. My personal life became better organized and I was able to afford an au pair girl to look after Stephanie. I was aware that I was not the sort of mother I'd hoped to be, but I gave her all the love and attention I could, and she'd adapted remarkably well. Cathy and I exchanged stories of inexplicable temperature yo-yos and our children were often together, with one of us as the minder while the other worked. My confidence was coming back – and I was becoming increasingly impatient.

One day, the sex thing struck me, rather like an irrational craving for chocolate after going a long time without it. I worked out that it was nineteen months, three weeks and four days since the last time, and that had been with Tom while I lay there in a 'I'll just wait till he's finished grunting' mood. I was thirty-three years old and had been living like a nun because there had been much more important things to worry about. I think it was seeing one of the secretaries talking to the religious affairs reporter that started me; their body language indicated the sort of relationship that would have shocked a bishop. To be perfectly candid, I began to feel randy and realized I was out of practice at what to do about it; I'd not had to attract a man for more than ten years.

87

My lifestyle offered limited opportunities. Most of my friends were women – usually single ones – and my social life was zilch. The moment I finished work I was dashing off to be with my daughter while the crowd went to the wine bar, and a night out with grown-ups was unknown. I'd been to the cinema eight times in the previous year, always taking Stephanie to the latest Disney or whatever; a meal out was a Big Mac with a lollipop for clearing my plate and a balloon to take home. I decided that I deserved a personal treat.

Malcolm Kendall was production editor, a position that involved forward planning, editorial budgets, costs, special projects, printing contracts, libel actions – all the hassle that Dennis or one of his cohorts should have been handling. He'd been Cathy's predecessor and the news desk was still his natural home; he would stay late to go through the stories, suggesting contacts we hadn't tried, having the library check something he remembered that could tighten up a piece. Cathy didn't like it, but he saved her skin a few times.

Malcolm knew me in the detached professional way he knew everyone, social drinks in the pub at lunchtime, me nodding when he was explaining how he wanted a piece tackled. He was so easy-going you had to remind yourself that there must be steel underneath for him to have got where he was. From time to time he would wander up to someone's desk and say, very quietly, 'My office, please,' and the rest of us discreetly watched the closed door until a very shaken journalist emerged. He was late forty-something, but only the slight paunch and spreading grey hairs gave it away, and he joked that he had reached the stage of working with journalists who hadn't been born when he began in the business. There were a wife and two children in Leicestershire, but he had a pied-à-terre in town where he stayed from Tuesday to Saturday nights. I know, I should have remembered how much Tom's adultery had hurt me, I should have found someone unattached. But it doesn't always work like that.

In my defence, I didn't overtly make a play for him – unless you count leaving my shirt unfastened a button too far when I walked into his office. He had no reputation, but I began to sense

88

that he was becoming ... intrigued, rather than interested, as though some new and unexpected possibility had appeared. Then I noticed that remarks about his wife and family, which he'd always naturally dropped into casual conversation, had stopped, and he seemed to make a point of joining me at lunch in the canteen when there were plenty of other people he could have sat with. The problem was, it went no further than that; every time I thought he was leading up to the suggestion that we might meet outside the office, he swerved away as though alarmed at where he had found himself.

Then came the time Stephanie was away with a family I knew; they owned a cottage on the Dorset coast where they spent most of the summer holidays, and I was to join them all for just the last two weeks. The sense of release was overwhelming – my life seemed to have been built around my daughter for ever – and I was able to enjoy the most banal pleasures, like going out in the evenings and not worrying about what time I got home, and lying in in the mornings. One Friday night a few of us went to the Swan With Two Necks, the *Register*'s semi-official pub. The crowd built up over a couple of hours, until Malcolm was standing next to me as I sat at the bar. Joining in the jokes and elliptical professional chat with the others, I paid him no special attention, but he'd have been terrified if he'd known how acutely I was aware of him.

'Another of those?' he asked, indicating my glass when it reached his turn to buy the round.

'I shouldn't ...' I said uncertainly. 'But there are too many things we shouldn't do. Thanks.'

And then I was part of the group round the bar again, delicately vulgar, swapping gossip, extravagantly welcoming Anthony when he arrived, enthusiastically agreeing when somebody suggested we should go on for a meal.

'All of us,' I insisted, turning to Malcolm. 'You as well. And you, Anthony. How many of us are there? Two, four, eight ... eleven ... fifteen. Harry, can you call four cabs for us? Thanks.'

As the landlord picked up the phone behind the bar, I'd committed Malcolm without him having a chance to refuse. I sat next to him in the taxi when we left, three of us on the back seat, making physical contact unavoidable.

Anthony took us to an Italian restaurant in Covent Garden where they knew him, which meant we were given the five-star treatment. They put several tables together, the waiters gave all the girls carnations and the owner handed out complimentary house wine. It was one of those spontaneous evenings that clicked, everyone relaxed, endless and increasingly noisy chatter, laughing insults thrown about, pressures of the day washed away in Chianti. I'd manoeuvred it so that I was sitting opposite Malcolm, talking to him no more than anyone else, treating him as though he was just another one of the crowd. It was a warm night and at one point I took hold of the lapels of my blouse and fanned them back and forth; I caught his eyes watching me and smiled at him ambivalently, then turned away again, loudly complaining that they were hogging the bread sticks at the other end of the table.

It was after eleven by the time we finished, dividing the bill, piling money and cheques on the tablecloth. Then we left in random groups, hunting for taxis. Anthony slipped away on his own, and the rest fell into geographically convenient parties, which left Malcolm and me walking down Long Acre alone.

'Where do you have to get to?' he asked.

'Barnet . . . Northern line. You?'

'Uttoxeter Street. It's not far from Euston.' He turned away as he spotted a cab, but it was already hired. 'We could share a taxi.'

'Fine . . . if we can find one.'

'Trafalgar Square'll be best.'

I thought of taking hold of his hand as we walked, but was uncertain of the response. We caught a cab outside the National Gallery, and as it pulled round the square he asked if I had time for a nightcap; he sounded rather engagingly hesitant.

'I don't want you to miss the last train.'

'It's all right. I can get another cab if I do.'

'Good. You can put it on your expenses if necessary.'

He could have sat further away from me, but only by actually going outside the cab. As I watched darkened London slip by, I

90

knew I was not in for instant rape. His flat was very small, a bedsitting room, bathroom and kitchen the size of a telephone kiosk all squeezed into the first floor of a terraced house, but it was well furnished and decorated. He explained how he'd bought it when he first started working in London and kept it on after ... white wine or red?

'Whichever's open ... This is a gorgeous chair.'

'It's one of a pair I picked up at a Sunday street market at Archway. The other's in ... Did you say white or red?'

It was like a Whitehall farce, with him stopping halfway through the sentences that led in the direction of Leicestershire. He poured the drinks, then asked what music I liked. He had jazz, classics, sixties rock ... the Beach Boys. I chose Johnny Mathis with strings and muted horns, the most romantically evocative album on offer. After that he didn't know what to say, except ask about Stephanie, who was frankly the last person on my mind at that moment – and I didn't know how to play it, either. The scenario was obvious, but after so long neither of us could remember either our scripts or our moves, and infidelity was an unexplored country.

'We're not very good at this, are we?' I said finally, when the conversation became totally meaningless.

'I'm sorry?'

'Well, you'll never win prizes for seduction and I've forgotten how to vamp.'

'Oh.' He looked embarrassed. 'I'm not used to this sort of thing.'

'I thought not.' I looked at him sympathetically. 'I can still catch that train.'

'Yes ... perhaps ... I'm sorry, Katrina, this wasn't a good idea. It just seemed so earlier in the evening. No hard feelings?'

I grinned. 'Unfortunately not. And I'd have been a pushover.'

'I'm flattered. You're very attractive. Frankly, I feel rather foolish.'

'It's OK, it's rather endearing. My experience of how husbands behave is somewhat different.' I finished my drink. 'I need to use your loo before I go.'

91

As I shut the door, the frustration hit me. His reluctance made him even more attractive. I'd got so close, and now it was the last train to Barnet, avoiding the drunks. Then Stephanie would be home again and I'd be locked back in the dutiful mother role with the celibacy price tag ... I saw myself in the mirror on the opposite wall; my cheeks were flushed.

I peed, then applied fresh lipstick and gloss, let down my coiled-up hair and shook it loose. Knowing I had to be certain of sending him over the edge, I took off my blouse and slipped my bra straps off my shoulders, pulling my arms through them so that only my breasts held it in place. I took a deep breath.

'Here goes nothing,' I told my reflection. 'He can hardly fire me.'

He was sitting with his back to the door when I returned, conscious that my bra was already easing down. I pulled it back half an inch.

'Can I say something? Don't look round. No commitments, no stupid demands, no favours at work, no threats ... OK?' He remained very still as I stepped round his chair and stood in front of him. 'Just me and you for the fun of it. The last thing I want is for us to fall in love. This is about something more primitive. Something I need.'

He stayed where he was, but his eyes moved and there was something that resembled relief in them. I pulled my bra down so that it dropped to my waist and sat on his knee. Within a few minutes, it was fantasy time on the carpet for a man of an uncertain age, captured in my urgent, gasping voice.

'There ... deeper ... Let me put my ... Just a minute, that hurts ... That's better ... I can stand any amount of that ... God, you're so big ... Is that nice? ... Lie still and let me ... I want to get on top ... Jesus ... Twist my ... You make me feel like a whore ... Not yet, I'm not ready ... Slow down ... Of course it's safe, you idiot, do you think I'd be letting you if it wasn't? ... Push! ... I want to feel it in ... harder ... I hope you're ready, because I ... Come on! ... Yes! ... Give it me! ... now ... all of it ... yes, yes, *yes*! ...'

When I finally rolled off him, I felt utterly fulfilled; abstinence makes the parts more tender. As we lay next to each other, he didn't say anything and I wondered what was going through his mind. Women have to accept that men instantly turn off after sex – one husband told me that the moment he'd finished making love he'd start thinking about something like painting the garage doors – but I knew that Malcolm's mind was occupied with surprised guilt and confusion and I had to inject some friendliness. I sat up, elbow on the floor, head resting on my hand and stared at him until he finally turned to me.

'Make me laugh,' I said.

'What do you mean?'

'Women like men who make them laugh. Didn't you know that?'

'I can't think of anything funny.'

'Oh, you're hopeless.' I stuck my tongue out at him.

'I could tickle you,' he suggested. That was better.

'No touching allowed,' I warned, moving away. 'Only words. Come on.'

He shook his head. 'Like what?'

'I don't know. How about "Don't try putting this on expenses"? Go on, say it.'

'All right . . . Don't try putting this on expenses.'

'Why not?' I demanded pertly. '"Sex with production editor: dinner eleven pounds seventy, taxi ten pounds, perfume twenty pounds . . ."'

'Twenty pounds?' he protested.

I waved my wrist under his nose. 'Smell that. I treated myself. What else? "Parking six pounds".'

'But you're claiming for a taxi.'

'Damn. I was hoping you wouldn't notice. All right, cross that out. So that's eleven . . . twenty-one . . . forty-one quid altogether. I'll forget the seventy pence.'

'But where's the copy?' He was catching on.

'What page is it going on?'

'How about sport?'

'Perfect!' I laughed. 'Indoors, of course.'

'Or the leisure section centre spread.'

'But Gerry will want photographs!'

'We'll do an artist's impression.'

'That won't work.' I giggled. 'We didn't stay still long enough.'

'You certainly didn't.' For the first time since we had walked into the flat, he smiled properly. 'How much is that on expenses?'

'Nothing, you idiot.'

'Good. I didn't want to bankrupt the paper.' He reached up and stroked my cheek softly. 'Why me?'

I turned his palm and kissed it. 'Now, because you make me laugh. Thank you.'

I seduced him with my body, but captured him with that conversation; it replaced guilt with amusement. I spent every night at Uttoxeter Street while he was in town and Stephanie was away, and afterwards he started visiting me in Barnet, discreetly leaving early to avoid embarrassing questions. But then I let them meet; she wasn't used to Mummy having friends who weren't other women, but she accepted it and he was very good with her. We began as hungry animals, we became affectionate lovers, we ended close friends; not a bad progress, that.

I made no overt demands on Malcolm; that would have been rewriting the ground rules I'd offered. But every time he saw my byline or a piece of copy with my name at the top it was a reminder of my existence as I behaved no differently towards him in the office. I discovered that there are a lot of attractions and delights for both parties if you're a willing and enthusiastic mistress.

The palace revolution came eighteen months later, when the chairman and his deputy found themselves voted off the board for resisting a massive investment in the company by Henry Cuningham III, a West Coast media mogul who wanted a stake in the UK and recognized that the *Register* was ripe for plucking. He bought the shares and support he needed to become chairman, then arrived in the office and glad-handed everyone before taking three minutes to tell Dennis Bruce he was out. His replacement was Charlie Taylor, graduate of the Murdoch school of brute journalism.

94

Once the initial shock waves had died down, everything went strangely quiet. Charlie ordered minor changes, but otherwise seemed to do nothing but stroll around the office; he became known as the Silent One at editorial conferences, rarely making any comment on what was being put forward. After four editions came and went there was a sense of relaxation, until I walked in one morning and could almost smell the atmosphere.

'What's happened?' I asked Anthony urgently.

'At this precise moment . . .' Not looking up from his type-writer, he paused to insert the precise word he'd been seeking '. . . nothing. However, the walls are ready to receive their oblation of blood.'

'Oh, God.'

'Don't be silly. Charlie won't get rid of anyone who's any good. And there are plenty of others to feed his appetites.'

The massacre was impressive. Five senior executives plus the features editor, chief photographer, deputy magazine editor, theatre critic, chief leader writer, the *Register*'s longest-serving columnist and a political correspondent were cut down, as someone remarked, in the prime of their expenses. There were also body bags for half the women's page staff and City desk, three reporters and four subs. Total payoffs were conservatively calculated at one and a half million. It started at eleven o'clock and by four o'clock in the afternoon there were notices on every board announcing new appointments, mainly from outside; Charlie was hiring his own henchmen. To my dismay, Cathy was moved to features, but Anthony remained in place and Malcolm was made managing editor; he quietly mentioned in the corridor that he couldn't see me that night because he had to have dinner with Charlie. I had no other opportunity to speak to him and went home, relieved that I'd survived. The next day I suffered a minor heart attack when Charlie's secretary said he wanted to see me. I was not a happy bunny.

'Sit down,' he said as I walked into his office. Still flecked with traces of Clydeside after working in London for most of his career, his voice sounded as if he gargled with grit. The legend was that he'd started as a fourteen-year-old messenger on the

Glasgow Herald and kicked his way up, never bothering to learn the concept of taking prisoners. He made me wait while he continued reading my personal file, deliberately holding it so I could see what it was. Finally he put it down and stared at me; he could make strong men put their hands in front of their crotches just by doing that. Somehow, I stared back.

'Malcolm tells me you're good. Are you?'

'I've held a job down here for long enough.'

'So have a few others who are knocking on doors at the moment.' He lit another in the endless chain of cigarettes that stretched from the moment he arrived until he went home. 'Starting next week, I want you to write a column for the op-ed page. Twelve hundred words, picture byline, choose your own subjects, but clear them with me first. Make it provocative. You've got six weeks to show you can do it. If you do, I'll confirm the appointment and you'll be on double your present salary. Otherwise, you're out. OK?'

I knew it couldn't just be Malcolm's recommendation; Charlie must have taken more notice of me than I'd realized ... and Charlie didn't do any favours. I managed to remain calm.

'OK,' I agreed. 'Thank you.'

'You won't be thanking me in six weeks if you fuck up. I want your first three topics on my desk before I leave here tonight.'

I was in serious need of a drink, but in those days the pubs weren't open at that time in the morning and I had to settle for coffee with Anthony in the canteen.

'Calm down,' he told me. 'He can't order your assassination.'

'You could have fooled me.'

'Stop it,' he said firmly. 'Your problem is that you're scared of flying. You've got to put Tom down.'

'What do you mean? I have done.'

He shook his head. 'No, you've not. Not completely. There's a tiny bit of you who's still his wife. That has to go.' His eyes hardened. 'If you mess this up, I'll never forgive you, Katrina. You've let yourself down too many times and you're very lucky to be given another turn.'

'Oh ... Well, it helps that you believe in me.'

I jumped as he slapped his hand on the table. '*You* have to believe in you. This hasn't happened just because Malcolm's put in a good word. Mr Taylor doesn't work like that.'

'Oh,' I said uncertainly. 'You know about me and Malcolm?'

'Don't be ridiculous, half the office knows. We are meant to be a profession that finds things out.'

'And we thought we'd been so careful.'

'Love's delusion,' he commented. 'Common complaint. The problem is that people will suspect this is a favour for the bedmate. That means you'll really have to prove you're good.'

'And then I fly?'

He nodded. 'And then you fly. Celebration dinner at Clapham Towers tonight. You bring the wine.'

London

Hamilton swiftly read through all of Leonard Drummond's entry in *People of Today*, retaining key facts. Born Ruislip, 1939; father an MBE; grammar school and Birmingham University; first book published 1976, shortlisted for Whitbread Prize 1987; married 1978, wife with impressive medical qualifications, one daughter; recreations walking, nineteenth-century literature and travel. Most importantly, he allowed his home telephone number to be published; Hamilton groaned with impatience when he got an answerphone, but held on for the full message and a woman's voice gave him a mobile for Dr Drummond. It was answered instantly.

'Hello.' Against the background rumble of traffic, there was a note of tension in her voice.

'Good evening, Dr Drummond. It's the *Sunday Register*. I'm sorry to trouble you, but—'

'The *Sunday Register*? What do you want?'

Hamilton scribbled 'Suspicious/nervous?' on his pad. 'I'm trying to contact your husband. We've got an advance proof of a controversial biography of George Eliot and we'd like to commission him to interview the author.'

'Who is this speaking?'

'My name's Steve Hamilton.'

'And why are you calling me, Mr Hamilton?'

'I got the number from your answerphone.'

'I assumed that, but I'm not my husband's secretary.'

'Of course not, but this is rather urgent. If you could tell me where Mr Drummond is, I—'

'He's away,' she interrupted.

'So we've been told. I believe he's in Wales. I thought you might be able to tell me exactly where.'

'I could, but I don't choose to. Now it's very important that I keep this line open. Please don't ring me again.'

'Where are you, Dr Drumm—?' She was gone. Hamilton looked at the purring receiver for a moment before replacing it. He could only assume that her aggression had meant she knew about the affair, but her initial tone and the speed with which she had answered had been that of someone expecting an important call. He returned to Kendall's office.

'Dr Drummond has just politely told me to get stuffed – and she's not saying where her husband is. My guess is that she knows exactly what's going on, incidentally.'

'That's nothing to do with us,' Kendall said. 'But at the moment he's the best lead we've got to find Katrina. Have someone get round there and hammer on the door.'

'She's not at home. I got her in her car.' Hamilton looked at his notes, recalling how she had sounded. 'She's uptight about something. She certainly didn't want to talk.'

'I warned you. If she knows about her husband and Katrina, this isn't her favourite newspaper.'

'It was more than that. My guess is that she was expecting a call from someone and said it was important to keep the line open. I can't see how that fits with her marriage collapsing.'

Kendall frowned. 'Could she have been in Wales? Or on her way there?'

'She could be anywhere.' Hamilton shut his notebook. 'Anyway, we're no nearer to finding Drummond. Have you checked Katrina's desk?'

'Security are sorting out a set of keys. I'll let you know.'

Judith Drummond knew that overtaking three caravans travelling in convoy needed more road than the hundred yards to the left hand curve. But she had already been delayed by them too long and it was miles to the next stretch of dual carriageway on the A303 across Devon. She pulled out and accelerated, glaring headlights, demanding to be let through. She was alongside the second caravan when the transporter appeared ahead of her, an immense wall of grey-blue steel and glass filling half the road. Its horn blared as the gap into which she could escape shrank like a door being slammed. For a terrifying moment she thought her impatience had been fatal, then threw herself forward against the seat belt as though her own movement would urge the car to greater speed. Distantly she heard an angry, frightened shout as the front caravan braked furiously, then all she could see was the transporter's radiator grille straight ahead of her, before it whipped out of sight as she screeched in front of the leading car. The road ahead was clear, but she was now right on the bend; as she swung the wheel, the Audi's tyres gripped the surface, slid sickeningly, then squealing rubber clenched the tarmac again. She gasped in relief, then glanced anxiously into the rear-view mirror as she sped on; it seemed for ever until the leading caravan appeared round the bend. At least there hadn't been a crash. Rubbing her shoulder where it had been banged against the car door, she accelerated again, ignoring the flashing headlights falling further behind. Nobody could have had time to take her number.

The phone call had agitated her. Why should the *Sunday Register* be trying to contact Leonard? She was instinctively convinced that Hamilton had been lying about wanting him to write for them. Or was that just suspicion? But if it wasn't to write something, what was the real reason? How much did they know about him and Katrina Darcy? How much did the press – prying, merciless, indifferent to human pain – know about her? About Teresa? What more could she do to protect her child?

Wednesday Evening

I drove into Penzance first thing to stock up at Gateway's; pre-packed salads, bread, fruit, milk, coffee, wine, vodka and another two hundred cigarettes. When I returned, Tuxedo was waiting for me. Back arcing like a bow, he stretched as I parked, then trotted over to the car, purring as he rubbed against my legs, tail quivering. His owners – a farm labourer and his wife – call him Sooty, but with that patch of white on his chest and the speckle of black at the throat he's always been Tuxedo to me. He'll stay here as long as I do, then find some other place where he can be indulged.

I bought all the nationals and the *Cornishman*. I've never quite forgiven it for going tabloid, but it still carries delicious pars of local gossip, although it's dropped the little line blocks of signposts with village names on them, sometimes with tiny photographs of the correspondents (surely they can't still be paid a penny a line?). Goldsithney Golden Age Club had an outing to Newquay; Marazion has suffered an outbreak of graffiti; Paul flower festival was another spectacular success; Hayle carnival went ahead despite 'a positively tropical monsoon' . . .

Does it matter a damn to these people that there could be another Cabinet reshuffle (*Times* and *Telegraph* splash)? Will it disturb their quiet lives if a right wing revolution convulses Hungary (*Guardian*)? Is the *Daily Mail*'s exclusive that some second-rate actress has changed boyfriends of the slightest relevance to them, or that the *Sun* can reveal that a minor television personality has a weight problem? One of my fellow columnists has become an instant authority on British architecture, despite the fact that she couldn't tell Victorian Gothic from sixties Brutal. And what will those people in the villages think

101

when all my success, money and glamour founder on a dead body in my London flat? Katrina Darcy at the centre of such a drama will certainly be news for a while, but the *Cornishman* will have much more important things to report.

Ted brought a dozen mackerel; I don't know how long he thinks I'm staying. He'd never expect money, of course, but there was beer in the fridge and we shared a couple of cans. Cornish to his bones, he used to own a back-street garage in Penzance, but he's retired now, dividing his time between his garden, fishing round Wolf Rock and taking package holidays with Madge; this year it was Florida to see the grandchildren. He's whippet-lean, skin brown and coarse as old rope, eyes like polished amber pebbles, and supremely contented. The world he sees on television is where mad people live. When he travels, it's scheduled planes, air-conditioned coaches, bland tourist hotels, guides to show him the sights. Reality is this little corner of Britain where he was born and will die; he'll have harmed no one and his family and friends will weep with genuine grief. The *Cornishman* will list the mourners and the floral tributes at his funeral and he'll be buried at Zennor, where his parents and baby sister lie in a family plot; there's room for Madge as well. He was, as always, garrulous, full of gentle gossip.

'Marigold Cottage has been sold for sixty thousand pounds. I didn't believe it, there's rot in those timbers you could stick your fist through. But Davy Miller works for the estate agents and he says it's true. Doreen Herbert fell and broke her hip three weeks back. Madge has been making her some of her special stew and I've been popping in to feed the dog. And have you heard about young Marian Faherty – her who married Tom Pollitt? Walked out on him. Living across in St Ives now – with some chap who taught her at school, if you please. I've told Tom he should get over there and sort it out. Mind you, we said it would never last . . .

I had to look away so that he couldn't see I was starting to cry. In London I've joked about him and the others I know down here, exaggerating their accents, mocking their values, incredulous that they can think lives that are so small can be so

102

important. I didn't mean it – I've always been very fond of them – but it was cruel ... No, not cruel, ignorant. An ignorance that sprang out of the conviction that my values had to be the right ones.

'And have you heard they're closing the school? Scandal, that is. There's people live ten miles away who don't have cars. You ought to write about that in your newspaper.'

But that's not news for us, Ted. We cater for Islington Person, who lives in a different little world.

The phone keeps ringing, but I never answer; the damned thing's like an umbilical cord I can't sever. There was an old boy on the *Stockport Courier* who could actually remember sending his copy back from a football match by pigeon. I press a key and a machine thousands of miles away has printed out what I've written before I've got myself a coffee. The news of John Kennedy's death went round the world in ten seconds in 1963; now we'd see the doctor reading the statement outside the hospital live on CNN. Everything's instant, throwaway, impatient for the next drama so that nothing becomes dramatic. It's not news, it's noise. And the noise expands to fill the space, which gets bigger and bigger. Did you know that in the very early days of the BBC they would sometimes announce there was nothing worth reporting on the radio news bulletin and play music instead? How naive. There's always news, there has to be, we've got eight pages or thirty minutes to fill. Entire channels are vomiting out nothing else.

And the most terrible thing is what it's done to people. There was a sickening story about a woman who jumped into the sea at Mont St Michel to save her daughter. Tourists watched her struggling, but they didn't help. Do you know what some of them did instead? Recorded it on camcorders and rushed it off to a television station – who used it. The woman drowned, but so what? This was news, and someone would pay money for it. Journalism has no pity, or humanity, or decency, or ... If I don't stop thinking like this, I'll end up jumping off those cliffs.

*

We've had remorse, tears and guilt; tonight it's anger, irrationally blaming everyone but myself. Why didn't I bring my passport? I could ring the bank and transfer funds, get over to the Channel Islands from here, then take off anywhere I want. Somewhere that drags its heels over extradition treaties; if only they weren't always places where it's so bloody hot. But I'd find a villa and invite *Hello!* magazine over to take the pretty pictures and write the anodyne words.

'Exclusive: Keri Darcy tells us her story from her charming home in the sun'. First par: 'Tanned and relaxed in a simple cotton dress, Fleet Street's top columnist sits on the sun-filled terrace to talk about why she left London. She insists that she is as innocent as the sweet-smelling bougainvillaea blossoms that cascade above her . . .'

One discreet par on the unpleasantness, then an extended plug for the next book, a hint that I could have found a new lover, some claptrap philosophy – 'Life is the classroom we can never leave' – the merest suggestion of returning because there's no reason not to, 'but there's so much I want to do here'. Then where would you like me to pose? Leaning against the railings of the balcony with a backdrop of the hills; in a bamboo chair by the window, typewriter next to me; picking fruit in the garden; sitting on the edge of the impeccably made bed, nudging the reader's subconscious towards imagined ecstasies; hair and make-up perfect, face now pensive, now composed, now touched with contentment, always blameless. Fifty grand is the going rate for that sort of garbage – but at least it doesn't pretend to be anything else.

And it will be a better image than a woman in her too-visible forties, smoking too many cigarettes, slopping around in jeans, sweatshirts and tatty espadrilles, hands stinking of raw fish, not bothering to mask the face lines because she doesn't care what she looks like. Talking to a cat.

I'm aching with tiredness, but I don't want to fall asleep again. I heard myself shout as I woke up, and the images keep re-playing across my brain, like a film in which a few frames have been lost each time I watch it again. At first I was married to Tom but still working in Stockport, and I couldn't understand what had made me give everything up and go back. Then there was a surreal bit involving a herd of giraffes in the Uffizi, then Stephanie was making love to me – the sooner those frames vanish the better – before Anthony just appeared and didn't know who I was. After that I was trying to feed a baby, but I had no breasts . . . I think I've just dreamt a whole textbook.

VERNON

It's a caricature of an age, him with scarlet braces showing, my dress with shoulder pads like an American quarter-back. Both holding tulip glasses of champagne (naturally), we're grinning inanely beside a life-size cardboard cut-out of me looking suggestive. It's vulgar, and now I find it embarrassing; at the time, I thought it was harmless. But there was so much we all thought was harmless then; we couldn't see that what gleamed so brightly was only an expensive bubble.

Nobody could have anticipated the eighties with their ruthless greed and the assumption that money came from a miraculous bottomless well, but it was very good time to be taking off. Thatcherism was definitely flavour of the month at the *Register* and the editorial policy was sell success. I wrote for the hard-faced, power-dressed women with balls; for the crowd who put their credit cards behind the bar, then shouted their conversations over Frankie Goes to Hollywood at full volume; for advertising executives with fat bank accounts and thin Armani suits; for all that I came to see later as the selfishness and delusion of it all. The Barnet house rose in value on an almost daily basis, dwarfing what Tom and I had thought was an appallingly high mortgage when we bought it, and he agreed we should sell. He moved to what was little more than a building site in Docklands at the time, and I bought a town house. According to the Post Office, the address was Swiss Cottage, but I could nudge it across the border into Hampstead for social purposes; the owner needed hard cash in a hurry, which enabled me to beat him down on the price. It was very late Victorian, probably built as a home for a City clerk and small family, with original bathroom fittings and new Swedish kitchen. It was also conveniently near the sort of school where I could send Stephanie without arousing sympathetic comments from other yuppies.

Charlie, whose contempt for the nouveau riche was total, still accepted that they were the sort of readers who bought the consumer desirables that attracted plump advertising accounts and reserved comments such as 'Thick as horse shit and not as useful' for the office. He'd given the paper an edge, bending its reputation for being an acceptable face of responsible journalism as far as he could without actually breaking it. Subtly written exposés of politicians' private lives or articles based on sex surveys were carefully balanced by concerned reports on the environment or inner-city drug problems. You had to understand how newspapers work to note the positioning; the latter were invariably placed on left-hand pages, while the former were on the right with better pictures. He introduced colour and a new sports section, resisted the temptation to add horoscopes, but constantly demanded upmarket competitions; nature notes that were almost as old as the paper itself were uprooted, and the age of the readers who protested satisfied him that he was right.

After my first six columns had appeared he called me in again and told me I could have another six weeks to prove I could keep it up. When I mentioned the rise, he said I hadn't earned it yet. I responded with an over-the-top anti-miners polemic, an attack on Help the Aged and a call for IRA terrorists to be executed. All were tempered by more-in-sorrow-than-in-anger comments and appeals to reasonable people to just think things through, but were laced with acid. For and against letters ran about one to three, but they arrived in very satisfactory numbers. The important thing was not to be liked – it was not to be ignored. The week after my second trial run ended, there was a note in my pigeonhole with Charlie's illegible hieroglyphic confirming the job – and the rise was backdated to when I'd begun.

'Thank you,' I said as I passed him standing by the lifts.

'The Lord giveth and the Lord taketh away,' he replied unexpectedly as the doors opened. His wit was rarely so literate – and it was a neat warning.

Anthony, whose position remained secure enough to refuse

writing anything that offended him, annoyed me with his attitude.

'You don't really mean this, do you?' he asked, holding the paper open at the piece on capital punishment.

I shrugged. 'Does it matter? It sells papers.'

'So do exaggerated mammary glands and elementary games for the stupid but avaracious.'

'I don't imagine Charlie's planning anything like that.' I didn't like the edge of reproach in his voice.

'I wanted you to reach your potential, not sell your honesty.'

'Butt out,' I told him crossly. 'You were the one who convinced me I could do this, but that doesn't mean you can tell me how.'

He dropped the paper into my wastepaper basket and wagged his finger at me like a scolding parent. 'I said fly, not lie. There'll be tears before bed.'

He walked away, and childishly I stuck my tongue out behind his back. I couldn't understand him. It wasn't professional jealousy, and I was acting no differently from countless other journalists. I should have remembered that he understood me very well.

Possibly in reaction to Anthony, more likely because I was acquiring a taste for the hedonistic, I played on my reputation in that tasteless decade. I became a controversial talking head on television chat shows, guaranteed to provide the contentious quote, which led to the first series of *Spiked Copy* on ITV. It went out at eleven o'clock in the morning and wasn't a great success, but Channel Four took it up for a late evening slot which meant we could harden it. A sycophantic women's magazine ran a profile on me and a left-wing female MP attacked me, which was an enormous publicity boost. Dazzled by it all – and a further rise plus a company car – I lapped it up. I could afford a full-time home help to look after Stephanie – when she wasn't on (by now private) school skiing trips, staying with friends in Dordogne *gîtes* or Tuscany villas, or spending time with Tom, which she was finding increasingly boring. Determined to remain the good working mother – several columns discussed this problem and

108

how to deal with it without letting your figure and complexion go to hell – I insisted she must be kept up until ten o'clock every night in case I got home early enough, and set aside every Saturday to give her quality time. The photograph for the profile was of me at home with Stephanie kneeling on the Indian carpet at my feet with her Harrods' doll's-house. We wore matching Laura Ashley dresses – trendy but not outrageous – to emphasize our closeness, and the caption read: 'Togetherness: Katrina insists that the happiness of being a mother is what really matters.' That attracted some nice letters.

Having long slaked the early passion, Malcolm and I had begun comparing slots in our diaries that seemed to grow further and further apart until we realized one day that we hadn't been to bed with each other for nearly four months and neither of us minded. We went out to lunch and I suggested we end it.

'Just this stage of it,' I added. 'We've played this very well so far, so . . . friends? You know I never wanted you to leave Carol and the children. It wasn't about that.'

'I know. I've appreciated that. You've been the perfect mistress. Every home should have one.'

I roared with laughter. 'My God, you've changed. You wouldn't have made jokes like that before I seduced you.'

'Did you seduce me?' he asked innocently.

'Your memory's going,' I said drily. 'Now I'll pay for lunch.'

Apart from finding we could put it down so comfortably, finishing with Malcolm unfastened a tie; it was as though if I'd had another affair, I'd have been unfaithful to him. Not that I instantly leapt into bed with the next prospect, but when the right opportunity arose I took it. Stephanie would have been about thirteen by this time and starting her adolescent social life; staying over with schoolfriends, or having them spend the night in Swiss Cottage, was increasingly common. I had freedom to do whatever I wanted. Did I become promiscuous? That depends on your yardstick. On my thirty-eighth birthday I calculated that I'd slept with as many men as there would have been candles on the cake if I'd had one; more than I would care to admit to my mother, but hardly *Guinness Book of Records* country. A couple had been around for a few weeks, most for less, a handful because it was a pleasant way to end the evening. I was very fond of several, but I didn't fall in love and had no desire to marry again. When one said he wanted me to have his children, I made an excuse and returned to the bedroom having taken an extra contraceptive pill just in case. In the morning, I told him I was going to Buenos Aires for ever.

I celebrated my tenth anniversary of leaving Tom with dinner at the Blueprint Café in the company of a television producer I'd been saving up for the occasion. That week's column was on divorce as a positive watershed, woman in a brave new world, never let the bastard beat you. There were letters from readers who said they'd found it inspirational.

I met Vernon Farrant in 1985 when he was among the guests at a party I attended in Notting Hill; I can't remember who held it, but it was a large house with an excess of bare wood and Athena posters, Thai food was the thing to serve, and a girl who'd discovered Buddhism sat in a corner and chanted a lot. He was the sort of Tory MP who looked as if he'd been grown from a culture dish in a laboratory at Central Office, interchangeable with any other smoothed, rehearsed dummy in a blue rosette. Whoever he was talking to, his eyes constantly worked the room and he never missed the moment for the polite acknowledgement, the gracious greeting. His wife, who appeared to be joined to him at the hip, contributed precise measures of conversation before deferring to him again. It was impossible that he should not express an informed opinion on any subject.

When I was admitted to the presence – you couldn't avoid it as they methodically quartered the place – all the right lines came out. Katrina Darcy of the *Sunday Register*? What a pleasure to meet me, he'd been so looking forward to it. First-rate newspaper. He'd been talking to my editor at a Downing Street reception only the previous week. Interesting man, self-made, very sound. My column seemed to be essential reading in the Farrant household, although I instinctively suspected he'd told the press office to provide him with a single sheet of topics I'd covered with selected quotes when he'd learnt I would be there that night. Similarly briefed, his wife asked about my daughter and which school she was at, admired my dress, then smiled as she was towed away. Her name, as far as I could remember, was Mary, suitably comfortable for his West Country electorate; it would have been a bad career move on his part to have married a Jocasta.

Frankly, I'd forgotten him within minutes and assumed I'd made no greater impression; I was unaware that his mind had a radar device that locked on to any opportunity. He rang me three weeks later to say he wanted to discuss a business proposition; if I was free on Tuesday evening we could meet at his town house ... Seven-thirty? My mouth made a little *moue* of cynicism as I listened; the Tories effortlessly supported family values and mistresses at the same time.

'What sort of business proposition?' I asked.

'One that could make you a great deal of money.'

'And what would I have to do for it?'

He gave a small laugh. 'Not what I suspect you're thinking. We'd both make money out of it. It concerns your book.'

That was a curve ball. It was five years since I'd written *Other Paintings in Other Rooms*, a novel about a woman who falls in love with her best friend's son, partly based on the experience of someone I knew. Anthony had complimented me when he read the manuscript, which meant a great deal. He'd praised my style and remarked that few writers were able to make the dramatic believable by combining it with the commonplace. At his suggestion, I'd sent it to an agent called Emma Sullivan, but she'd never been able to place it. There'd been a couple of appreciative letters among the rejection slips, but it wasn't quite right for the market, their list was full, perhaps next year ... All the standard excuses. Emma had complained that they couldn't recognize quality when they were hit over the head with it, and promised to keep trying, but it had been at least a year since I'd last heard from her. Drabble and Farrant were a new firm that had risen out of the destruction of the print unions and computer type-setting; their list was a mixture of disposable lifestyle books colour printed in the Far East, television spin-offs, sports annuals and paperback fiction. Not the sort of house that won literary awards, but spectacularly successful. I didn't know Emma had sent it to them.

'You've read it?'

'One of our editors has, and I've read her assessment. That's what I want to talk about.'

'I'll see you on Tuesday evening.'

I was ecstatic. I didn't delude myself that *Other Paintings* was a masterpiece, but it was probably the best thing I'd ever written. I dug out my own copy and read it again that night. There were changes I'd want to make, but there were phrases I'd got absolutely right, passages in which I'd managed to catch emotion in words, bitter humour, real pain. It said things I really believed, and I felt I'd betrayed both myself and the friend it had happened to by not pushing Emma harder to get it published.

Any residual doubts that Vernon was only using it as bait to get me into his bed were dispelled when I checked with our Parliamentary sketch writer about his private life; the mistress, a Yale politics student working as a Commons researcher, was securely in place. I looked him up in *Who's Who*; born 1943, Uppingham and Balliol, married Mary Vera Wilbraham 1968, elected 1979, two children, on overseas aid committee, chairman of Drabble and Farrant, Garrick and Carlton clubs, hobbies reading and numismatics, homes in Eaton Square SW1 and the Old Manse, Tavistock. Definitely Thatcher's child.

His wife opened the door at Eaton Square when I arrived and spent precisely the right length of time with us to be polite before asking me to excuse her; the children were still young enough to enjoy their bedtime story. The journalist had been given exactly the correct image, in case it should ever prove necessary. Vernon completed it by telling her he would be up shortly to kiss them goodnight.

'Another drink?' he suggested when we were alone.

'Thank you.'

He was different from when I'd met him at the party, with another, more relaxed, social face. He was wearing brogues, cavalry twill slacks and an expensive fine wool sweater, a prosperous countryman entertaining at his elegant London home. His wardrobe was a collection of uniforms for all occasions. He handed me my glass then sat opposite me, picking up a file from the table beside his chair.

'Now, about your book,' he said. Small talk had been dealt with in the previous ten minutes.

'I'm delighted you're interested in it.'

'We're not.' He sounded dismissive.

'Oh.' I smothered surprise with coldness. 'I must have misunderstood you. I thought you liked it.'

'I didn't say that.' He opened the file. '"Worthy but uncommercial" is the final assessment. It's the sort of thing written by *Guardian* columnists and published by Virago.'

'They've turned it down.'

'That surprises me . . . but so have a lot of others.'

'I still think it's good. I think people would buy it.'

'Maximum sales of, say, fifteen hundred in hardback if you're lucky, and remaindered in a year. Hardly the cutting edge of success.'

I put my glass down. 'Mr Farrant, I don't like having my time wasted. If you think it's useless, why did you want to see me?'

'I told you. To make a proposition.' He took a plastic envelope from the file. 'We want you to write something else. Two hundred thousand words – the Americans judge value for money by weight – to be published in the autumn, so we need the manuscript by April.'

'April? That's only three months away.'

'So it's about two thousand words a day. Any journalist can manage that, but not all of them can go the distance for a book. You've shown you can.' He stood up and gave me the envelope. 'Read this. It's been drawn up by our marketing people. I must say goodnight to the children.'

There were three sheets of paper, the first defining the target readership – B2 and C1 males and females, in the twenty to thirty-five age range, income £15,000 to £30,000, impulse book purchasers at W. H. Smith or airports, ITV viewers. The second

113

sheet showed the marketing. Advertising in tabloid Sunday magazines and *TV Times*, posters and dump bins at high turnover retail outlets, pilot television campaign in Granada area followed by LWT if response figures were right, author interviews to be placed in supermarket giveaways. Under estimated cost it read: 'Initially £50,000. Additional to be approved by board.'

The third sheet began with the 'Preferred author profile'. A woman, aged no more than forty, who already had a visible public presence (preferably television) and photographed well. If married, husband must be kept in background. London-based essential. Underneath was the plot.

Working title: 'The Leopardess'

*Central character: Woman, rich, twenties, bisexual, ruthless. Name to be agreed in advance. Redhead desirable. Unmarried. Drives custom-built sports car, red or black and knows how to fire a gun.**

Background: English, born in London, educated Roedean (and perhaps Switzerland/France). Family home in Sussex, she has apartments in Chelsea or similar and Manhattan. Only child, mother dead, father head of international conglomerate (jewellers/fashion?), offices in London, Rome, New York, Paris, etc. The best addresses.

Storyline: Father in wheelchair and losing control of business. Company backed by unidentified Arab money is secretly planning to buy him out, but he doesn't appreciate what is happening. Girl discovers this and sets out to stop them. Exotic locations, opulence, scenes by private swimming pools, etc., no major character to drive anything below a BMW. Frequent mention of top designer names, soft porn passages every fifty pages on average. Most straight, but lesbianism must also be included. Troilism and bondage acceptable if carefully worded (editor will tone down if necessary). No more than one coloured person should be included. If Americans appear, can on no account be villains unless politicians. Financial details minimal and easy for readers to follow.

She saves the family business, but her father dies. There must be a point near the end when she cries and says something on the lines of 'I did it all for you, my darling Daddy' to give necessary touch of humanity. She then takes over the company.

* Expert advice available on firearms and cars, or can be added at editing stage.

114

Vernon returned while I was reading. 'And what makes you think I'm going to write crap like this?' I asked.

A gold lighter glittered in his hand and flame licked at the tip of a slender cigar. 'Would a forty-thousand-pound advance be persuasive?' That was a year's salary at the *Register*. 'Half when you sign the contract, the rest when you deliver. I think you'll find your agent will advise you to accept. If we've got our sums right, you should earn out within twelve months or so, not allowing for the possibility of a TV mini-series. I have all the right contacts there.'

I spotted what seemed a way out. 'Can I use a pseudonym?'

'No. Your name's important. We don't want someone completely unknown and have to sell them from scratch.'

'Sell them?' I repeated. 'So I'll be a product?'

'Isn't everything? The thing is to be a successful one. If it offends you, we have two other authors in mind. One writes for a middle-market tabloid, which is actually a better background, but we don't know if she can produce a book. And she doesn't have your television exposure.'

I looked at the storyline again, cynically calculated, exploiting people's willingness to be seduced by sex, a famous name and blatant hype. Vernon waited, and I heard him expel quiet smoke. This was the man who'd written a piece for the *Daily Mail* just before the last election calling for girlie magazines to be removed from newsagents' shelves because they could corrupt teenagers. But who would remember that?

'I want to think about it,' I told him.

'Don't take too long. We have a deadline. I need someone signed up by the nineteenth. So you've got ... say, two days to decide.'

As soon as I got home I rang Emma and almost ordered her to meet me for lunch the next day. She was disappointed *Other Paintings* was being turned down yet again, but hard-headed about Vernon's offer.

'Forty grand is one hell of an advance, and I'll be going for a two-book contract with noughts attached after that.' She knew

115

from the look on my face that I was still uncertain. 'I'll tell you what. I'll try for a deal in which they agree to publish *Other Paintings* as well. You'll have to use another name of course, but—'

'Why?' I demanded. 'That is my book.'

'Darling, get real. The line they'll want to use will be "The New Katrina Darcy Blockbuster" not "A Sensitive Novel of a Woman's Love". People don't buy tins of beans to find caviar inside.'

I looked at her dubiously. 'So you think I should do it?'

'It's up to you, but you're throwing away serious money if you say no.' She gestured through the window at the crowds on the pavement. 'What are they into out there? *Dallas. Dynasty.* It's the envy syndrome. What makes you so superior?'

Forty thousand. For starters. I could laugh off the embarrassment. My friends would know I was only cashing in the way everybody was. They would read *Other Paintings in Other Rooms* and know the truth. I could sell the Swiss Cottage house and buy a flat nearer the centre of town, my own holiday cottage, Stephanie could be sent on that skiing holiday in Aspen without my having to juggle money . . .

Before then I'd changed so slowly the process had been indiscernible; now I made a deliberate decision. Vernon had completed what I had begun myself. I combined my holidays with a sabbatical plus a couple of weeks' unpaid leave. I called her Starr Xanadu (the editor approved) and crashed it out with a week to spare.

Other Paintings in Other Rooms was published, but they spent less on the publicity than they did on the jackets for my sex and shopping sagas. It got very good reviews in papers that ignored me otherwise, and there were requests for interviews with Helen Southall. But in my contract with Drabble and Farrant I'd had to accept a clause that I was not to be identified as the author under any circumstances, and enquirers were put off until they lost interest. Vernon had been right; it was remaindered in less than a year, and I was offered three hundred at a tenth the retail price; in one afternoon I signed the same number of copies of *Eligible*

Lovers at a shop in Birmingham and the paperback of *White Queen, Black Knight* briefly topped the best-seller lists. Vernon sent me a Cartier bracelet engraved with the message 'Better profits in other plots'.

I did eventually sleep with him, not as his mistress, but for the few days we spent at a hotel in Siena, where they assumed I was his wife. It was a casual indulgence for both of us and rather enjoyable; whatever Vernon does in life he does very efficiently. There was nothing more to it than that, but after he started to move up the Westminster ladder I occasionally teased him about it. He didn't like that; he hates the thought that anyone might have power over him and his ambitions. I'm one of his significant others.

London

Kendall could still persuade himself that Katrina might walk in at any moment, dismissively apologizing before insisting that the second op-ed page be pulled so that she could fill her own space, indifferent to the chaos it would cause to the production schedule, threatening to complain to Charlie Taylor if she was refused. She had been allowed to make her own rules for a very long time.

'There you are.' There was a metallic click as the security guard succeeded in opening the drawer. 'Now the top one's done, the rest are OK. See?'

'Leave it, please,' Kendall told him, then waited until he was alone before looking himself. The largest drawer, at the bottom, contained two out-of-date telephone directories, an empty wine bottle and an old pair of rope-soled shoes; the middle one appeared more promising, but the papers in it were only press handouts, kept for no discernible reason, and proofs of one of Katrina's novels, the title sheet looped with cup stains. The top drawer rattled with half-used ballpoint pens, paperclips, bits of costume jewellery and a broken Swatch; there was also a *Sunday Register* desk diary and several envelopes.

The diary was empty, apart from occasional telephone numbers, mainly attached to names he recognized; Drummond's was not among them. Two of the envelopes contained press invitations, one of them from nearly five years previously, another was a letter of complaint from a reader with 'Lunatic' scrawled across it in Katrina's writing, another an unpaid private telephone bill. Then he found the photographs, with a brochure from a hotel in Tuscany. There were four of them, a view of the hills, Katrina standing outside the Basilica in Florence, and two of her with

Vernon Farrant, one on a hotel balcony, the second by a swimming pool. Kendall put them in his pocket.

'Nothing in her desk,' he told Hamilton as he passed the secretary's office. 'I didn't think there would be. She doesn't leave personal stuff lying around. Still no luck with tracking down Drummond?'

'No, because I can't think of anyone else to call. I got back to Emma Sullivan and asked her to try other writers she represents. One of them might know.'

'Let's hope so. I've thought of another couple of people I can contact. I'll tell you if anything turns up.'

Kendall first checked the hotel brochure; the tariff quoted was for four years previously, before Farrant had been made a junior minister. The balcony photograph meant nothing; they could have been guests at a party. But in the one by the pool they were lying beside each other on sun-loungers, his hand resting on her bare thigh, glistening with tanning oil. That Katrina had gone on holiday and presumably slept with her publisher was hardly surprising; he'd helped her to make a great deal of money. But Farrant's predecessor at the Department of the Environment had been sacked after a scandal, and the government was not in the mood for any more. Certain newspapers would pay a lot for the pool picture – and Charlie Taylor would certainly use it. Kendall opened his personal contacts book, then rang an unlisted number.

'Mr Farrant, please. It's Malcolm Kendall at the *Sunday Register*.'

'I'm sorry, Mr Kendall, the minister's in his constituency.' The secretary carefully used Farrant's correct, shiny new title.

'Thank you. I'll try him there. I've got the number.'

'I'm afraid he's having dinner with the West Devon Farmers' Union this evening. Is it urgent? He has a mobile phone with him, of course. I could ring and ask him to call you.'

'No, it's all right. I'll try tomorrow. Thank you.'

Kendall hung up and thought for a moment, then punched the speedcall button for the paper's Parliamentary editor.

'Harry? It's Malcolm. Heard any whispers about Vernon Farrant?'

'Saying what?'

'Skeleton in the cupboard – mistress-shaped.'

'He was knocking off an American political student who was working in the Commons, but that was years ago. She's back in the States now and he paid her enough to keep quiet. The *People* were on to it a while back, but even they couldn't make her talk.'

'Nobody else?'

'Not that I know of. What have you heard?'

'Just a rumour,' Kendall said dismissively.

'Who's it supposed to be with?'

'Don't know . . . I thought you might.'

'Not a word. Anyway, Farrant's got a grip on the greasy pole now and he's not going to let some indiscretion get in his way. He wouldn't have a prayer if it came out. How strong are the rumours?'

'Very vague. Just thought I'd check.'

'Well, tell Charlie to make sure he's got hard facts before he prints anything. Farrant would sue for funny money because he's got too much to lose. Someone on the 1922 committee told me he's building up favours to be paid back at a leadership election one day.'

'Has he got a chance?'

'When you look at some of the people who've had it, any bugger's got a chance. Be bloody careful on this one, Malcolm. He'll stamp on anyone who gets in his way.'

On the *Daily Mirror* a reporter was negotiating with an anonymous caller.

'If it's good enough we'll pay, but I can't make promises until you tell me what this is.'

'I'm letting you have it exclusively.'

'Fine. So what is it?'

'Five thousand?'

'It'll have to be bloody good for that.'

'I can make it good. I've slept with her.'

'So? You're not the only one.'

'But I'm prepared to talk about it. Graphic details.'

120

'We'll want to use your name. Anonymous is no good.'

'That's what costs money.'

'Five grand's a hell of a lot.'

'You'll get your money's worth. Like how she practised a few of the things that happen in her books?'

'Did she?'

'I think I could remember it like that.'

The reporter was becoming interested. Katrina Darcy's disappearance was the Saturday morning story; salacious personal revelations would be what sold on Sunday.

'How did you know she was missing?' he asked.

'I work at her hairdressers. Someone from the *Sunday Register* called us today asking if we'd seen her. The boss mentioned it to me. Said they were worried. I reckoned it could be a story.'

'How often did this happen with you and her?'

'Just the once, about three years ago. I'd chatted to her in the shop, then one night we met at a party. Next thing, it's back to my place.'

'How old were you?'

'Twenty-seven. I was one of her toyboys.'

'OK, but we're not promising five grand until we know what we've got. We'll want all the details plus pictures of you lying on your bed looking sexy with most of your clothes off. Right?'

'No problem.'

'Where can we meet you?'

'Come round now. I'm at home. I presume you'll still be interested even if she turns up.'

'Probably. Why haven't you told this story before?'

'I was waiting until it was worth selling.'

LEONARD

It's a dreadful photograph. I was so concerned with getting in the disused windmill in the field behind, I didn't realize I was taking him with a telegraph pole sprouting out of his head. I was too far away as well, so you can't really make out his face except to see that he's laughing. He was joking about the weather; wind and rain were scouring East Anglia and the sky was like the inside of a dirt-grey igloo. I have other pictures of him – a 'Register' photographer took a marvellous shadowed portrait to go with the profile Anthony wrote – but this was taken on that particular day and at that particular time in my life.

The first time we met, he insulted me. We were two of the authors on a weekend at Bredon Hall Hotel in Gloucestershire, where people were prepared to pay a hundred pounds plus hotel bills for workshops, author panels, readings – and profitable signing sessions. I was the trash bestseller, included to pull in the mass audience, and my agreement with Drabble and Farrant demanded public appearances. Apart from Beth Hope, the travel writer, Leonard was the only one there I hadn't met, although I knew his books; intelligent, ambivalently funny novels, often written from a woman's viewpoint. We first spoke at the reception on the Friday evening when he was trying to avoid being cornered by a professor from a Midlands polytechnic hoping to supplement his lecture notes with an earnest discussion of motivation, influences and deconstructionalism.

'Thank God, another author,' he said as he spotted the bright yellow identifying badge on the front of my dress. 'I'll be safe with you.'

'Who from?'

He waved his wine glass vaguely round the room. 'The great

British reader. Lovely people, but they will insist on asking you what you *meant* by something. Half the time I can't remember writing whatever it was.'

I grinned sympathetically. 'They quote bits as well, don't they?'

'All the time. But never anything you thought was good.' He looked more closely at my name badge. 'Although it doesn't really apply in your case, does it?'

'What do you mean?'

'I started reading *The Leopardess* once. Gave up at chapter three.' He smiled. 'Admit it. It's bloody awful.'

Perfectly capable of knocking myself among friends, I shouldn't have been offended, but irrationally I was. We'd only just met.

'I outsell you.'

'So does Jackie Collins. And Barbara Cartland. And . . . Need I go on?'

'You're fucking rude,' I told him. 'Piss off.'

'We're doing a panel together tomorrow morning.'

'And I'm going to slag you off.'

'I may cry.'

What I can't capture is the way we were talking, like a couple of Noël Coward characters where there's a great deal of affection beneath the bitchiness. I knew he was right, and the way he said it wasn't offensive. The subtext was: 'You're cashing in on being famous, and good luck to you. But we're both intelligent enough not to pretend to each other.' They sat us at the same table for dinner that night and he put someone down when they dismissively told me that anyone could write bodice rippers. Leonard suggested they tried it.

'Katrina's an author,' he said. 'Are you? Writing anything is bloody hard work.'

Afterwards I thanked him, adding that I was surprised, when he obviously recognized my books as trash.

'I'm allowed to say that,' he replied. 'I'm another writer. He's a reviewer, who can only write about books, which any fool can do. You must have noticed how many do so. Anyway, you can write very well . . . Helen Southall.'

123

'What?' I was delighted. 'You've read *Other Paintings*? God, I can count people like you on one hand. It was remaindered after ten months.'

'It was strangled at birth by your publishers. A friend lent me a copy – and there are people in the business who know you wrote it. You should do more like that.'

'Perhaps I will one day. I'll send you one from the pile in my study. Signed.'

'That will be a nice thing to have.'

It was a good start, although I didn't think any more about it. There was another man passing through my life at the time, and Leonard showed not the slightest interest.

About six months later we met again at somebody's book launch at Hatchard's in Piccadilly, ending the evening with a group of others exchanging chat, gossip and slander at the Academy club in Beak Street. There was a lovely loquacious woman telling stories about her family that could only have happened in Ireland, and a journalist who insisted on talking about the book he was going to write; when he said he would be demanding a £100,000 advance Leonard remarked that writers needed their fantasies. Anthony and Toby arrived after attending a first night and joined us (it was as a result of that meeting that Anthony did his profile on Leonard). We left just after midnight, and he asked me if I wanted a lift.

'Are you safe to drive?' I asked.

'Perfectly. Those gin and oranges didn't have any gin in them. I've got to get back to Harrow. Where are you?'

'Bayswater Road.'

'Right direction. Come on. I'm parked just off St James's.'

It was a warm night in early spring. Central London is wonderful in late darkness, still trembling with secret activity, pockets of shadowed quiet, graceful houses stroked by street lamps in silent squares; it seems even better seen through a haze of alcohol. I was on my own again by then, and became slightly impatient when he didn't even try to hold my hand. I might have made my own move, but we reached his car and the moment passed. Driving up Park Lane, he began to sing, about skylarks and September being April.

'Ah, they don't write 'em like that any more,' he said.

'What is it?'

'Theme song from *Spring in Park Lane*. Anna Neagle and Michael Wilding, romantic confusion and virginal brides. My mother wept. Now it's gasping press-ups and instant climaxes by the second reel.'

'It's the way people behave – or are you a lost romantic?'

'I sometimes think I am. It must be my feminine side.' He accelerated in front of a coach at Marble Arch and into Bayswater Road. 'I used to work along here. Haymarket Group, Lancaster Gate.'

'I didn't know you'd been a journalist.'

'It didn't last long. My father died and left me enough to quit and write full time. After that I married Judith, who's a very successful woman.'

'Judith?' It was a name that triggered memories. 'I used to know a Judith. She was one of my teachers at school.'

'This one's a doctor. Well, a specialist now. World authority on skin diseases.'

'Sounds gruesome.'

'Fortunately she doesn't bring her work home.'

'Do you have a family?'

'Just one daughter. How far now?'

'Where are we? Next street past the hotel and almost immediately on the left . . . Would you like to come in?'

'Better not. I've got to be at Heathrow at the crack of dawn. British Council trip to Brazil.' He turned and stopped outside my flat.

'Bring me back some coffee.'

'I'll try to remember . . . Goodnight.'

He leant across and lightly kissed my cheek, the only physical contact we made, as meaninglessly polite as being greeted by a casual acquaintance. My earlier disappointment had grown. He was eminently suitable for a relationship, athletic fifty, good company, intelligent, handsome without conceit. And, I reflected as I stepped out of the car, apparently very married. Pity.

There was no coffee, but I did receive a postcard from Rio; the Christ of the Andes with the message, 'There's certainly an awful lot of temperature.' I couldn't interpret it as a come-on, and got on with my life.

We met a couple of times before East Anglia, once at a reception at the French Embassy – I can't remember why we were both there – the second time when we ran into each other outside Selfridge's and went for a pub lunch in Carnaby Street, over which he asked a lot about me and appeared genuinely interested; I felt afterwards that being with Leonard was rather like being with Anthony, which was a great compliment to him. Three weeks later, he rang me at the *Register*.

'I've just been reading the bumf on this library weekend at Norwich and spotted your name.'

'Pardon?' I flicked open my desk diary. 'When is it? All right, I've found it. I didn't realize it was so close. Are you going as well?'

'Yes. I wondered if you'd like a lift.'

'I hadn't even thought about getting there. Thank you. That's kind. Can you pick me up?'

'Sure. About ten o'clock on the Thursday? See you then.'

I scribbled his name in my diary . . . Then added a couple of question marks.

They put the writers up in the Maid's Head, which must have knocked a hole in the county council budget, but they made us work for it. Leonard and I did no events together, and the only time I was alone with him was immediately after lunch on the Saturday, when we skipped the Germaine Greer session. We walked round the cathedral and he began to . . . It sounds such a posy word, but it's the nearest I can think of . . . to flirt with me in the cloisters.

'Stand in that archway. I want to take a picture of you . . . Left a bit so I can get the spire . . . Look to your right, I want your profile . . . Fraction more. That's it.'

126

'I didn't realize you were such a fussy photographer,' I said.

'Stay still.' The shutter clicked and the motor wound on. 'I am when I'm taking pictures of something beautiful.'

I turned to look at him. 'Like a fifteenth-century spire, of course.'

'Something like that ... Stop there! Now smile ... Perfect. Come on, let's have you standing respectfully by Edith Cavell's grave.'

He bought me a scarf I admired in the gift shop and I insisted on buying him a tiepin in return, then we had tea in the cathedral restaurant. Later on, I reflected that in a couple of hours we had covered a lot of ground. As we stepped outside again, the wind buffeted us and he glanced up.

'It looks black over Willy's mother's.'

'I'm sorry?'

'Old country saying. Don't you know it?' He pointed to where a mass of thunderclouds was starting to block the sky with charcoal. 'Willy's mother is very unlucky with the weather.'

The first fat drops plopped down as we reached the hotel, and I gave my final talk to a background of racketing thunder. By the time we left at six o'clock it was seriously torrential; as we drove out of the city he had to drop down to a crawl because the wipers couldn't cope and the local radio was giving the first flood warnings. We persisted for about twenty miles, then were flagged down by a road block; a river had broken its banks and it was impossible to get through.

'Is there another route?' Leonard asked the streaming policeman standing by the car. 'We're trying to get to London.'

'You could go back to Norwich and see if there's a train, but half the county's under water. Might be all right in the morning, but I wouldn't count on it.'

'Thank you.' Leonard wound up the window and looked at his watch. 'It's taken us more than an hour to get this far. God knows what time we'll get back to Norwich.'

'And there might not be a train,' I pointed out. 'Looks like we're stuck. We passed a sign for a hotel a mile or so back. Let's try there.'

Any resemblance to a romantic comedy film was shattered by the Cranford Crest. According to the script, it should have been an historic coaching inn, run by a warm, elderly couple smiling knowingly at each other as we sat by the open fire in soft focus and fumbled our way to falling in love to hummable selections from Rachmaninov. In fact it was hideous. Modern, sterile, flocked wallpaper and carpets relentlessly matching. The immediate impression as you walked through the door was of a furniture catalogue, with trouser presses and kettles in the bedrooms for making morning tea. Muzak was endemic and inescapable. The teenage receptionist was obviously being knocked off by the manager, and the only other guests were a party of Japanese; the barman told us they were planning to buy a Jacobean manor house nearby and turn it into a golf course and conference centre.

'Double room?' The receptionist sounded as though she didn't care if we wanted to spend the night in the car park. 'The Tudor and Regency Suites are available.' You could hear the capital letters.

'Which has the four-poster bed?' Leonard asked.

'Both of them.'

'Such historical verisimilitude.' Irony was wasted on her. 'Neither, thank you. Two singles.'

I paused as I examined the damage to my hair in a mirror in the lobby; it had been a twenty-yard dash from the car protected only by a newspaper held over my head. I felt disappointed, but, since we'd been in the cathedral, he hadn't made even the most oblique suggestion to cause me to expect anything different.

'See you in the bar,' he said as we reached our rooms, mirror-image doors facing each other in a dreary corridor lined with reproduction fishing prints. 'There'll be prawn cocktail and locally caught trout on the menu, and whatever we order they'll push the Beaujolais Nouveau.'

'Undoubtedly.' The disappointment of the lobby was still with me. 'See you in the bar, then.'

'OK.' He unlocked his door. 'And put on that dress you wore on Friday evening.'

That was more promising, but still low key. It struck me that he'd never made sexually suggestive remarks to me, the sort of politely coarse banter most men and women casually exchange. When I found I still had a pair of clean knickers in my case I wondered if it was my desire rather than his imagined intentions that made me feel pleased.

He was already in the bar when I went down, flicking through a copy of *Country Life* (all the right magazines were provided, including several on motoring, and a note in my room discreetly referred to an adult TV channel; there had to be a contraceptive machine in the gents). On the table beside him was his whisky and a vodka and lime.

'Thank you,' I said, taking the plump matching easy-chair next to his and picking up the glass. 'You notice what I drink.'

'I notice a lot about you.' He beckoned the barman, who brought us two menus (green leather covers embossed in gold with the company's logo). 'They say the trout is off, which shows a rare degree of honesty, and soup of the day is French onion. Shall we risk it? There's not a lot they can do wrong with a packet.'

The Japanese delegation walked in, identical suits, polite smiles and suggestions of bows, then gathered at a table near the fireplace, talking in secretive, urgent tones as though their master plan was to buy up the whole of Norfolk and transfer it to Tokyo as an East Anglian theme park. We ordered our meal and Leonard turned to me.

'Nobody would ever think that half an hour ago you looked like a drowned gerbil – and that dress suits you. Versace?'

'School of.' I caught a drift of expensive aftershave, then jumped as the wind howled viciously and rain machine-gunned the windows just behind us.

'It's all right.' He took my hand, which was resting on the chair arm. 'The storm gods are angry, that's all.'

He kept hold of my hand as we talked until they called us through to the restaurant, and suddenly it was so *comfortable*. I'd been chatted up, leered at, mauled by wandering hands, ducked clumsily aimed kisses, endured all the garbage that women have to put up with. Now I was being courted by a man of incredible charm and was overwhelmed by it. Dinner was . . . dinner. It could have been the best that Quat' Saisons can offer or the worst of a greasy spoon. I was conscious only of Leonard, amused and amusing, flattering and attentive. There was so much . . . companionship to it. The word struck me as strange, because by the time we were having coffee and brandy in the lounge I was ready to let him do anything he wanted with me. The Japanese smiled goodnight on the stroke of eleven o'clock, and the barman pointedly asked if we wanted anything else.

'No, thank you,' Leonard told him. 'We're going to bed.'

As we reached our rooms again, he glanced at each anonymous door in turn. 'Do we toss a coin?'

'What's your view like?' I asked.

'Almost invisible in this weather, but there are trees and a distant church I saw by lightning.'

'Definitely yours, then. I drew the car park.' As he inserted the key, I felt . . . not so much aroused as incredibly happy (and exquisitely, faintly drunk). And all he'd done as we walked upstairs was to hold my hand again.

'Well, Mr Drummond,' I said archly as he closed the door. 'You certainly take your time.'

'I'm sorry?'

I nodded towards the bed. 'Most men I know are interested in bonking rather sooner than you.'

'Oh dear.' He sounded dismayed. 'My sex does piss me off sometimes.'

'What do you mean?'

'I mean I don't want to bonk you, Katrina.'

'Then what, pray, are we here for?' I laughed. The situation was ridiculous. 'To admire the view?'

'If I'd just wanted to bonk you, I'd have tried to do it a long time ago.' He put his arms around me. 'I want to make love to you.'

'But it will include the bed?' I asked uncertainly.

'That's the general idea. But you must have noticed that I've been making love to you in all sorts of other ways for some time.

130

If I go to bed with someone, I want it to be a person I've got to know, not just a woman.'

'Oh . . . But you still didn't ask for a double room.'

'No.' He reached behind my neck and unclasped my pearls. 'That would have meant I assumed that for no other reason than that we were marooned in a hotel for the night you'd suddenly be panting for me. I grew out of that attitude some time ago.'

I sighed. 'Christ, bloody few men do.'

'Ain't that the truth?' Carefully, he removed my earrings. 'So when we arrived here, I expected no more than the pleasure of your company for the evening. But things . . . developed. And here we are. So now . . .' still holding me, he moved back a couple of paces '. . . we turn off the light because there's enough from outside and at my age half-light is prudent. Then you kick your shoes off . . . Where've you gone? Oh, you're down there . . . and I reveal why I carefully avoided anything on the menu containing garlic. The escargots would have been frozen, anyway.'

I was laughing with delight as he kissed me.

It was ages before he'd undressed me completely, caressing each new area of flesh he revealed, making gentle jokes, rubbing my bare feet when I told him I liked that, recalling times we'd spent together . . . Oh, he was touching me very deeply. For a while I even stopped feeling randy; I just wanted him to hold me and stroke me and . . . love me. By the time he entered me, I needed him so urgently it was a delicious agony.

'I presume this is safe,' he murmured.

'I wouldn't give a damn if it wasn't. I just want you to stay exactly where you are for the next three hundred years.'

'It's very tempting, but I may have to move occasionally . . . If you'd like that, of course.'

'Oh, I think I might find it . . . Christ!' I shuddered and locked my arms and legs urgently around his body.

'But I didn't move,' he whispered.

'You didn't need to.'

And when I die, if God says I can have just one moment of my entire life again it will be what happened about ten minutes later. I thought I was dying at the time.

Eventually, I became conscious of the rain again, of the spasmodic savagery of the wind, that the bed had been designed by computer to accommodate one standard-size Western human being, of the smell of pungent air freshener, of the fact that I needed to go to the loo. Leonard was right on the edge, face down; his breathing had slowed but was still very deep. Softly, I ran my fingers down his back and he made a purring sound.

'And did the earth move for thee?' I asked.

His voice was half muffled by the pillow. 'If we look through those curtains, we'll probably see Wales outside.'

I giggled. 'I bet it's the Empire State Building.'

'Very phallic. Anyway, let's not try for California. They've got enough problems without us compounding them.'

'San Andreas, you're an amateur . . . Sorry, I need a pee.'

'Fold the lavatory paper back into a little point. It's compulsory.'

When I returned, he was lying with one arm behind his head. 'This is not a convenient bed for two people to sleep in.'

'It is if they're friendly. Turn on your side and we'll play spoons.' As I fell asleep, I remembered the first time Judith made love to me, and the contentment afterwards of simply being close to each other.

In the morning, Leonard hung the 'Do Not Disturb' signs outside both our rooms, and we made it only just in time for the final serving of Sunday lunch. The rain had stopped but the floods were still going down, so we decided to stay another night. We went for the walk where I took the photograph, and back at the hotel he told the receptionist we'd decided to move into the Regency Suite.

'I hope there's nothing wrong with your rooms, sir,' she said. God, she was dense.

'Not at all. But we may never find a Regency four-poster again.'

'It's standard in all our hotels, sir.'

'Of course it is. How stupid of me. We'll bear that in mind.'

He started quoting the opening chapter of *Emma* – he knew most of it by heart – as we made love. I made sure he didn't get past page two.

*

It lasted just over a year. I'd have been happy to leap into bed with him every afternoon and all weekend, but he spread it out so that each time there was an excitement of meeting again. Weeks would pass when we didn't even speak to each other, then there would be a phone call or a card. Sorry he'd been busy or away or whatever; he'd missed me. Was I free for lunch or supper on . . . ? I cancelled a lot of engagements at the last moment. I bought all his books and read them over and over again, but I didn't want the writer, I wanted the lover who understood women. God doesn't make enough of those.

I can't remember dropping overt hints, in fact I'm sure I didn't, but I knew this affair wasn't going away, not for me at any rate. He never talked about his marriage, but I sensed distance in it; his wife certainly spent a good deal of time abroad. I may have started sending out signals without realizing it, but there was nothing coming back. Whatever, for the first time since the false dreams of Tom, one person mattered more than anything else, and this time I knew what I was doing. Happiness is a deceptive magician.

Christmas found me in the classic mistress at home alone while he's with his family situation, which triggered my carefully phrased hints in the New Year. When he didn't respond, I began to tease him, then my frustration started to surface and we argued. It was going wrong, and I couldn't understand why. We loved each other – we *liked* each other, which was equally important – and we'd crossed a lot of bridges. I couldn't understand his reluctance to commit, or identify the sense of remorse that accompanied it. I pulled back and the tenseness went away.

During the summer, I wanted us to spend a week together in Paris while his wife was away, but he said it was impossible, without explaining why. Then, in late September, he rang and asked me to meet him one Saturday afternoon in Kensington Gardens, but would give me no reason. He was waiting on a bench overlooking the water near Peter Pan's statue.

'Why've you dragged me out here?' I asked. 'You could have come to the flat. It's bloody chilly.'

'I wanted you to meet someone.'

'Who?' He appeared to be alone.

'Teresa. My daughter.'

'Oh.' Abruptly, I sat down next to him. 'You might have warned me.'

'I couldn't find a way of saying it.'

'Saying what?'

'What I'm going to have to say now. She'll be back in a minute. Marion's taken her to feed the ducks.'

'Who's Marion?'

'Her nurse.'

'Nurse? I thought she was about fourteen.'

'She's fifteen next month.' He took hold of my hand. 'I've started to feel bad about how I've decided to do this, but it's too late now. It was never the idea that we should fall in love.'

'But we have, haven't we?'

'Yes. That's the problem . . .' His hand went away. 'Here she is.'

She looked nearer ten than a teenager as she approached round a curve in the path, mystified, glazed eyes in a mindlessly happy face, clumsy walk, hands floppy. She was wearing a woollen bonnet tied beneath her chin, and mittens with strings attached dangled from her wrists. Her coat gave the impression of an awkwardly shaped parcel wrapped as well as possible. She was dribbling slightly and the sounds she made when she saw her father were incomprehensible to me.

'Did you see the ducks, Teresa?' he asked her. 'What did they say?'

I could feel tears of shock and pity starting as she made mangled noises and turned to look at the water again, bewildered they weren't there to show him.

'That's right. They say quack, quack. Clever girl.'

Limping slightly, a woman had walked up behind Teresa; as soon as the child realized she was there, she grasped her hand and made infantile kissing faces at her. She was about fifty, although white hair made her look older, wearing trousers, low-heeled shoes and a trench coat.

'This is Marion,' Leonard said. 'Teresa's nurse. Katrina Darcy, a friend of mine.'

'Hello.' She took out a tissue and stooped to wipe away saliva. 'We'll walk down to the bridge and Teresa can drop stones in the water.'

'Thank you, Marion. We'll set off back soon. I'll find you.'

For several minutes we were silent after they left us, then Leonard leant forward, arms resting on his knees.

'I have a prepared speech.'

'Let's hear it.' I was taking an enormous amount on board.

'You probably think it's inexcusable using Teresa like this, but she doesn't understand and I needed you to see her. She's the way she is because Judith and I shouldn't have had children. Genetic accident country. By the time we found out, it was too late. The result, for a very long time, has been a sexless marriage—'

'Why?' I interrupted. 'There was nothing to stop you making love.'

'Perhaps not, but people react in different ways. Judith became committed to her career and me to my writing. The shared commitment was Teresa. Marion's her third full-time nurse, but we both feel we owe her everything we can give. Her condition is our fault.'

'It's nobody's fault. It's—'

'That's how we see it.' He spoke sharply. 'Everyone we know tries to impose their own brand of logic, but it's pointless. All right?'

'I'm sorry.' I was resisting what I feared was coming. 'Go on.'

He raised his head and looked across the park towards the distant traffic. 'So we did the mature, intelligent individuals bit and agreed we would be faithful to the marriage because that meant we would be faithful to Teresa. Her understanding's very limited, but she would know if we ever split up and it would distress her.' He glanced over his shoulder at me. 'Don't try logic again. On the question of being faithful to each other, we agreed it should be like having separate friends. Close friends. Judith attends medical conferences all over the world, and I have the lecture tours and promotional trips. The rules are simple. Always bring back a present for Teresa, and only talk about the business side. It's worked so far.'

'Why are you telling me this?'

'Because the space . . .' he waved his hand back and forwards between us '. . . is getting too small. I didn't mean that to happen. There haven't been many affairs – you know the way I think – but the others just ran their course. This one kept going.'

'Yeah.' I ground my cigarette out on the path. 'You are a bastard, Leonard. You can even end this in a way that means I can't hate you.'

'It's not an act.'

'I know it isn't. I'm sorry. I've suddenly started hurting a lot, but by God you've always been honest.' I looked at him. 'I really thought that . . . Oh, what the hell.' I laughed defensively. 'Whatever happens, we'll always have the Cranford Crest.'

'And a lot more.' He squeezed my hand. 'If it helps, I hurt as well.'

I shook my head. 'Don't say that. What you have to learn, my love, is that there's a limit to how much understanding a woman can cope with.' I didn't know you could be so near to crying without actually doing it. 'We'll see each other again, though? Please.'

'Of course, but let's leave it a while. Anyway, I must lock myself in a room and finish the new book.' He stood up. 'Now I've got to take Teresa and Marion home.'

'So we say goodbye by Peter Pan.'

'Yes.' He looked regretful. 'I didn't think of that. Lousy choice of location. Another poor kid who couldn't grow up. Sorry. Take care.'

We kissed very gently and held each other for a few moments; then he walked away towards the bridge. He waved to his daughter and the nurse helped her to wave back. I watched him going away until I couldn't bear it any more, went home, howled a lot and drank too much. There are times when all that life grants us are the clichés.

London

Possible leads for pages three and five of the *Sunday Times* had collapsed, giving the mystery of a celebrity's disappearance greater urgency; Richard Harvey had reached the stage where Katrina Darcy being found would be a major irritation. He had put three reporters on to the story, one to research the background, the others to chase what few facts were available. There was no shortage of contacts, but nothing more than guesswork and rumour was emerging until somebody remembered Tom Darcy.

'For Christ's sake, he's next door on the *Times*.' Hamilton threw an internal phone directory at Penny Conrad, who had returned empty-handed from visiting Katrina's flat. 'Get on to him.'

'I thought they split up years ago.'

'They did, but there's a daughter, so they must have kept in touch over her if nothing else. Even if he doesn't know where she is, he's got to be good for a quote.'

'Won't he give the story to the *Times*?'

'We'll have to risk that. Anyway, it's too late for them to do a proper job on it for tomorrow. Just don't tell him anything we know.'

She checked the directory, then dialled the extension. 'Is Tom Darcy about?'

'He's just gone on his break. Who's calling?'

'Penny Conrad on the *ST*. Is he in the canteen?'

'Probably. Can anyone else help?'

'No, it's OK.' She rang off and turned to Harvey. 'I can catch him on his break. What does he look like?'

'Tom Darcy? Tall, mid-fifties, small grey beard—'

'Raddled,' added the girl next to him. 'And he's got seriously wandering hands. Wet your lips and he'll tell you anything.'

'Man of my dreams.' Conrad commented.

She crossed to the main block, taking the lift to 4A. As she entered the self-service area, she spotted Darcy carrying his tray through to the pay desk and collected a coffee for herself while he found a table. In the restaurant she couldn't see him at first, but then realized he must be in the smoking area behind the slatted wooden partition. He was sitting alone beneath one of the abstract prints that lined the wall, reading the *Evening Standard* open beside his plate; he had the resigned, defeated air of a middle-aged journalist going through the motions of a career leading nowhere until he was offered acceptable terms for early retirement.

'Tom Darcy?' The way his eyes flicked down to the outline of her breasts and back again appeared automatic, even subconscious.

'Yes. I've seen you around, haven't I?'

'Probably. Penny Conrad, *Sunday Times*. Have you got a minute?'

He gestured with his knife. 'Sit down. What is it?'

'It's about Katrina. We're trying to get in touch with her, but she seems to be away. I wondered if you knew where she was.'

His face, which had been interested, went blank. 'No, I don't. My very famous ex-wife and I don't have anything to do with each other. Why do you want her, anyway?'

Conrad hesitated. 'Off the record?'

'If you want.'

'She's disappeared. They're panicking at the *Register*, and we're doing a piece on it. We thought you might know something.'

Darcy shrugged. 'She's probably screwing someone.' There was a distinct bitterness, unexpected so long after the marriage had ended.

'But everyone says she wouldn't go off without letting them know.'

'I know her better than that. She does whatever she wants.'

'So you can't help?'

138

'No.' He began to eat again. 'I last saw her ... It must be a year or so ago ... That's it, our daughter's eighteenth birthday.'

'Do you still see your daughter?'

'When she feels like it.' Bitterness had turned to self-pity, and Conrad felt he might produce at least a quote if she could encourage him to talk.

'How long were you married?'

'Too bloody long.'

'What happened?'

'Once she'd finished using me as a stepping stone, she went her own way.' He looked at her. 'She was a junior on a bloody weekly when she met me. I was the one who got her on to the nationals. As far as I'm concerned, she's a cow.'

'Aren't you worried that she's missing?'

'The only thing that worries me is that she'll turn up again.' His eyes challenged her to take offence.

'Can you help us to contact your daughter? She might be able to tell us where—'

'Leave it out. I don't want to talk about it. All right?'

Conrad sipped her coffee, watching him over the rim of the cup. He was angry.

'Why is this so heavy?' she asked. 'You broke up a long time ago.'

'Who says it's heavy?'

'You're making it sound that way.'

'Somebody might fuck you up one day. You don't forget. Is that it?'

She hesitated. 'Quote on the record? You know, former husband mystified.'

Darcy gave a small, sardonic laugh. 'How about "I don't give a shit if the bitch is alive or dead"?'

'You're telling me I can quote you as saying that?'

'If you want.'

Conrad stared at him thoughtfully. 'She really got to you, didn't she?'

Darcy said nothing but pointedly turned over a page of the

139

paper and started reading. Conrad stood up. 'Sorry to have troubled you.'

'You haven't.'

She returned to the *Sunday Times* concluding he was unable to cope with his own inadequacies, but still adjusting to the level of his hostility. One of her women colleagues, who had once worked with Darcy, gave part of the explanation.

'Tom was a star on the *Mail* until he blew it. His future's been behind him for years. He resents the fact that Katrina is right up there – and she's done it on her own – but the sickest thing is that he's got a major hang-up about the fact she can still pull almost anyone she wants. Pitiful or what?'

'You're joking,' Conrad protested. 'He hates her for that?'

'Believe me. I've heard him in the pub. You'd be amazed how spiteful he can be.'

'The way he was looking at me, I bet he cheated on her when they were married.'

'Of course he did. It was years ago and I've forgotten the details, but he was perfectly happy as long as Katrina was a doormat and he could screw around. He's never forgiven her for fighting back.'

'He told me we can quote him as saying he doesn't care if she's alive or dead,' Conrad recalled.

'Wrong – he'd prefer her dead.'

Thursday Evening

The weather was so good this afternoon that I had to go out; it could be a long time before I can walk between the hedgerows of these lanes again. I picked wild montbretia that flickers in orange flames among the dark green of hawthorn, ivy and convolvulus; chatted to a group of cows that inquisitively wandered up to a gate I was leaning on and fed them grass; smiled at a young couple with rucksacks and serious shoes walking hand in hand; waved to a man who passed me on a tractor; picked up a plastic bag someone had thrown away, because it offended me; scratched my hand probing for early blackberries; cried for a while at one point; nearly went into a church, but what for? It was probably locked, anyway.

I wonder how it will end here? A car driving up, a CID officer from London showing me his identification, the formal caution, a silent policewoman for propriety's sake, a courteous request to accompany them after I've called my solicitor and packed? Tuxedo will be cross when I shoo him out but within an hour he'll have forgotten me again. Somebody will have tipped off the pack and I'll get out of the car at – I don't know where my local police station is – to whirring motor drives, icelight of flash, television cameras probing like rigid tentacles, and unanswerable shouted questions.

'Where've you been, Katrina? Was anyone with you? How are you feeling? Can you give us a statement? Have you spoken to the editor? Who's your lawyer? We want to talk to him. Look this way! Give us a smile! Wave! Have they charged you? What with? Where are you going to stay? Did you give yourself up?'

People who hardly know me will sell tit-bits, anecdotes they've twisted into smut. News editors will slaver when the bisexual line

141

comes out and start killing to find a girlfriend, preferably young and pretty who'll pose with her lips slightly apart because butch lesbians don't excite their male readers. The tabloids will get out the chequebooks to buy the exclusive, but they'll want blood for their money. None of them will be interested in the truth, because the truth is long and complicated; they'll want sensation, simplistic guilty confession, remorse, just enough sex to titillate without offence in a family newspaper. Agony and confusion that is tearing me apart will be crushed into six words in the headline and my entire life will have to fit into five instalments of fifteen hundred words. And their readers will lap it up, the tedium of their lives alleviated by tragedy where they feel no pain. A few may be sympathetic, but others will write letters calling me a bitch, ungrateful for everything I've enjoyed while they can't manage, their conviction of my wickedness making them feel superior. Understand? What's understanding got to do with it? This is journalism, not help.

God, this is maudlin – and hypocritical. How many lives have I distorted into a good read? The fact is that I've murdered someone; I didn't mean to, but I did it. Now I'm hiding from it and finding excuses not to go back; I've got the spiteful courage to hurt, but I'm screaming at the thought of the same pain being turned on me.

This evening I went and looked at what I call the Sun Stone. From the end of the garden I can just see the tip of the little cove that ends in a tall, tapered rock, bleached by the weather. When the falling sun's right, it lights it for about ten minutes through a gap in the hills and it blazes like a sallow frozen flame. I wondered how long it would be before I watched it glow and fade again. When I'm not angry, I'm sentimental.

ANNA

She's leaning against the wall of the Chelsea Embankment and bleak winter light has got into one side of the frame, throwing her figure into an ochre silhouette, the sort of atmospheric image that art editors love. You can't make out what she's wearing, but it was rust-red culottes, tan leather boots and the patchwork suede waistcoat I bought her in Covent Garden market. Her face is almost completely lost, but I can still see the nose that was fractionally too long and irritated her so much. She was my completely unexpected lover.

The people overlap in my life, of course; she arrived in the Leonard period, played her own part, then was important in what happened afterwards. Anna Probert, fourteen cousins in the Rhondda, a 2:1 in combined English and American Studies at Aberystwyth, appeared scatty but cat-clever underneath, funny, ambitious, wanted it *now*. After moving to London, she worked in PR for a while before joining the *Register*, taking the editorial secretary's job as a foothold in journalism after failing to land any of the graduate entry reporter vacancies. I shared her with three other writers and the picture editor.

'What's your ambition, then?' I asked her shortly after she arrived. She'd made no secret of virtual instant impatience with what she had.

She shrugged. 'Your job'll do.'

'Don't hold your breath. Now get me a coffee from the canteen. Cream, no sugar.' She amused me.

She was incredibly shrewd; within a couple of weeks she'd sized up everyone in the office and when I asked her for a rundown on some of them her accuracy was startling.

'Malcolm's shy, and I bet he used to stammer. Anthony's a

143

sweetie, and he sees right through people. Mark overplays the hard bastard act because he's unsure of himself. Fiona's an intellectual snob and I wouldn't trust her, Trevor's a crawler, Roger's a dreamer who only fires on three cylinders and Sally's just passing the time until she meets someone who'll marry her and give her a houseful of kids.'

'How do you work that out?'

'Child-bearing hips. My sister's got them.'

I laughed. 'Idiotic logic, but you're right. What about me?'

She pursed her lips. 'Truth or discretion?'

'Try discretion, then I'll tell you if I want truth.'

'OK . . . Disappointed about something, but you keep it hidden.'

'You could say that about almost anyone,' I remarked.

'But nobody would think you've got anything to be disappointed about. Star columnist, books, own TV programme. So the disappointment must be a big one.'

'Grandmother a witch, was she?'

'So I'm right.'

'Maybe.' Surrounded for years by people who paid me compliments, I wasn't accustomed to 25-year-olds who spoke their minds. And I did suffer periods of disappointment, although without knowing what brought them on. I decided it must be middle-age disillusion, an awareness that I was playing the second half, speculative reflections about roads not taken. Perhaps a realization that I'd spent my life in the most ephemeral of professions – the first stirrings of the cynical journalist – and somewhere up ahead was old age, some sort of summing-up, inertia after endless activity. I wasn't prepared to recognize more than that. In any event, at that stage I was warmed by secret dreams about me and Leonard, which would completely transform the picture.

'Do you want truth?' she added.

'Another time. I'm going out.'

'Of course you are.'

A lot of our conversations were like that, invariably finishing with an equivocal comment and enigmatic look from her.

*

144

She began writing pieces to fill panic holes in the magazine section or feature pages, dateless so they could be held on file. Fiona resisted for a while – editorial secretaries were meant to do nothing more for publication than a round-up of imaginative Christmas presents for under ten pounds – but she finally used one of them. When I was next in the office I found a cutting on my desk, which Anna had signed.

'My first piece, autographed,' she said. 'For you. It might be worth money one day.'

'I'll treasure it for ever.'

'Don't be so bloody condescending. What was the first thing you ever had in a newspaper?'

I thought back a depressingly long time. 'Two pars about a WI coffee morning in the *Stockport Courier*.'

'And look where you've ended up.' She stuck her tongue out at me. 'Watch your back.'

'Get out,' I told her, laughing. She began putting her cuttings up on the wall by her desk, but stopped when she ran out of space.

Anna was always complaining about being hard up, with the rent on her Chiswick flat taking up most of her salary, which is why I decided to offer her the chance of some money on top of her extra writing work.

'Here you are,' I said, putting the proofs of *Who Katy Laid Next* on her desk. 'Check that for me and it's worth a hundred quid.'

'What is it?'

'My new book.'

She looked surprised. 'Do you have to do your own proof reading?'

'Theoretically. They send it out to a professional reader as well, but I'm supposed to check it myself. Here's the typescript. Make sure they've not left anything out.'

'Classy title, dodgy grammar,' she said sarcastically, flicking through the opening pages. 'I won't expect A. S. Byatt.'

'Don't. I've got to return it in two weeks . . . And I don't want a literary critique. It won't stand it. At least it's not too long. They're blowing up the type size to give them enough pages.'

Three days later it was back on my desk, typos, mispunctua-

145

tions and occasional insertions from the original neatly marked –
she had minute but impeccable handwriting – with a note on a
postcard from the Tate Gallery: 'I demand £150; it's putrid!
Incidentally, you can't spell millennium – the root is anno, which
means there are two ns – and you don't know the difference
between "like" and "such as". It doesn't matter, of course; I can't
imagine your readers do, either. You've also got a cock-up
(plotwise, not sexual, which makes a change) in Chapter Seven.
I'll explain when I get back from Wales. Love, Anna.'

I read the chapter again but couldn't see anything wrong with
it. I nearly returned the proofs, but fortunately hung on to them
until she returned.

'What's the problem with Chapter Seven?' I demanded.

She came and stood next to me, turning to the middle of the
chapter. 'Look. After they spend the night together, he flies
to Acapulco. Right? Then she's screwing his father when he
phones from Singapore. You're so anxious to get in another
couple of pages of soft porn and perfect climaxes, it's all
happening on the same day. Christ knows how she found time
for Harvey Nichols.'

'Are you sure?'

'Check it yourself. Your readers must be fairly dense, but even
they might notice that.' She pointed with her pen. 'Anyway, if
you put a couple of sentences in here, you can buy yourself as
much time as you need to move him a few thousand miles. Send
her to a health farm for colonic irrigation. It's about the only
bodily experience you haven't put her through.'

'All right. Thank you. That's worth a hundred and fifty . . .
and lunch.' I don't know why I added that. Anna became silly.

'Lunch? God bless you, lady. Long life and all happiness. Just
a crust'll do. I'll wear me best.'

'As long as it's not Welsh national costume. Book a table at
the Criterion for Friday.'

'Don't I get the Ivy?'

'No, you bloody don't.'

*

She was one of those people I instinctively liked, conscientious, good at her job and intelligent company. Everyone got on with her, and one of the reporters had been seen out with her a couple of times. She still had provincial edges, but she was working hard at smoothing them. Her clothes sense had certainly improved. For lunch she wore a Vivienne Westwood dress which she'd bought in a nearly-new charity shop in West Kensington and carried an extravagantly fringed Persian shawl from Camden market, which complemented it rather well.

'It's only the Criterion,' I said when she arrived that morning and I instantly felt bad, as though she had made a special effort and I was putting her down. I should have known her better.

'I know.' Her mocking ennui was exquisitely pitched. 'If it had been Langan's, I'd have dressed up. Still, we might see someone vaguely famous slumming it.'

The only person we actually saw was Emma, my agent, who was lunching with an independent television producer.

'The Americans rang to say yes just before I came out,' she said as she paused at our table. 'Megabucks. They're faxing a draft contract for us to argue over. I'll call you.'

Anna looked impressed as she walked away. 'Congratulations. I'll keep my opinions about your books to myself in future.'

'I don't mind,' I told her. 'I know they're rubbish.'

'Why don't you write something better? You could.'

'Too much like hard work – and I wouldn't make as much money.'

I can't remember our conversation particularly. She told me about her background, which was nothing remarkable apart from the fact that she had a brother who was a radio actor I'd never heard of. We discussed the business, but she'd been picking mine and others' brains since day one, so there was little new there. She asked about me and I gave her a few selected highlights, then we just chatted. We were finishing the second bottle of wine when she threw me.

'Were you ever married?'

'Once. A long time ago.'

'What happened?'

147

I shrugged. 'It didn't work . . . What about you? Anyone lined up?'

She replied in an exaggerated accent. 'Oh, a boy in the valleys pines for me something rotten. Wants us to marry in the bethesda, then live in a semi in Swansea and have kids called Megan and Ifor. There's lovely.'

I grinned. 'Does he come to see you in town?'

'He did once, but it was really to watch London Welsh play Pontypridd. He couldn't understand it when I didn't want to go with him. He was legless when he got back and I made him catch the last train to Cardiff. The penny still didn't drop.'

'Home keeping youth have ever homely wits,' I said, pouring her another glass of Médoc, then my hand shook and I spilled some as she spoke again.

'Anyway, I want to go to bed with you.'

I put the bottle down before I dropped it. She had made it sound as though she was suggesting we went window shopping in Regent Street when we'd finished.

'Pardon?'

'You heard.'

'But . . . Look, I didn't realize you were gay, but what makes you think I am?'

'Look at me.' She leant her arms on the table, bringing her face closer to mine. 'Now tell me you've never made love to a woman.'

Slate blue eyes challenged me to deny it. I suddenly remembered how I'd assessed her when she started with us; not beautiful, but with the ability to look stunningly pretty. Her hair, raven black with the sheen of the bird's feathers, was parted in the centre then fell to below her chin before flicking inwards, framing and emphasizing pink cheeks and dusty ivory skin. Her lips were thin, but she brought them out with dark lipstick. When I didn't reply, she simply nodded.

'Would you have told me this about myself if I'd asked for the truth whenever it was we had that conversation?' I asked.

'I'd have been elliptical, but you'd have got the message.'

'Anyway, you're out of date.' I moved away from her slightly.

148

'It was . . . Christ, you can hardly have been born. I was seduced by a teacher. It's never happened since. I'm resolutely hetero now – and there's a serious fella. OK?'

'Pity. You're very attractive.' She sat back in her chair. 'OK. Worth a try . . . I'd like a pudding, please.'

Anna's orientation surprised me – her dates with the reporter had just been a chance to be taken out for a movie and supper, with the hapless romeo of the valleys a convenient excuse to deflect standard manoeuvres – but I was more amazed that she had seen indications of it remaining in me. Judith had been ecstasy as well as trauma, but that had been my one excursion into lesbianism. I knew women whom I thought attractive – Fiona had knockout legs, and there was a blonde in display advertising with a figure designed for sin – but it was a detached appreciation, like admiring something they wore or a new hairstyle . . . Anna's perception could be disturbing.

I've just deleted four pages of things that happened over the next few weeks; the important thing is where we were going, not how we got there. At the end of April I was sent tickets for the first night of a West End show, which happened to be on her birthday, and I invited her to come with me. Afterwards, I ran her home and she asked me in for a drink. There had been nothing at all to suggest that the Criterion lunch was anything but history.

Her flat was one half of the ground floor of a post-war semi, minute kitchen built on to the sitting room at the back, and the bedroom at the front. The loo and bathroom were shared. She put on a tape of . . . I think it was Ella Fitzgerald . . . then we sat in facing armchairs, talking about the show and others we'd seen. I was thinking of leaving when she kicked off her right shoe and stretched her leg across the space between us, rubbing her toes against my shin. I pushed it away.

'It's like riding a bike,' she said softly. 'Once you've learnt how to do it, you soon pick it up again.'

'No way, lady,' I said crossly. 'I only swing one way now, and I told you there's someone who matters – a lot.'

'OK.' She shrugged and stood up. 'Sorry. Won't try again. Promise. Another drink?'

'No, thanks. I don't want to be stopped on the way home. Anyway, nice evening. Glad you enjoyed it.'

'I always enjoy being with you ... Oh, slap my wrist!' She did so. 'I'm fast. I'm a bad lot. I'll go to hell. Call me Dolores like they do in the stories.'

'Goodnight, Anna,' I said firmly. 'Find someone else.'

Leonard played his scene with Teresa the following September. I cried a river, then told myself that I had to shake it off. I began to work like fury and although there was sex available (there always is unless you're green with two heads), I wasn't interested. I didn't tell anyone what had happened – I'd kept Leonard a very secret part of my life – but one morning I found an envelope on my desk and inside was a card from Anna with the message 'Get Well Soon'.

'What's this about?' I demanded. 'I'm not bloody ill.'

'Tell me about it,' she said drily, throwing away a pile of junk mail. 'You've got chronic something. Heart all right, is it?'

'No.' I sighed. Caught off-balance, the idea of being able to talk to someone brought immense relief. 'I thought we grew out of this sort of thing. Like measles.'

'But measles is very nasty in grown-ups.' She frowned. 'Or is it "are nasty"? It sounds wrong either way.'

I grinned; smiling was still tricky. 'Want to be a sob sister? I appear to need one.'

'Sure. I'll supply the hankies.'

'Thanks. Tell you what. Supper at my place tonight. We'll send out for pizzas.' I held up the card. 'When did you guess?'

'I didn't guess. Something happened about three weeks ago. Yes?'

'Almost to the day. You're a shrewd little bitch.'

I was at the stage when it only needed someone's affectionate attention to swamp my emotions. That night I poured it out diluted with red wine and all she did was listen, nod in sympathy, remain silent whenever I wept, softly coax out the pain. It was half-term and I'd agreed to let Tom take Stephanie away, so I could invite Anna to stay, but she didn't make the slightest move towards me, slept on the sofa and brought me tea in the morning.

'Sorry it's early,' she apologized. 'But I need to pop home and change before work. I'm due in at ten.'

'I'll give you a lift,' I offered.

'Don't be silly, but you can pay for a taxi. I'll call one. See you in the office.'

Fifteen minutes later she left, calling goodbye. When I went into the kitchen she'd cleared away everything we'd left the night before and washed up. Taped to the fridge door was a large piece of paper with a childish smiley face drawn on it with a yellow marker pen and there were flowers on my desk when I arrived at the office that afternoon. She was so clever; I longed to be hugged. We made love for the first time a week later, and her experience made up for my lack of practice. I never imagined I'd do that again – but I'd never imagined I'd have fallen in love the way I had with Leonard. Gradually we moved from victim and helper to friends and – all right – eager bed partners. The Celts are very passionate and what started as a form of ultimate comfort became an exquisite lust. It was exactly the sort of relationship I needed, no commitments or promises to break, no vulnerability of the heart, no exposed defences. It became . . . uncomplicated fun, satisfying and wickedly decadent, something to smile over inwardly and which gave a secret ambivalence to certain conversations when we were with other people. We were very discreet and no one suspected a thing.

It was a gorgeous autumn (except when I took her to Cornwall and it bucketed down), London painted with browns, golds and cinnamons, crisp foam of leaves beneath our shoes as we walked, brass-bright sunshine in diamond-cold blue skies, stretched shadows pencilled across parks in the afternoons. By winter it had become familiarity, by early summer it was fading. I felt enormously grateful to her for helping me through, but there was nowhere for us to go and the sex had lost its frisson and novelty. She accepted the situation as willingly as I did, and I bought her a new Westwood dress as a goodbye present. She left soon after for a feature writer's job with one of the group's magazines. Their offices were in Clerkenwell and we saw each other only occasionally. She left good memories, among the last I have.

London

The tabloids would have been more satisfied if Katrina Darcy had been a teenage actress in a soap opera or the supermodel girlfriend of a rock star, but in August they were grateful for anything. There were enough pictures available that made her look glamorous, and references to blatant sex scenes in her books went well with a shot of her stooping out of a taxi in a low-cut dress as she arrived at a film première.

'Nice tits . . . How old is she? . . . Forties? . . . Reminds me of my first wife; I used to wish she looked like that. Anyone got this in colour? Tell them we'll pay five hundred for it exclusively . . . Anything with anyone famous? . . . David Mellor? Better than nothing. Get hold of some of her book covers. There was one of a redhead with a tiger or something on a leash . . . No, that's crap. Makes her look too old . . .'

The urgency was for the exclusive angle, the indiscretion of a friend, the malice of an enemy, the suggestion of something lurid. Drugs? Possible, but no sign of a line on that. AIDS? She's been putting it around enough. Been careless? Check the clinics. Run off with the lover? Obvious, but who is it? Wasn't there a piece in the *Mail* Diary a while back about her being seen out with . . . what's his name? Rupert something. Does that chat show for the brain dead. No, hang on, we ran a piece last week about him getting engaged. Talk to him, anyway. Isn't there a daughter somewhere? Find her . . .

Stories for early editions began to take shape, occasional gaps in information filled with speculation prejudiced to agendas.

From the *Daily Mail*, scheduled as the second lead on page five. Largely rewritten by a sub-editor from three reporters' copy. A

153

previously unused photograph from the paper's Diary file, showing Katrina Darcy with Daniel Day Lewis at a reception, was to accompany the piece. Headline: 'Why has Katrina done a Suzi?'

> Best-selling author Katrina Darcy has copied one of her exotic heroines, Suzi Sinclair, and mysteriously disappeared.
>
> Katrina, 46, failed to turn up at the *Sunday Register*, for which she writes a weekly column, yesterday and executives at the paper admitted they had not seen her for several days. There was no reply at her luxury London apartment and efforts to find a secret cottage she owns in Cornwall were continuing.
>
> Suzi, the oversexed wife of a media magnate, is the central character in *Eligible Lovers*, which sold 100,000 copies in paperback and became a TV mini-series attracting eight million viewers. In the controversial book, she vanishes after murdering her lesbian lover, later turning up as the mistress of a Japanese prince.
>
> Rupert Rose, host of *Rose's Pick*, used to be her regular escort. Speaking from America last night, he said: 'I haven't seen her for more than a year. I hope she's OK. We were good friends, but she had these moods and I think she sometimes got fed up with being famous.'
>
> Bettina Warwick, whose own bodice rippers rival Katrina's success, commented: 'Everyone paints us as deadly enemies, but we've always got on with each other. One thing is certain – Katrina is a professional. If she's missed a deadline, it's because she's got a very good reason.'
>
> Justin Hammond, producer of Katrina's Channel Four programme *Spiked Copy*, added: 'We're due to meet next month to discuss the new series. I last saw her a few weeks ago and if anything she was happier than I've known her for ages. I can't imagine what has happened.'
>
> Katrina, who started her career as a *Daily Mail* reporter,

is one of Britain's leading women journalists, commanding top-of-the-range fees for her work. She has been a long-time close personal friend of *Sunday Register* managing editor Malcolm Kendall, 57, and accompanied him to a Liberal party conference where they stayed at a four-star hotel. Last night he was said to be 'very upset' by her disappearance.

From the *Sun*, pencilled in for page eleven. Entirely the phrasing of the home subs' desk after six rewrites. The accompanying photographs were to be a headshot of Katrina Darcy and a deep, three-column of Jackie Hilman wearing a wet T-shirt. Headline: 'Kinky Kate Pulls In Her Klaws'.

Bonk-busting bestseller Kate Darcy, whose sizzling sex sagas make Miss Whiplash look like a virgin, has vanished.

Britain's queen of soft porn was last seen a week ago and nobody knows where she is. Her swish £250,000 London flat is empty and a close friend said last night: 'She's just disappeared.'

Fortysomething Kate, blonde newspaper columnist and TV star, has had endless glamorous toyboy escorts, including pin-up chat show host Rupert Rose, now living with Hollywood wonderbrat Jessica Martine.

'I haven't seen Katrina for more than a year,' Rupert, 29, said from his Bel Air hotel. 'I don't know where she can be.'

The couple once spent a fortnight together in Jamaica, when fresh oysters were delivered every day to their beachside love nest.

Kate's biggest hit was *The Leopardess*, the adventures of sexpert Starr Xanadu, which featured steamy three-in-a-bed, rubber bondage and lesbian sessions.

Busty Jackie Hilman, who played Starr in the mini-series of the book – due to be screened on Sky TV next month – said: 'We had to cut out most of what Kate wrote or it would have been banned. I don't know where she learnt some of those things.'

Last night, Kate's bosses on the *Sunday Register* admitted that their star writer, said to earn more than £150,000 a year from books, TV and newspapers, made her own rules.

'I'm sure she's all right,' one added. 'But obviously we are worried about her.'

One of Kate's other books, *Eligible Lovers*, was attacked by a vicar as 'smut, sensation and sinful' – but it still sold all over the world.

From the *Guardian*, suggested for the foot of page three. By a Cambridge politics graduate who usually wrote Parliamentary sketches, unchanged by the subs. No picture. Headline: 'Fact and fiction after erotic author writes Fleet Street a story'.

Katrina Darcy, who combines a career as a provocative commentator and broadcasting personality with the profitable writing of licentious trash novels, has mysteriously gone absent without leave.

The *Sunday Register* columnist's failure to arrive at the office – hardly an unknown phenomenon in journalism – was described by colleagues as unprecedented, and the tabloids were enjoying a welcome late summer news story, scarce facts magnified by suggestions that touched the higher lunacies of kidnap, suicide and hideouts with assorted lovers.

Ms Darcy, 46, has achieved the rare distinction of having followers in both Hampstead and among the Rottweiler-owning fraternity of Essex. Her Sunday column and Channel Four programme, *Spiked Copy*, attract the chatterati with a combination of controversy, wit and good conversation. Her books – shamelessly exploiting the bubble reputation of media celebrity – are ruthlessly calculated to appeal to the sexual fantasist, indeed fetishist. Ecstatic bodies are described in meticulous detail, and guaranteed simultaneous satisfaction for all eagerly consenting parties are among their many fictions. Two television adaptations had to be severely censored from the originals.

The cynical observer would suspect a publicity quotient to such a disappearance, but it does not appear to coincide with the publication of a new opus or any other endeavour. Malcolm Kendall, managing editor of the *Sunday Register*, sounded concerned. In a statement released last night, he said: 'Katrina Darcy is a committed professional. We have neither seen nor heard from her for a week, and there appears to be no explanation. We are making extensive inquiries and trust that she is safe and well.'

Mr Kendall declined to enlarge on his statement, but a close source said: 'Katrina has never allowed her personal life to interfere with her work. This is very out of character.'

Several newspaper editors will appreciate Ms Darcy remaining out of character until the dog days of August have passed.

STEPHANIE

Her photographs appear on page after page, twenty years chronicled in fractions of seconds. Inquisitively peering round the hood of her pram outside the Barnet house; the pale angel in an infants' school nativity play; looking tiny and gripping my hand for reassurance as we stand next to the statue of Guy the gorilla at London Zoo; a portrait taken on impulse when I spotted a photographer's stand in a supermarket; buried in the sand at Newquay; self-conscious fourteen in her first full-length frock when I took her to a film première; both of us on skis at Val d'Isère; outside the flat with the car I bought her. I'm sure I had some of her with Tom, but they disappeared.

I want to say something right at the beginning, even though it may be only balm for my conscience. I really was a good mother at first, playing peek-a-boo, alert to her needs, reading the right books to her, making daisy chains, sitting cross-legged on the living room carpet at Barnet, arms out wide to encourage those first excited, stuttering steps towards me. Even when Tom left, Stephanie was the centre around which my life had to rotate. That didn't just stop, it gradually changed, and I could blame things outside my control. She grew up in the eighties, when all that mattered was money and what it could buy; and why shouldn't my daughter have had what other children enjoyed? It wasn't her fault my marriage had collapsed. Tom's contribution wasn't sufficient, so I made up the difference. But it was an accelerating treadmill; whatever I bought her was replaced by the next fashion craze, the new thing to possess and flaunt. And I felt increasingly entitled to a life of my own, which meant more effort, eating up further areas of my time. Any woman who's been in the same position knows it's never an easy balancing act.

From where I was standing, she slipped from childhood to young adulthood without passing through adolescence. Teenage turmoils barely touched me; the various house mothers I employed must have dealt with them. But I always made sure she had the best I could give her (all right, buy for her). I paid for every extra her schools offered; she was certainly a more experienced traveller than I'd been at her age. Her clothes cost me a fortune and she had regular appointments with my hairdresser. I often took her to the theatre – freebie tickets were always landing on my desk – and for years *Peter Pan* was compulsory at Christmas. And I made time for her, never enough, but as much as I could spare. I could actually draw up a scenario to show that things that happened later simply weren't my fault ... Of everything I've tried to write, this is the worst part.

For her eighteenth birthday I hired the immense cellar at Sammy Mac's wine bar in Covent Garden with a wild disco, free champagne and buffet by Suzanne Carstairs, *the* caterer that year. The cake was made by Fortnum and Mason, a flamboyant peak of frothy icing to represent a mountain. Eighteen dark green candles were placed like pine trees on its slopes and there was a tiny glass cable car; inside it was the key for the Golf GTi which was my present to her. She invited most of the girls from school and there were sixty or so of our – my – friends. Tom came as well with Celia, his second wife, a geography teacher in Greenwich; they'd married five years earlier, but this was the first time we'd met. It made the evening perfect when I saw the tightness of the leash she kept him on.

While I was dancing with Anthony to one of the occasional ballads they played to give us all a rest, he, as ever, spoke his mind.

'Wonderful party,' he said. 'Who's it for?'

'What are you talking about?' I was on about my third bottle, brain floating in bubbles and conscious only that everyone was having a marvellous time. I'd been watching Stephanie doing the twist with a West Indian pop artist who lived near us as other dancers made space around them, electric with energy, eyes sparkling, the centre of attention. The contrast between the

159

pudgy tar baby I'd once found eating soil and the slender, sexy blonde in a plum purple crushed velvet cocktail dress and black Gucci stilettos had amused me.

'I mean it's as much your evening as your daughter's.'

'And why not? It's a milestone for me as well. Stephanie thought it was a great idea . . . Stop being such a party pooper.' I pulled his hair to show affectionate annoyance, then kissed his cheek. 'She adores the necklace you and Toby gave her. Hatton Garden. Very generous.'

'We've known her a long time. She's a sort of favourite niece.'

'She couldn't have had better uncles . . . and I couldn't have had better friends.'

'Yes, you could,' he said.

'What on earth do you mean by that?'

'It doesn't matter.' His tone meant it did.

I'd hoped she'd go to university, but money only buys small classes, not a willingness to work. At parents' evenings her teachers had warned me about under-achievement, and I'd done the dutiful mother bit by talking to her. She'd promised to buck up, but only in a 'get off my back' way, and I accepted that school was starting to bore her. It was no problem. There were plenty of jobs, and I had all the contacts to give her a start – once she decided what she wanted to do. Modelling was considered and discarded, and journalism was out because she said she didn't want to be constantly compared to me. Acting appealed, but meant studying again once she had managed to gain the entrance qualifications. Public relations or advertising were the only acceptable options, but the best openings demanded degrees. Finally, she agreed to join an agency in Soho – not one of the high-flyers – as the office junior; the incentive was that one of her predecessors had become a copywriter with J. Walter Thompson. The salary was basic, but I could supplement it, although I drew the line at paying for her own flat. She worked there for a few weeks, complained she was bored spitless, then walked out and went to work in the trendy dress shop near the office where she spent most of her money. I made some token arguments but let her get on with it. She didn't need a career unless she wanted one and could afford to play the hedonist until she grew up.

Then, abruptly, she went out of control, going around with a crowd of hoo-hah Henries and Sloane wannabes, disappearing without letting me know where she was, then calling from somewhere unexpected – Paris was the classic, and on one mystifying occasion Ipswich – to say she'd run out of money and could I make arrangements with a local branch of my bank. At first I was only mildly cross, but then I became impatient. When she walked in one night to announce she'd been breathalyzed by the police after driving into a wall, I went for her.

'And you expect me to pay the fine and the repair bill? And for taxis while you're banned? Get real, Stephie. I'm getting pissed off with you.'

'Makes us even, then, doesn't it?'

'What are you talking about?'

'I mean *you* get real!' Instant anger flared out of part-sobered drunkenness. 'I'm sick of being the daughter as fashion accessory.'

'And what exactly does that mean?' I demanded.

'You really don't know, do you? No, of course you don't. Jesus.' She sighed warily. 'There's no point in talking about it.'

'No,' I insisted. 'Come on. Sit down. Let's have this out, whatever it is.'

'Don't try and sound as if you mean that.'

'I do mean it. Obviously everything I've done for you hasn't been good enough, so let's get it in the open. I'm listening.'

'You're *listening*?' she repeated. 'What's brought this on?'

'I'm your mother. I always listen to you.'

Her eyes went wide in mocking wonderment. '*You* always listen to *me*? This is bloody surreal.'

'Perhaps if you just started . . .?' I was becoming irritated with her. 'We might get somewhere.'

'I'm not counting on it, but . . . OK, I'll try.' She sat down and looked at me as though I was some stranger she was trying to sum up. 'I've got about a million starting places for this.'

161

'Try the beginning,' I snapped.

'The beginning. It's as good as anywhere. But it won't get through to you.'

'Try me.'

She flopped back in the chair and for a brief moment I thought she was going to cry, but she controlled it. 'Can you remember when you picked me up from nursery that afternoon and took me to Amanda's? They lived on a farm somewhere.'

'Of course I do. I'd just ... Well, you know what had happened. It was the start of Daddy and me splitting up.'

'I know that, but I don't mean do you remember doing it or what *you* felt like. I mean what it was like between us. You and me. I knew something was wrong because you wouldn't talk about Daddy. But you made it all right. You took me to a fair one afternoon and bought me candy floss and I had a ride on a silver horse, and you were ... there! And after we went back to Barnet, I didn't mind staying with all those people when you were working, because I knew you'd come back the moment you could. And you never let me down. You were interested in me, wanted to know what I'd been doing. It changed when we moved to Swiss Cottage. You just weren't around any more.'

'You know what happened with my job. We needed the money the *Register* paid me,' I argued. 'And I always made time for you.'

'Exactly ... You *made* it. I was a regular note on your fucking Filofax. "Saturday, lunch to five o'clock, Stephanie." Do you have any idea how often the phone rang those afternoons?'

'They were business calls,' I answered defensively. 'You've never complained about how much money I made – and you've certainly had your share of it.'

'Terrific.' She sounded defeated. 'It was obviously easier signing cheques at Hamley's than talking to me.'

'Why haven't you told me this before?' My voice betrayed I was into attack as defence.

'I have.' She stared at me accusingly. 'I've been trying to say it for years. You've never listened before *and you're not fucking listening now!*' She stood up and ran out, and I heard her bedroom door slam.

It should have been taking-stock time, the start of disenchant-
ment, of recalling things Anthony had said that I'd dismissed.
There'll be tears before bed. But, God forgive me, I was furious.
I was admired and envied everywhere I looked, and the bloody
daughter I'd knocked myself out for was a little ingrate. (Thinking back, I was reacting exactly the way men do in such
circumstances.) All right, I thought, she can learn to hack it for
herself, she can make an effort for a change instead of me
spoonfeeding her. My mistake, I told myself, had been not
making her stand on her own feet. She was a spoilt, selfish . . .
Oh, I was brilliant at self-justification.

The following morning she stayed in bed, and I left a note for
her on the breakfast bar. I'd pay for the car to be repaired, but
the fine was up to her; if she got banned she was not to use my
account with a local taxi company. I was cutting my monthly
standing order into her account by half; if she wanted any more,
she would have to convince me she deserved it. Everything else
remained the same. She had a home to live in which didn't cost
her anything and there was always food in the freezer. It was the
time of the short, sharp shock.

(Confession isn't a form of catharsis here, a plea that if I admit
I was psychologically incapable of helping the child I betrayed
I'll somehow expunge the guilt. When I started this I promised
myself I'd tell the truth, however much it belittled me, whatever
people would think. Of all the people I've tried to write about,
Stephanie's the heaviest one. Perhaps I'm really writing all this
for her.)

She wasn't at home when I returned from the office, but the note
had gone so I assumed she'd read it. Charlie Taylor had invited
me round for supper with his wife and some *Register* contributors
that evening, so I was only in for as long as it took me to shower
and change; I came back shortly after midnight and the flat was
in darkness. Not sure if I should engage the security lock, I
looked into her room. The bed was empty and the wardrobe
doors open; I turned on the light and saw that it was virtually
empty.

'Where the hell have you gone?' I said aloud. A handful of special treasures – signed photograph of Duran Duran, ring tree her grandmother had given her, the surviving teddy bear, the James Dean mirror – had also been taken. It was too late to start ringing round her friends, but she had to be with one of them. Irritated – I was battle-hardened to unexplained absence – I left it until the morning, which is when I found her note by the telephone.

'I've moved in with Alison; you know the number. Don't bother calling me, I'll be in touch when I've got my head sorted. Stephie.'

'When you're bloody broke more likely,' I muttered, as I punched in Alison's number. At least she was one of the more intelligent of her friends, a trainee with a design company, struggling with a mortgage on a flat that was too big for her. I was about to give up and try later when it was answered.

'Stephanie?'

'No, it's Alison. Is that Katrina?' All of them had always called me by my first name.

'Yes. Is she there?'

'You've just missed her. She's gone to work.'

'I gather she's moved in with you.'

'Yes. She arrived last night. She was in a state but didn't want to talk about it.' I had to grant the girl that she sounded concerned.

'There's no great problem, Alison,' I told her. 'We had one of those talks last night, that's all. It seems that she doesn't want to live here at the moment. I'm not over the moon about that, but it's not a big deal. She's old enough to do what she wants. Anyway, let me give you some advice. Make sure she pays her rent. I know you need the money.'

'We've sorted that.' Distance, even distaste, had entered her voice. 'Stephanie's already given me a cheque.'

'I'll make sure it doesn't bounce.'

'I'll rely on Stephanie to do that, Katrina. She's a friend of mine. Would you like me to give her a message?'

'Just tell her I called and that I'm not best pleased with her.'

164

'I see,' Alison said quietly. 'Message received and completely understood, I think. Goodbye, Katrina.' She hung up.

She played it extremely well, saying nothing I could have taken offence at but making it perfectly clear what she thought. At the time I regarded her as a sarcastic young woman who was too sure of herself. She and Stephanie should get on very well, I reflected; my grandmother used to have an old saying about them coming round without water.

I let Stephanie slip away because I didn't value her, and was convinced in my blind, insufferable arrogance that she would return on my terms. The worst thing was that I told myself it wouldn't concern me if she never came back. But I *did* start as a good mother, and tried to become one again. Let me keep that.

And those are my Significant Others. Except for Vernon, I loved all of them in different ways, at least for a while, and Tom was the only one I came to hate, but that diminished into indifference, which is crueller. Anthony once pointed out that there's nothing on our birth certificates or contracts of employment that makes any reference to happiness. They don't mention love, either.

I'm exhausted. Joe Mellor would have told me to wrap this up in three hundred words, then knock out the police briefs before popping across the road to Maureen's for his beef sandwich. Well, I've finished now. Long journey, strange roads, wrong destination. Christ, I'm writing for the sake of it. Twenty past three on Friday; I made the deadline, Joe.

Full point . . . ends.

London

The *Sunday Register* had settled into a torpor of low activity. Most of the reporters had left and about a dozen sub-editors were completing the Friday schedule, final parts of the business section, inside sport, three news pages. Voices were subdued and the thump when a messenger dropped a bundle of pre-printed colour magazines on the floor seemed an intrusion into discreet tension. Kendall, who had appeared abstracted as he approved the final content and appearance of pages, was alone in the editor's office watching a skein of starlings above the trees across the river, waved like a giant speckled scarf against a gleaming gold and lime sky. Nearly a hundred feet below him a barge slid through reflected oyster twilight that lit the river and he heard Big Ben toll eight-thirty; almost nine hours since Miranda Webb had first mentioned Katrina's absence. His initial bewilderment had imperceptibly hardened into fear, the unknown capable of conjuring anything in the mind, held at bay by the superstition that imagining dreadful things was somehow a talisman that prevented them from happening ... He turned as the door opened.

'Hello, Anthony.'

'Has she turned up?'

'No. I tried to get you on your mobile, but—'

'I left it here. I didn't think I'd need it.'

'I couldn't have told you anything, anyway. We've tried everywhere we can think of.' Kendall crossed to the editor's cabinet. 'Scotch?'

'With water.' Delamere seemed to slacken, as though he had persuaded himself Katrina would have been found and the reality that she was still missing deflated him. 'People don't just vanish.'

'I'm afraid she seems to have done.'

'No leads at all?'

'Only one possibility we still haven't managed to check out . . . Leonard Drummond.'

Delamere looked surprised. 'How do you know about that?'

'Her agent told us. I assumed you knew. He's apparently somewhere in Wales. I can't see Katrina just going off with him without telling us, but . . . Well, it's about all we've got left.'

'Where in Wales?' Delamere asked.

Kendall handed him his drink. 'We don't know. Steve tried calling his wife, but she wouldn't tell us. Of course, if she knows about him and Katrina, she won't be in the mood to co-operate.'

Delamere stood up. 'I'll talk to her. I'm afraid I'm not interested in Mrs Drummond's feelings at the moment.'

'Good luck. Steve's got the number . . . and it's Dr Drummond.'

'I know. Katrina told me.'

Hamilton was working on another draft of the story – so far little more than a series of negatives – when Delamere reached the news desk.

'I want Drummond's number.'

'Hasn't Malcolm told you that—?'

'Yes, he has.'

'OK.' Hamilton pushed his pad towards him. 'Top one's the home and the other's her mobile, but I don't think you'll get anywhere.'

'I'll use charm.' Delamere picked up the phone and punched in the home number; after only seconds he rang off and tried the mobile.

'Dr Drummond? My name's Anthony Delamere. I'm sorry to trouble you, but it's very important that—'

'Is it about Marion?' The question was instant and concerned.

'I'm sorry . . . Marion?'

'Yes. Who are you?'

'I'm a journalist, Dr Drummond. A colleague of mine rang you earlier to ask if he could contact your husband, but you

167

refused to say where he is. I'm afraid it's become rather urgent that we—'

'That's not my concern. Now please get off this line. I—'

'No,' he said sharply. 'And if you hang up, I'll hold it open. I'm sorry, but I mean that.'

'Mr Delamere, if you don't get off this line immediately, I—'

'Just tell me where I can contact your husband and I will.'

'This is intolerable! How dare you—?'

'Dr Drummond, there's no point in us wasting time arguing. You want to keep this line clear, we need to contact your husband.'

'And why is it so important?'

'That would take too long to explain. You'll just have to accept my word that it is.'

'For God's sake, I . . .' She sighed impatiently. 'All right. He's at Cardiff University. English department. Satisfied? Now will you—?'

'Thank you, Dr Drummond.'

Hamilton raised an eyebrow as Delamere hung up. 'If that's charm, what's nasty like?'

'At least I know where he is. See if there's anyone in the English department at Cardiff University. Let me know.'

'She's still on the road?' Hamilton asked.

'Yes. I heard a car horn.'

Delamere looked at the first word he had written down. Marion, the woman Katrina had told him about, the child's nurse. Why had Judith Drummond asked about her so urgently? He left Hamilton asking directory enquiries for the Cardiff number and went to his own office where he called up the Register group list of home addresses on his screen and did a search for Probert. When he rang, he got an answerphone and an invitation to leave a message.

'Anna? It's Anthony Delamere. Can you call me the moment you get in? Believe me, it's extremely urgent. I'm at the office. Thank you.'

He drummed his fingers on the receiver as he thought. Katrina was missing . . . Judith Drummond was somewhere in her car . . .

And very anxious to leave her line open and ... What had happened with the nurse? Trying Anna was a shot in the dark, but she might have some ideas. Nearly nine o'clock on a Friday evening. She was probably out, maybe all night, almost certainly until late. Through the glass he saw Hamilton crossing to the editor's office and followed him.

'She's not with Drummond,' the news editor said. 'Or if she is, no one's seen her. I told a porter it was a five-star emergency and he rang the head of the English department at home who's just called me back. He says Drummond's been there all week, apparently alone.'

'Did you speak to Drummond?'

'He's not there at the moment. Martin Ross is over from the States – you know him? Won the Pulitzer last year. Drummond's taken him to see friends and they're staying overnight. Not due back until tomorrow afternoon.'

'Where are the friends?' Delamere asked.

'Drummond didn't say.'

'Just a minute,' Kendall said. 'Could they have gone to see Katrina? How far is it from Cardiff to ...? But that would still mean she'd gone to the cottage without telling us. Shit.'

Delamere picked up the whisky he had left on the desk. 'When do we expect to hear from this freelance?'

Hamilton glanced at the wall clock. 'I called him about six-thirty. He reckoned an hour or so to Penzance, but when I rang him with the instructions Emma gave me he said the traffic was bad. Then he's got to find the place ... It still should be any time.'

'And if she's not there?' Delamere said.

'Then we've run out of options ... apart from her mother. We haven't tried there in case she gets worried.'

'Katrina hardly ever goes back to Manchester, anyway.'

'I'll call her if the freelance says Katrina's not at the cottage.' Kendall looked at Delamere sympathetically. 'Sorry, Anthony, this isn't getting any better, is it?'

Delamere stared into his glass, then spoke as if to himself. 'She's not been seen for a week, she doesn't appear to be with

Drummond, nobody knows how to reach Stephanie, her agent can't help . . .' He swallowed half the whisky. 'There's something else, but I can't see if it's connected.'

'What is it?'

'The first thing Judith Drummond asked me was if I was calling about someone called Marion. I know from Katrina that she's their daughter's nurse. The child's handicapped. Drummond sounded panicky, as though she was waiting for news.'

'But what's it got to do with Katrina?' Kendall asked.

'God knows. Perhaps nothing. But it seems we're not the only people worried at the moment. The only person I can think of who might be able to help is Anna Probert. Remember her? She was a secretary here for a while. She and Katrina were good friends.'

'If we'd known that we'd have called her.'

'They didn't make a big thing about it.' Delamere sounded dismissive. 'It would take too long to explain, but—' He broke off as the green phone on Kendall's desk rang.

'Yes . . . for Christ's sake, I've said we'll let PA know when we have any news. Just watch the wires and don't waste my time.' Kendall slammed the receiver down. '*Daily Telegraph* checking for their second edition. Who the fuck gave them this number? Go on, Anthony.'

'Anna and Katrina both know Marion. The details don't matter. Anna's not at home at the moment, but if we can get her . . . Oh, for God's sake!' The green phone rang again and Hamilton picked it up.

'What is it?' he snapped.

'Steve Hamilton? Mike Hay, Plymouth Network News. I'm at the cottage. She's dead!'

'What!' He put his hand over the receiver. 'It's the freelance. He says she's dead.'

'Put him on intercom,' Kendall ordered.

Hamilton pressed the key. 'Say that again.'

'She's dead!' The distorted voice sounded excited in the loudspeaker. 'Someone's bashed her head in!'

'Are you pissed?' Kendall demanded.

170

'No . . . Who's that?'

'Malcolm Kendall. Managing editor. You're on intercom. Now what the hell's going on there?'

'I don't know! I just found her, and . . . Look, you just asked us to check if she was here. You didn't say anything about—'

'We didn't say anything because we didn't know. Now calm down.'

'What do you mean, calm down? Someone's murdered her!' Hysteria was entering his voice.

'You're certain she's dead?'

'She felt cold and there's blood all over the . . . Mr Kendall, I'm calling the police. There could be a murderer round here somewhere.'

'Have you seen anyone?'

'No, but—'

'Is there a car outside the cottage?'

'What? Yeah . . . dark blue Rover. I can see it from here.'

'That's hers. Where are you?'

'In my car with the doors locked. There's a pub on the main road. I'm going to wait for the police there.'

'Just a minute. You're quite safe in the car. When did you arrive?'

'About ten minutes ago. I rang the bell, then went round the back. There was a window open and I looked through and saw her on the floor.'

'Did you go in?'

'Yes. I thought she might have passed out. Then I saw the blood.'

'And there's no one else in the cottage?'

'I didn't hang around to find out. I—'

'Are you absolutely certain it's Katrina Darcy?' Delamere's voice was rigid. 'Well?'

'I've only seen her on TV, but it looks like her.'

'Did you look properly? Did you turn the light on?'

'It wasn't dark.'

'It's starting to get dark in London and you were inside the cottage. Did you *really* see her face?'

171

'Yes ... well, sort of. I didn't hang around. For God's sake, it's her cottage, isn't it?'

'That doesn't prove anything. Was she wearing a ring with a large tiger's eye stone? It would have been on her right hand.'

'I don't know! I didn't look.'

'What *did* you look at? All you know is that there's someone lying on the floor. Are you even certain she's dead?'

'Look, you're not here and I am!' Hay shouted. 'I'm not going back in there! As far as I'm concerned she's dead, and if she isn't Katrina Darcy I don't know who the hell she is. Now get off my back!'

'All right!' Kendall gestured the seething Delamere to stop, then leant towards the intercom. 'I'm sorry about that. We're all on edge here. Obviously didn't know anything about this or we wouldn't have sent you. When you speak to the police, give them the direct line number you've got and tell them to call me. Now you'd better get to the pub.'

'Just a minute,' Hamilton added. 'Mike, it's Steve again. Treat this as an exclusive. Don't ring anyone else, and I'll make sure you're all right. A thousand ... OK?' Kendall silently indicated approval.

'Fine ... thanks.' They could hear Hay's nervous, heavy breathing. 'If I find anything, I'll let you know.'

'Just call the police.' As Kendall closed the line it was imposs-ible to disentangle shock, disbelief and grief from his face.

'You need another drink,' Hamilton said quietly.

'We all do. You all right, Anthony?'

Flushed with rage seconds earlier, Delamere had gone very pale and his voice was a monotone that still carried the imperative of an order.

'Get me down there.'

'It'll take hours.'

'Not by private plane it won't. Charter one.'

Kendall nodded. 'Sort it, Steve.'

Delamere remained silent after Hamilton had left, making no response as he accepted his refilled glass.

'You're thinking it's not her?' Kendall asked quietly. 'Who else could it be?'

'I don't know, but until I see her for myself I'm not accepting the word of some hysterical freelance.'

'I'll come with you.'

'There's no need. Anyway, you'll have enough to do handling the calls. Whatever's happened, this won't be anyone's exclusive. The police will release it and I rather suspect our Mr Hay will realize he can make more than a thousand pounds by calling a few people.'

'I'll prepare a statement,' Kendall agreed. 'And what about Katrina's family? Even if it's not her, there's still a body in her cottage.'

'Stephanie's living with a friend in Islington, but I don't know who it is. As well as her mother, there's a brother somewhere in the north too. He might be on her personnel file. But you mustn't contact anyone until you hear from me. All right?'

Kendall nodded. 'I hope you're right, Anthony.'

'So do I.' He finished his drink. 'I'm going to see how Steve's going on with that plane.'

Left alone, Kendall found his mind reverting to practicalities as he called Charlie Taylor's villa in Crete. Delamere could be right that it wasn't Katrina, but ... A suitable tribute to a respected columnist, two sentences would be enough at this stage ... Sympathy for her family, full co-operation with the police ... tragedy ... horror ... sensation. News.

'Charlie? Malcolm Kendall. We've got a crisis.'

Taylor listened in silence. 'Right. I'll come back, but there isn't a plane until the morning. I'll let the chairman know ... You OK?'

'Just about.'

'Aye.' His sympathy had a detached economy. 'I'm sorry, Malcolm. You were good friends.'

'We're still not positive it's her.'

'I hope it's not, but ...' He paused. 'Who's working on our story?'

173

Kendall sighed. 'Steve. We're on top of it, Charlie.'
'Good. Call me the moment you hear from Anthony.'

Kendall's direct line rang again half an hour later. 'Mr Kendall? Chief Inspector David Cheeseman, Devon and Cornwall CID Cambourne. We've been given your number by a Mr Michael Hay. I believe he's already been in touch with you.'
'Yes. Do you have any more details?'
'Not at this stage, sir. I'm just about to set off. However, the body's in a cottage which we believe is owned by a Miss Katrina Darcy, one of your employees. Is that correct?'
'Yes . . . and Mr Hay says it's her body.'
'I'm not responsible for what he says, sir. Officers from Penzance are at the scene and have confirmed the discovery of a body, but we don't know who it is.'
'But Miss Darcy has been missing all week. We've been trying to locate her.'
'Have you advised the police?'
'No. We only realized today. But nobody seems to have seen her in London since last Friday.'
'I see. We need the names of her next of kin just in case. Do you know who they are?'
'Yes, her daughter, her mother and a brother.'
'No husband?'
'Not now. She was married, but that was some years ago. We only seem to have her mother's address. Someone will let you have it. I'm not sure where her daughter's living at the moment. We're trying to find her.'
'Thank you, sir, and if you know where her former husband lives I need his address as well. I'm sure you appreciate that I must ask you to make no contact with any of these people yourselves.'
'I understand . . . and one of my staff is flying to Cornwall tonight. He's called Anthony Delamere. He's coming as a friend of Miss Darcy's, not a journalist.'
'Then he may be able to help us with formal identification. When does he expect to arrive?'

174

'We're still arranging his plane. I'll let you know.'

'I'll have a car pick him up, sir. If you call Penzance 278564 with the details, they'll give me the message. The code's 01736. The only other immediate question – and this is still assuming it is Miss Darcy, of course – is if you know of anyone who has made threats against her.'

'No. I'm not saying she didn't have enemies, many people do in this profession, but they don't murder each other.'

'We're not treating it as murder until we know a great deal more, sir,' Cheeseman warned. 'But there've been no threats?'

'Not that I'm aware of.'

'Very well, sir. I may be sending officers to London to talk to you, and I'll see Mr Delamere when he arrives.'

Kendall hung up and waved Hamilton in. 'That was the police. Have Sally call this number and tell them where her mother lives.'

'Have they confirmed it is her, then?'

'No. I'd like to think it was someone else, but I can't imagine who. Anthony'll find out. How's the plane going?'

'He leaves from Radlett in about an hour and a half.'

'An hour and a half!'

'They've got to find a pilot and get clearance from air traffic control, Malcolm,' Hamilton told him. 'Once he takes off he'll be at RAF Culdrose in about three-quarters of an hour.'

'Culdrose? What about . . . What's it called? Airfield near Land's End, I've flown to the Scillies from there . . . St Just. That must be nearer.'

'They say the runway's too short. Culdrose is on the opposite side of Mount's Bay, but it can't be more than about fifteen miles. Anthony's gone home to grab some things and is going straight on to Radlett, so he should be in Cornwall . . . say, eleven-thirty to midnight.'

'All right, if it's the best we can do. The police are meeting him, so let them have the details.' Kendall paused as the news desk secretary knocked at the door and, unusually, waited before entering. 'What is it, Sally?'

'I'm ringing round hotels,' she said. 'Anthony'll need somewhere to stay. It's the holidays and they're all full, but I'll find something. I'll let you know and you can call him when he gets there.'

'Well done,' Kendall said. 'We hadn't thought of that.'

'I had.' She blinked rapidly. 'I'm so sorry, Malcolm. It's awful.'

'Well, we don't know how bad it is yet. Thanks.' Kendall watched as Sally returned to her desk. 'Katrina always liked her.'

Hamilton felt uncomfortable; since the death of his wife and son he had allowed nothing in his personal or professional life to touch his emotions.

'Did the police tell you anything?'

'They've only just reached the cottage. Officially, it's not murder at the moment, but they must be thinking that way. It was a waste of time offering Hay that money. This can't be kept quiet.'

'Of course it can't,' Hamilton agreed. 'Everyone's known for hours that she's vanished. But it was worth a grand to try to keep ahead of the pack a bit longer.'

Kendall glanced at him. 'Good piece . . . as we say.'

'Yeah.' Hamilton hesitated. 'I know this is bad for you and Anthony, but I need decisions on how much space we're giving it. I'm assuming splash and page three, drop Nineties Britain for tributes and obit, possibly a piece on op-ed. I've got standby pics, but we'll need one of the cottage. I'll send a reporter and photographer down. We'll be fucked up on the news story if someone's charged before tomorrow, but—'

'Steve, we don't know for certain it's Katrina.'

'I realize that, but if it is then we have to—'

Kendall held his hand up. 'Go easy on the professional bastard bit at the moment, will you? Charlie's let me have a tribute and I'll write another statement. Release them both to PA if we get confirmation. When the calls start, tell them we're saying nothing else at this stage. In the meantime, just get on with it. Jesus!' He laughed bitterly. 'I've just remembered what an American editor said about Marilyn Monroe. He regretted her death as much as the next man, but she sure did the press a favour by doing it in August.'

Book Two

Chapter One

Journalists talked about the story long after it had ceased to be news, its sensation, great angles, incredibility, their personal scoops. They used all the headline words – hate, death, sex, murder – but rarely spoke of it as a tragedy; emotion is never part of any professional discussion. There are thousands of words on newspaper databases, background pieces, vivid reporting, interviews with the grieving and the malicious. Much of what was written was invented, but it was a great read. Television rights to *Fatal Deadline*, a paperback published less than a week after the court case, were immediately sold. Within its limits it was a good book, a powerful storyline charged with the urgency of high-speed journalism. It was presented as the true story, but it wasn't; it was just those surface aspects of it that were known and had sufficient drama. It read like a newspaper, was as easily digested and as easily discarded.

Too complex for the simplicities of journalism, the full story went back years into many lives, but its drama really started when the affair between Anna Probert and Katrina Darcy finished. Katrina felt no identifiable sense of loss, but discovered that being on her own was unbearable for reasons she couldn't explain. To compensate she became brittle, as though she had the urgent fizzling of a sparkler. She went out at every opportunity, taking lovers with a casual greed; an affair with a reporter from the *Sunday Times* lasted a while, but otherwise it was 'You're nice, let's do it, and what was your name again?' But she worked harder as well; apart from her column she did several celebrity interviews for the *Sunday Register* and pre-recorded a *Spiked Copy* special that the producer said would be put forward for a Bafta award. Her agent negotiated a large advance for another book, which she began dictating into a tape-recorder and hired an agency typist to write it out. She discovered that depression only crept in when she wasn't doing anything, so she made sure that never happened.

When the sparkler burnt out, she was shaken to see what its frantic dazzle had prevented her from recognizing; it scared her that after so many years she could be so vulnerable. Having become visible, the unbelievable truth began to colour everything. She became impossible to work with – even to come near – and this climaxed with her hurling a potted plant at Anna's successor one afternoon when she brought her a chicken sandwich without mayonnaise. The secretary slammed the door behind her, and Katrina Darcy was left in her glass box in the corner, aware that everyone in editorial was watching her. Furiously, she pulled down the Venetian blinds and stood by the window, arms tightly folded against an ecstatic form of fear.

'Get out!' she snapped as she heard the door open again.

'I'm just checking that you haven't jumped. My car's parked somewhere down below you.'

Her shoulders dropped; there was a promise of comfort in the voice. 'No. Not yet. Come in and help.'

Anthony crossed the room, put his hand beneath her chin and turned her face to his, examining it like a concerned doctor. 'Too many late nights with too many wrong people for too many wrong reasons.'

She started to cry. 'I don't know what's the matter with me.'

'Then we'd better find out. I'm going to tell Charlie you need a couple of days off, then I'm taking you home with me. Talk, supper and a bed for the night – alone, for a change. I've seen this coming.'

'Why didn't you say something?'

'You weren't in the mood to listen. You haven't been for a long time. Now fix your face. You can fax your column in.'

In the car he said nothing, and when they reached Clapham he simply sat her in the garden with a Pimms, before joining Toby in the kitchen; through the open door she could hear them chatting as they prepared supper against the background of

180

Classic FM. It was a warm afternoon, and she lay back in the deck chair and closed her eyes, grateful for the space they were allowing her to face what she had been running away from. If there was not something wrong with her heart, there was something seriously wrong with her head.

'Still alive out there?' She opened her eyes to see Anthony on the top step, wearing a linen apron with 'Kiss the Cook' stamped in red on the front, holding a partially peeled avocado.

'Yes, but I could manage another of these.' She held up her empty glass.

'Only one more,' he warned. 'In vino melancholy.'

He came out with the Pimms jug, pausing at the edge of the lawn to pick up a wooden trug basket with a hand fork lying in it.

'There you are.' He refilled her glass, then handed her the basket. 'Now you can weed for your supper.'

By the time they ate, she was ready to let everything pour out. The two men exchanged glances when she told them about Anna, as if silently acknowledging something they had previously talked about, and Anthony nodded as the real problem began to emerge. As the kitchen dwindled into twilight, neither of them spoke, and Toby only moved to turn on the Tiffany lamps. Their eyes rarely left her.

'So that's it,' she said finally, having repeated herself, become tearful, acknowledged all the reasons why she should be able to accept and survive. 'I've spent three hours saying what a sub would have cut to one sentence. I'm bloody in love with Leonard.' She smiled weakly. 'Thank you. You're the loveliest men I know.'

'Barring one, it would seem.' Anthony tipped his chair back to take another bottle of Chablis from the fridge. 'Anyway, you know house rule number one. No advice. Only observations.'

'OK, but before that . . . You knew about Anna?'

'I made an educated guess from seeing you together in the office a couple of times,' he replied. 'It must have been the early days when you couldn't completely control your excitement in public. I mentioned it to Toby, but as you'd never told us you

181

were once gay, I thought I must be wrong. Now it makes sense. It was a very extreme reaction to Leonard ... but you didn't realize that, did you?'

'No. It just ... happened.'

Anthony sniffed. 'Well, it's over and you're left with this. Frankly, when I met Leonard he seemed no different from any other of your endless inamorati. Then I began to suspect he might be. What you've told us explains a lot. But he won't leave ... Judith, was it? ... because of the child, and in fairness to the man he *was* honest about it.'

'I know.' She picked the foil wrapping off an Elizabeth Shaw mint and began to fold it into a cup, a hangover from her father's habit. 'Do you know what the worst thing is? The thought that he's found someone else by now. I feel incredibly jealous about that.'

'And that,' said Toby, 'is a new emotion for you.'

'Is that all it is?'

'That "all" is a great deal.' Anthony sounded rather serious. 'When did you last envy anybody anything? It's an immature passion, and you of course are totally mature. I underestimated Mr Drummond. He really has peeled layers off you.'

She sighed. 'And left me naked to mine enemies.'

Anthony rapped the base of his glass on the table. 'House rule number four. Thou shalt not fall back on quotations. Find your own words to say it.'

'OK,' she agreed. 'I love him, I want to grow old with him, and if I can't die with him, I want to die before him – and the thought that I can't have him is ... driving me out of my mind. It's totally stupid, or ...' She suddenly laughed. 'Or this is menopausal and I really should be using it as material for my column, then start taking the tablets to get me through it and thank God I've got you two.'

She put her elbows on the table, hands together as if in prayer pressed hard against her lips to stop herself crying. 'But at this precise moment, that's not helping and ... and I can't bring myself to believe there'll be a time when it will. Help me out here, you guys.'

182

'We can't, darling,' Anthony said gently. 'Nobody can. We can help in all sorts of other ways, but you got yourself into this and have to find your own way out. It's the same for everyone.'

'The worst thing is I can't control it,' she said wearily. 'It makes me feel so bloody inadequate.'

'The next new emotion must make another appointment.' Anthony stood up. 'Anyway, bed, cocoa if you want it, and you can choose anything from the household soft toy collection as a friend to cuddle in the night. There's no point in you talking any more at the moment. Repetition only creates more confusion. We'll wash up.'

Katrina smiled in gratitude. 'All right, Uncle.' She glanced at Toby, then back to Anthony. 'Do you two have any idea how much I value your *kindness*?'

'Kindness is love's younger sister.' Anthony looked surprised. 'Good God. That sounds like a quotation, but I don't think it is. I just made it up. Now, off to bed.'

At the time, their comfort seemed a catharsis, an opportunity that allowed her to accept that someone had breached her defensive armoury of independence; however reluctantly, she had to repair it, not pretend it wasn't there. Then what they did in helping her to recognize her feelings became a bridge she raced across. After staying with them for a couple of days she felt she had got some sort of perspective, but it was a fragile one and collapsed within two weeks when she was in a taxi and saw Leonard Drummond turning out of Shaftesbury Avenue into Dean Street, heading towards the Groucho Club. There was a woman with him and Katrina instantly hated her; she resented anyone who shared a moment of his life if she wasn't a part of it. As the cab drove on, all she could see on the pavements were couples, families with children, items, affairs; holding hands, laughing. The renewed realization of how much she wanted one man was terrifying.

It was Friday, so she had to go back to the office and write her column, but her mind could only crash out one of the jaded, regularly recycled themes (women as breadwinners after partners are made redundant, absolute desperation country). When Miranda Webb complained it was ninety words under, she told her to put an extra line of head on it and left. She went straight to the Groucho – without knowing that he'd been going there – but the girl on reception said he'd left about twenty minutes earlier. The next thing Katrina was conscious of was staring in the window of a bookshop on Charing Cross Road, only able to remember one particular thing she'd told Anthony and Toby; she was far past the stage of just wanting Leonard in her bed, she urgently needed him in her life. She went home and rang Harrow. A woman answered.

'Oh . . .' She had not thought of anything further than the pleasure of hearing his voice. 'Is Leonard – Mr Drummond – there?'

'I'm afraid not, but he should be back shortly. Who's calling?'

'It's a friend of his. Is that . . . Mrs Drummond? Or is it Doctor?' She tried to make it sound lighthearted.

'No, she's away at the moment. I'm Marion Blake, Teresa's nurse.'

'Oh, yes, we've met. Well, only briefly. In Kensington Gardens. It's Katrina Darcy. You've probably forgotten.'

'No, I remember. It was last September.'

'That's right. Could you ask Leonard to call me? It's about his new book. I want to do a piece about it for the *Sunday Register*.'

'I'll give him the message.'

'Thank you . . . Oh, and tell him I'm at home. He has the number.'

She felt illogically delighted that his wife was away. There'd be nothing to stop him coming to see her. That night . . . For God's sake, slow down. Lunch tomorrow. The article line would be enough to persuade him, and once she'd got him on her own, surely . . . She banged her forehead against the wall.

'Stop it!' She was crying with hopelessness. 'He loves his daughter. She needs him, she needs both of them. *You can't have it!*' An enormous sob left an ache across her chest. 'Don't be such a sodding, bloody fool! Grow up! You screwed him, and it was marvellous, and . . . Oh, just let him ring back, God, and I'll build you a cathedral.'

Half an hour later on the clock – three days in her mind – he did. 'Hello. How are you?'

'Fine. I saw you today. On Shaftesbury Avenue around lunch-time. There was somebody with you.' No small talk, just who the hell is she?

'Lucy. She handles my publicity at Cooper Bradlock. They're planning a splash for the new book.'

'Oh.' She felt disproportionately relieved. 'I wondered if she was a friend.'

'We get on with each other. Anyway, what have you been doing?'

'Usual things. Earning a living, a few interviews, dancing with strangers . . . missing you.' She mentally despaired at her inability to control her tongue.

'Oh.' She frantically tried to persuade herself that there was a note of sympathy, reciprocation, even relief, in one syllable. 'Marion said something about an interview.'

'Yes . . . I'm sorry, darling, that just came out.'

'Lucy said it would be good if we could get a piece in the *Register*. She'll be sending you an advance proof.'

Was he gently deflecting or stumbling in her direction? 'I'll watch out for it. Leonard, let's meet. Neutral ground. I need to talk to you. Not on the phone . . . please.' There was a silence, then a surge of relief.

'All right. I've missed you as well.'

'Tomorrow?' She was being too eager, but couldn't prevent it. 'Somewhere we've never been . . . Kew Gardens?' Why on earth there? she wondered. Hearts and flowers?

'Not tomorrow, I have to spend the weekend with Teresa. But I've got a recording with the Beeb at White City Monday lunchtime. I could be at Kew by two-thirty. Main gate on whatever road it is?'

'I'll be there . . . I love you.'

'I know.'

*

185

She was there at two o'clock, forty-six years old and excited as a child waiting for a treat. A couple of students walked past, arms round each other, her head snuggled against his shoulder, totally together, and Katrina watched them walk into the gardens with a warmth of shared experience. Leonard arrived at 2.49; she couldn't remember when any man had last kept her waiting. As he paid the taxi driver, she went over yet another version of what she wanted to say.

'Sorry I'm late,' he said. 'The interview over-ran.'

'That's all right.'

They kissed with the casual affection of friends and a sense of shared apprehension. Kew was quiet, apart from planes passing over flying into Heathrow, and for no logical reason they went to the Cactus House. For a while they talked about what they'd each been doing, news of mutual friends; he told her about his book. Finally, he took the first step.

'We couldn't put this down, could we?'

'I certainly couldn't. I didn't know about you.'

'I kept telling myself it was impossible and . . .' he smiled wryly '. . . and that we're both supposed to be too intelligent to start playing Mills and Boon. This would be farcical if it didn't bite so deeply.'

'Seriously stupid,' she agreed. 'But we're both here.'

'Yes. By our age, one would have thought that the chemicals would have dried up.'

'Perhaps it's not chemical.'

'Whatever, it's just as potent. I'll have to stop rubbishing romantic films and sentimental songs. Very bad for the image.'

'We could play it as a film scene,' she suggested. 'How about I walk towards that door over there, the camera watches from behind your head, and if I close it behind me, that's it? Roll credits over a craneshot of me walking back to the gate, then pull-up for a slow panorama of London and a lonely guitar theme. No sequel, of course.'

He smiled. 'Or I call your name five paces from the door. You stop, don't turn round, start to walk on, then stand still and hold

186

out one hand. Cut to close-up of me taking hold of it, then the same craneshot, but with the two of us and a lot of violins.'

'Shall we go for it and see which we get?'

He shook his head. 'No. I haven't just travelled from Television Centre to get here today.'

'Christ, how corny!' She was laughing as she protested. 'You ought to be in bad scriptwriting. Have you been rehearsing that line?'

'It was one of several. You can have the others if you want.'

'No, thanks . . . and I'll spare you all of mine.' She looked at him hesitatingly. 'But what about Teresa?'

He picked up a fallen leaf from by his feet and began to tear it into strips.

'I've used her as an excuse. It was easier than saying I couldn't handle the commitment. Sorry. I can now.'

'But you think she'll be all right, if you . . .'

He dropped the green fragments. 'I can't see why not. She'll be confused at first, but . . . well, ordinary kids have to put up with situations like this. She'll have Judith and Marion and I've got all the time I need to see her.'

'That's important,' she agreed. What was really important was that he was prepared to put her first.

'What about yours? How will she react?'

'Stephanie?' She shrugged dismissively. 'Don't ask me, I'm only her mother. She's living with a friend in Islington now.'

'Does she know about us? I only met her the once.'

'I don't imagine she's even thought about you. I'll tell her when we next speak. Don't worry, she won't want to be a bridesmaid.' She squeezed his hand. 'This is just us. Thank you.'

'No need.' He looked round as though making sure they were alone, then whispered, 'I've got a confession to make.'

'What?' she whispered back.

He put his lips against her ear. 'I've never kissed a woman in a cactus house.'

She turned his head and hissed back. 'Have you ever screwed one?'

'It must be very uncomfortable.'

187

'Agony,' she agreed. 'So why don't we use my bed instead? I changed the sheets this morning.'

They talked a great deal before he went back to Harrow. Katrina was very careful, aware he was still coming to terms with something that transcended his feelings for Teresa, and yielded everywhere she had to. He was sure Judith would not make waves over access and they agreed he had to meet Teresa alone; seeing another woman in her father's life would bewilder her. Standard problems of the house and financial support were irrelevant. They both had money and his wife was not going to make excessive demands in any event. He would insist on paying the nurse's salary and Katrina could provide a ready-made home until they bought somewhere. They discussed Sussex, somewhere on the South Downs so he could take Teresa to the seaside . . .

'When will you tell Judith?' she asked.

'I'm going to Cardiff on Saturday for three weeks as a short-term writer in residence at the university,' he replied. 'I'll talk to her before I leave. Teresa's fifteen now and the situation's changed. It's not the reason it was for us staying together.'

'How hard will she fight you?'

'I don't know. Perhaps not as much as I expect.' He took hold of her hand. 'Don't worry. I'll handle it.'

Chapter Two

What had always struck Drummond about Judith was her
control; she had a detached intelligence that could separate the
most complex situations into distinct black and white, one of
which she chose and rarely abandoned. She had been a virgin at
twenty-nine when she first agreed to sleep with him and, looking
back, it was as though she had made a dialectic decision that she
had reached the point in her life when it was time to experience
lust. She had become a passionate lover, even a demanding one,
but then Teresa had been born and she had immediately
rationalized to her own satisfaction that their daughter's demands
must override their desire. Judith could even channel love in the
direction she wanted.

'There were other women before me,' she had said. 'And you
told me you often remained friends after you stopped sleeping
together.'

'But you're my wife.'

'Then I should be a very good friend, shouldn't I? Anyway,
I've given this a great deal of thought. I feel guilty about Teresa.
We both should. It's because of us that she'll never have the sort
of life we take for granted, so we have to give her everything we
can. I don't just mean what we can buy, I mean she must always
have us. We owe her that.'

'I agree, but it makes no sense to stop sleeping together.
Neither of us knew that our genes would—'

'Then we should have taken the tests. I knew enough about
the possibilities, even if you didn't.'

He began to understand; she had let herself down pro-
fessionally, as though she had failed to make certain checks
before authorizing a course of treatment. It was not a question

189

of logic, it was a matter of betrayal. With another woman, he would have reasoned she would eventually change her mind, but not with Judith in such circumstances.

'Do you still love me?' he had asked.

'Yes, and I'll be your wife everywhere but in bed.'

'I'm not sure that will work.'

'It's going to have to for Teresa's sake. I accept you'll want sex, but that has to be kept separate. You go away a good deal, and I'm not going to ask questions as long as you always come back here and are her father.' Unexpectedly, she had smiled. 'Not many women offer their husbands those sort of terms.'

'And what about you – or can you simply turn your body off?'

'I have at the moment, but . . . well, I know how hormones work.'

'So you're saying we'll just be casually unfaithful.'

'Not casually, I hope; I expect you to use discretion. The most important thing is that we must never be unfaithful to Teresa. Think about it, Leonard.'

Whatever he'd thought would have been irrelevant; Judith had made the decision for both of them. And it had worked better than he could have imagined. They were successful in their careers, good hosts and welcome guests at dinner parties, escorting each other to medical or literary events, sympathetically admired for their devotion as parents. And Drummond had recognized that many men would envy him if they knew the truth. It had been more than a year before he had found a lover, chosen by a rule he continued to follow; he would not attempt to take any woman to bed until he knew enough to write at least a thousand-word description of her. Over fifteen years there had been five of them (it would have been six, but in one case what he finally wrote contained too many warning signs). They had lasted, on average, eighteen months, all had been enjoyable, each had left good memories; two had become characters in his books. It was impossible to quantify what was different about Katrina; she was intelligent, attractive, easy company, satisfying when naked . . . but so had the others been. One day it could be

190

explored in a novel; now it was a mountain he had never expected to have to climb.

And he had not expected the emotion with which Judith reacted. He had rehearsed answers to reason, pitting his mind against hers in intellectual arguments; what he faced was initial disbelief and dismissal that became bitter fury as he insisted that she listened. Suddenly she was an emotional, vulnerable woman; for the first time since he had known her she actually cried. He came very close to saying he would stay, but discovered that he had crossed too many lonely bridges. He left for Cardiff without Judith waving him goodbye; that had never happened before. When he reached the university he phoned Katrina and told her it was all right; equally importantly, he needed the reassurance of hearing her voice.

'Come down when you've settled her, Marion. I want to talk to you.'

Teresa's nurse looked up from helping the child into her pyjamas. 'What's the matter?'

Judith smiled. 'You are so good at spotting the tone of my voice. I'll tell you downstairs.' She ruffled her daughter's hair and allowed her hand to be grabbed with an urgent affection. Only she, Leonard and Marion would have understood the garbled, distorted pleading to share a picture book.

'Look at it with Marion, darling, and you can tell me about it tomorrow.'

More misshapen sounds said she would tell Daddy as well.

'He's gone away. You know that. He gave you a big kiss and said he'd bring you a present. Now Marion will turn off the light when the big hand's pointing to the rabbit and then you go to sleep like a good girl. Promise? Goodnight, precious.'

In the drawing room she poured a drink and sat in the gold-upholstered French scrolled-arm chair by the window, suddenly drained. Several women she knew had gone through what she was facing, but any fears that it might one day happen to her had been dismissed. She had ceased to think how she would react, because after so long there was no reason why it should ever arise; there was every reason why it shouldn't.

'Fast asleep.' Marion closed the door quietly. 'I've changed the batteries in the child alarm, incidentally.'

'Thank you. Help yourself to a drink.'

Over five years, Marion Blake's relationship with her employers had changed. At first she had been just another nurse, efficient and caring, accepting that employing her meant they were using their money to give their daughter something more on top of what they provided. Then she had grown to like and admire them, and in Judith's case it had developed into affection and friendship; sometimes she felt like a favourite sister who had moved in to help.

'Come on, then. What's the problem?' she asked. 'There's something on your mind.'

'Leonard's told me he's leaving.'

Marion momentarily paused as she poured her drink; she had never heard the sting of controlled tears in Judith's voice before.

'He can't mean it.'

'I'm afraid he does. He told me on Tuesday night and we've been arguing about it ever since. He's moving out when he gets back from Wales.'

'But . . .' Taking the matching chair opposite her, she saw how drawn, even suddenly older, Judith's face was. 'Tell me about it.'

'He's met someone else, and . . . well, he swears he's in love with her.' She pushed a strand from her pale silver cap of hair back into place. 'I thought that if this ever happened it would have been years ago. Not now after it's worked for so long. I might have handled it better when I was expecting it.'

'Has he told you who it is?'

'Yes, which makes it worse in some ways. I know there have been others, but he always stuck to the agreement and kept them out of our life. This time he's told me her name.'

'Do you know her?'

'No . . . Well, I've never met her, but . . .' She smiled without humour. 'I always make a point of watching her television

192

programme. It's Katrina Darcy. The journalist. I assume you know her.'

'Of course.' Marion did not admit having briefly met her with Leonard. 'But he must know it will break Teresa's heart.'

'He's persuaded himself it won't.' Her face crumpled. 'He wants to marry her, Marion! I can't cope with it!'

'Oops.' She stood up and put her arms round Judith's shoulders, the way she had so often comforted Teresa. 'This isn't like you.'

'That's what's terrifying me. No it's not . . . you know what I mean.' She sobbed against her sleeve. 'I've got to stop him, but I can't!'

Marion held her for a few moments, then gently released her and returned to her chair. 'How long have they known each other?'

Judith took a handkerchief from under her cuff and wiped her nose. 'He says he met her . . . I can't remember how long ago . . . at a writers' weekend somewhere. They've been having an affair for a year or so.'

'But he's had affairs before. What's so different this time?'

'He says he can't explain it. Perhaps it's his mid-life crisis. I've told him I don't mind if they continue being lovers, just as long as he stays with me and Teresa. But he won't listen.'

'What are you going to do?'

'What can I do? I've got nothing to fight him with. Christ, if he hadn't been so reasonable. He says he'll pay your wages and make an allowance for Teresa as well, he'll see her as often as possible . . .'

'Couldn't you prevent that? It might make him think again if he thought he'd lose her completely.'

'How?' Judith demanded. 'He's her father. A court would give him access. And I wouldn't look good if I refused, would I?'

Marion sipped her drink as she thought. 'What about talking to her? Surely if she understands how much hurt this will cause, she'll—'

'He says he's discussed it with her already. If I approach her now, she'll realize I haven't been able to make Leonard change his mind and . . . God, she must be a bitch! She's so desperate to have him, she doesn't give a damn about his daughter!'

'There's got to be something you can do.'

'What? Pay her off? She's probably earning a fortune. Appeal to her better nature? She can't have one. Threaten to kill myself?' Judith sniffed loudly and swallowed. 'I even thought of that last night. Then I realized I'd have to kill Teresa as well and . . . Shit, Marion! I can't stand being helpless! I don't know what—' She broke off at the sound of a child's frightened cry from a loudspeaker fixed to the wall by the door. 'She's dreaming again. It's all right, I'll go. You've had a long day with her. Get me another drink.'

'Don't let her see that you're upset.'

'Don't worry. I won't.'

As Marion poured two more glasses of wine, listening to soft assurances over the alarm system, she was as much shaken by Judith's reaction as by the fact that Leonard was prepared to abandon Teresa. Judith had often reminded her of her mother, but with an intellectual edge; strong, resilient, convinced everything would be all right if she could just get through the next three days – which she always did, of course. Judith wouldn't break, but it was shocking that she should have been bowed down so much. She recalled her surprise when she had met Katrina in Kensington Gardens, and had wondered if Leonard had deliberately arranged it. It had been his suggestion that they went out together that day, but why had Katrina arrived after he had said he would sit on the bench while she showed Teresa the ducks? It could have been chance, but it had not been the sort of afternoon to take a casual walk alone . . . and he'd been unusually quiet in the car driving home. That had been more than a year ago, and now he was saying he wanted to marry her; it was a cruelty of which she would never have thought him capable.

But there was an ironic dimension to the situation that Judith knew nothing about. And could that somehow be used to make Leonard change his mind? Marion had long known that she loved Teresa as much as she could have loved a daughter of her own, and her feelings for Judith ran deep, an alleviation of her

194

own loneliness. Was there a way in which she could protect them both? She began to see it was possible, but only if she could threaten and make clear she would carry out the threat. If there was no choice, someone would have to be hurt to prevent a greater pain. She heard Judith saying goodnight to Teresa again, but it was several minutes before she came back downstairs. The tears had been washed away and her make-up restored; Marion recognized the composed, highly competent woman again.

'Sorry about that.' She sounded self-conscious. 'But I've been bottling it up for three days. Very unlike me.'

'Yes,' Marion agreed. 'So . . . ?'

'So I'll have to find something. I can't imagine what it is at the moment, but Leonard simply cannot leave. That's all there is to it. Perhaps I could sleep with him again and see if that works.'

'Do you want to after all this time?'

'Frankly, no. I've told you, I must have grown out of it early in life. But if it will keep him here, I'll do it.'

'I don't like the sound of that,' Marion said. 'It's sex for the wrong reasons.'

'No, it isn't. I'll lie back and think of Teresa.'

'And if it doesn't work?'

'Then I'll end up hating him even more than I hate her.' Judith picked up a copy of the *British Medical Journal* off the settee. 'I shouldn't have dropped it all on you, but you happened to be nearest. I feel better now. Thank you. Are you going out this evening?'

With other women, Marion would have turned them back to the problem, but Judith Drummond was in control of herself again and quite capable of becoming impatient.

'No. I've got a couple of letters to write and must iron name tags on Teresa's new school clothes.'

'Fine, and I want to read a piece in here then finish that paper for Copenhagen next month . . . and we'll take Teresa to Brighton tomorrow. Can you make a picnic first thing? If we set off early, we should miss the traffic. I need to get out.'

When Marion checked Teresa on the way to her room, she had twisted round in bed and was hanging over the edge; it was

195

only a year since it had been agreed she no longer needed a cot. Other parents would have placed her in a home for the handicapped and visited her at weekends; if they'd wanted, the Drummonds could have afforded the best there was. Instead, they sent her to an expensive special day school, treated her as far as possible like a normal girl – and had never abandoned her. It was a selfless love, repaid only in a teenager's infantile gestures that had warmth but no comprehension. Marion tucked the sheet and blanket firmly into place and gently kissed Teresa's forehead.

'It's all right, my poppet,' she whispered. 'Marion will make it better.'

Chapter Three

Lovers find their private songs by chance; in Leonard and Katrina's case it was 'Come Rain or Come Shine', for no other reason than that they had heard it on his car radio one night. She was humming it to herself in the office on Monday morning when Anna's successor said there was a call for her. Mildly irritated – she expected people to read her column, not express opinions on it – she asked who it was and what they wanted.

'Hang on . . . Just a moment.' The secretary muted the phone again. 'Marion Blake? Teresa's nurse?'

Her immediate reaction was incomprehension, then sudden terror that something might have happened to Leonard overrode questions as to why the nurse should be ringing about it. 'Put her through . . . Hello? Katrina Darcy. What's the matter?'

'I'm sorry. In what way?'

'Is Leon . . . Mr Drummond all right?'

'As far as I'm aware. You know he's away, of course.'

'Yes, but . . .' She stopped, uncertain how to continue. 'So how can I help you?'

'I want to talk to you.'

'What about?'

'It's not something we can discuss on the phone. It'll be best if we meet.'

There was an understated determination in her voice. Katrina tried to visualize her but failed. 'I can't imagine what you can possibly have to say to me.'

'No, but you must know what it's about.'

In other circumstances the obvious suspicion would have been blackmail, the threat to tell his wife about the affair. But that would never have mattered and was completely irrelevant now;

197

he'd told Judith that he was leaving her. What did anything have to do with the nurse? Leonard had always said how much they valued Marion, how much she cared for Teresa, that her presence would help to heal the pain of his absence. Could she also have been his lover? No, that was ridiculous.

'If this is to do with myself and Leonard, I frankly can't see that it's any of your business.' She edged her voice with resentment at the woman's interference.

'In a very important way it is. Look, this is going to be difficult for both of us, but I am serious. Are you free for lunch?'

'If I am, I can't see why I should have it with you.'

'Believe me, there's a very good reason. Please. It will save a lot of heartache.'

She must mean Teresa's heartache – so it might be best to at least respond. Perhaps the nurse wanted to talk about how Katrina could help, but why should that be difficult? She could only find out by agreeing.

'Let me check my diary. Yes, you're lucky. Did you have anywhere in mind?' Mild sarcasm underlined a distance between them which might prove necessary.

'Do you know the *Queen Mary*?'

'What? The liner?'

'No. The old steamboat moored by Waterloo Bridge. It's a bar and restaurant now. I thought it would be convenient coming from your office. If the weather stays fine, I'll be outside. Two o'clock?'

'I'm not sure I'll recognize you.'

'I'll know you. Thank you.' She rang off.

Katrina immediately tried to call Leonard in Cardiff but was told he'd finished his morning lecture and left the university for ... He hadn't said where. They weren't certain when he would be back, but they could pass on a message ...

'It's all right. I'll try again later.' It might be better to establish what she was dealing with before she spoke to him.

The nurse had left no impression that day in Kensington Gardens; Katrina's attention had been concentrated on Leonard and Teresa and she had taken no notice of her, except to register that she and the child appeared close, which was what she'd have expected. They had barely spoken and they'd been in each other's company for little more than seconds. Marion Blake began to take on the menace of the bewildering. Katrina nearly rang back to demand exactly what it was about before they met, but that could have indicated apprehension, yielding ground the nurse might exploit.

Walking through the ship's bar she did recognize her, despite the sunglasses, spotting her through the open door, sitting alone at a table on the sunlit deck. She was wearing a pale mauve linen trouser suit and cream shirt; Katrina noticed that her hair, whiter than she remembered, had been cut by someone who knew their business; she was obviously paid well. As Katrina reached the table she looked at her watch.

'Something's cropped up, so I can only spare you half an hour,' she said pointedly.

'That should be enough.' The voice was as cultivated as her appearance. 'I've eaten, but you can get something at the bar. Drink?' A second glass stood next to the wine bottle.

'I haven't got time to eat.' Wariness was masked by false impatience as she sat down. 'I think the best thing is for you to say whatever it is you have to, Miss Blake . . . Is it Miss?'

She nodded, then unexpectedly smiled as she poured Katrina's wine. 'You still don't realize, do you?'

'Realize what?' Game-playing was infuriating.

'It's hardly surprising. Prepare yourself,' she warned. She put down the bottle then took off her glasses, and for the first time Katrina saw her face properly, older but still remembered with a spasm of the heart. Instinctively, she closed her eyes, convinced that when she opened them again she would see something different.

'But why do you call yourself Marion?' It was the most banal but immediate of endless questions.

'Because Leonard's wife is called Judith and we agreed it would confuse Teresa. It's my middle name. Don't you remember?'

199

'I don't think I ever knew it . . . and what about Blake? You didn't get married, did you?'

She laughed slightly. 'I haven't changed that much. It was protective cover. Another girl – she was before you – told her parents about us in a belated fit of conscience. They reported it and I lost my job. The word got around and several interview boards obviously knew all about Judith Hurst, so I adopted my mother's maiden name.'

Katrina was still adjusting. 'What happened to . . . I've forgotten her name. The one you went back to?'

'Chris. The one I'd still be with.' Her eyes held remembered sorrow. 'She died in a car crash. I was with her. The doctors managed to save my legs, but . . . Well, the pain's been tolerable so far but it will get worse and the trousers aren't a fashion statement.' She touched her hair. 'This is the other legacy.'

The glass of wine she'd poured was suddenly needed. 'But why did you become a nurse?'

'I just became tired of teaching, and . . . I'm not sure. Perhaps it was something to do with being in hospital all those weeks. I left the NHS six years ago and went private. A year later I landed the job with Judith and Leonard.'

The boat rocked slightly as the wake of a passing pleasure cruiser licked its sides. 'But why didn't you tell me who you were when you rang?'

'I thought about it, but . . . Well, I was a drama teacher, remember.' For a brief moment she smiled again, but then looked regretful. 'Anyway, I'm afraid this isn't meant to be a reunion.'

'Then what is it about?' Amazement at an incredible coincidence was replaced by apprehension again.

'I'd have thought that was obvious. It's about Leonard leaving Judith for you. She told me after he left on Friday.'

Katrina moved back fractionally. 'I told you on the phone. That's none of your business.'

'And I told you it is, which means I don't want it to happen.'

'You don't want it to happen?' Katrina stared at her. 'For Christ's sake, don't tell me you're in love with him.'

200

'Of course not, although I admire him. My concern is Teresa.' She rubbed one thumb against the other palm, a remembered subconscious gesture of uncertainty. 'I don't know the best place to begin this, but let me tell you something I don't think you know. Judith and Leonard haven't slept together since—'

'I know all about that,' Katrina interrupted. 'Do you think we don't talk to each other?'

'But has he told you they still share the same bedroom? Single beds, but whenever they're both at home, which is most of the time, Teresa knows she'll find them both there in the morning. And that's very important to her.'

'How can anyone know what's important to her?'

'I do.' She picked up her wine glass and rotated it between her fingers, as though she needed something to occupy her hands. 'I'd done very little work with handicapped children when I first met Teresa, and I almost cried at the tiny things that made her happy. But then I realized she *was* happy. As long as she had everything she needed, all the things she lacked didn't matter. And one of the most essential things she needs is her parents . . . both of them.'

'Leonard knows that,' Katrina argued. 'He'll see her as often as he can. He's thought a lot about this.'

'Then he's not thinking straight, which is unlike him.' She put the glass down and refilled it. 'So I want you to think for him, and tell him he can't leave her.'

'Oh, no.' Katrina almost stood up and walked away. 'I've had bad times as well. I've got a case of need here.'

'So has Teresa – and she can't do anything about it.'

'I know that, and I'm sorry, but . . . Oh, this is impossible!' She bit back comments about intolerable interference. 'Look, I appreciate how you feel about Teresa as much as Leonard does. She'll miss him at first, but her mother will be there and she'll have you. For God's sake, what would it be like if he died?'

'But he's not dying. He's . . .' She reached across the table and took hold of her hand. 'Katrina, please. I knew you and Leonard were having an affair when I met you last year. That was no problem. Judith told me a long time ago about their arrangement over that sort of thing. Just settle for being lovers. Long-term lovers if you want. Why not? That won't hurt anyone.'

'Because ...' Katrina pulled her hand free '... because that's not enough now. For either of us. These things happen. It matters. OK?' She was dismayed at what she was being put through, but she couldn't give way.

'Teresa matters to me,' Marion said. 'And to Judith.'

'I know she does. Teresa's lucky to have someone as devoted as you, but ...' Trying to argue would achieve nothing. 'I'm sorry. Leonard won't change his mind any more than I will. Believe me. It's taken us a long time to get where we are.'

'So you're saying I'm wasting my breath with arguments? Being lovers isn't enough.'

'No, it isn't.' The denial carried more force than she had intended. 'If you just think about it, Teresa won't ...'

'Can't you see that it's hideously selfish?' For a moment, she was the impatient teacher again from a lifetime before. 'The one person you'll hurt is the one who can do nothing to defend herself.'

'Back off!' Katrina flared into defensive anger. 'I don't need bloody moral blackmail. She'll be all right.'

'Teresa deserves a damn sight more than "all right"! She needs to have her father at home to love her!'

'So do I!'

A man at a nearby table glanced up at the sound of their raised voices then returned to his mobile phone conversation. Katrina momentarily wondered if ... No, she was not prepared to take on another personal hurt to protect a child she didn't know. She lit a cigarette and turned her head away, watching a train slide between the girders of Hungerford Bridge into Charing Cross, trying to compose herself.

'I'm sorry,' she said finally. 'I appreciate how you feel, but we're not going to get anywhere. There's a great deal you don't know about Leonard and me. We've come a long way to get where we are.'

'Oh, spare me your love life. I've read enough about your affairs in the gossip columns.'

202

'This is different. Very different.'

'Of course it is.' Marion looked sceptical. 'You always were a romantic. Anyway, if you won't listen to reason, I'll have to use other means because, believe me, I'm as determined as you are about this.'

Her handbag was on the bench seat beside her; she opened it and took out two photocopies. 'Here.'

The first was of a photograph they'd asked a tourist to take of them with Katrina's camera the day they'd spent in Chester; the Diamond Jubilee Eastgate clock was visible in the background. They were laughing and holding Tudor dolls; Katrina remembered she'd bought Anne Boleyn. The second was what she'd written on the back, with kisses after her name: 'To my dearest darling Judith, who taught me to speak the language of love. Katrina'. It had taken a long time before she'd been satisfied with the words.

'You said this wasn't a reunion,' she said, unable to understand.

'It's not.' Marion held up her hand as she offered the photocopies back. 'Keep them, I've got the original. Now listen, because I've spent a lot of time thinking about this. If you won't agree to accept a perfectly good alternative relationship with Leonard I'm prepared to protect Teresa with everything I've got. You say he can handle leaving her, but can he cope with me letting our affair become public knowledge? I don't like journalists very much, but I think they'd be interested.'

It was too much to absorb at once. 'What are you talking about?'

'Do I have to spell it out? Leonard leaving Judith for you is a news story, isn't it? You're both well known and it's good scandal. And if they then discover you've been a lesbian, and he's abandoned his handicapped daughter ... Well, you're the professional. You tell me. Won't they go overboard?'

Staggered at what she was so calmly threatening, Katrina could still imagine the headlines. 'GAY KATE SPLITS HEARTBREAK FAMILY ... HOME ALONE WHILE DADDY DATES BONKBUSTER LOVER ... TEARS OF A CHILD WHO CAN'T BEG "COME BACK".' The subs at Wapping and Canary Wharf would use those for starters. The pack would be staking out Harrow, snatching pictures of Teresa as she left for her special school, terrifying her as they shouted questions at her mother, finding other parents who could be tricked into talking. Leonard would never allow it. They had discussed the possibilities of publicity, but decided it was unlikely to be a problem. Writers lack the news value of showbusiness stars and Teresa need never come into it. But with lesbianism tossed out as bait . . .

'I don't believe you,' she said. 'One moment you say you want to protect Teresa, the next you'd let her become a freak in a media circus.'

'Teresa won't be hurt by it. She can barely read and can only comprehend her very small world. The only hurt she'll suffer is losing her father – and the publicity will make him hate you much more than he'll hate me. Frankly, I don't care if he does hate me. I don't like him for what he's planning to do.'

'And what about his wife?'

'Judith and I have become good friends, and take that look off your face, it's not like that. She feels he's betraying Teresa, and will fight this her own way, but she's admitted to me that she hasn't got enough weapons. I haven't told her about us yet, but I will if you leave me no choice. And I'll tell her what I've just said. She'll know it will be enough to stop him.'

Katrina began to stand up. 'I'm not listening to this. You're unreal. Leonard will sort it when he gets back.'

'I wouldn't count on that. You don't know him as well as you think.' Of all the things she'd said, that hurt Katrina most. 'And don't go, because I haven't finished.'

Shocked enough to grasp at anything that offered a way out, Katrina thought for a moment that Marion was hinting she could be bought off. She sat down again.

'This is in case you need any more convincing,' Marion continued. 'But I need to explain something first. I'm a member of Ziggy's. Do you know it?' It was a long-established lesbian club near Soho Square.

'Not personally, and I can't see the relevance of your sex life.'

'Believe me, my sex life is all in the past,' she replied. 'But

Chris and I were almost founder members, and I have some very good friends there. They held me together after she was killed. The male fantasists would find it very disappointing. There are members older than me and we just meet for a drink and a chat, tell the youngsters what it was like in the Dark Ages. There are couples who've been together for years – we celebrated a twenty-fifth anniversary the other month—'

'I presume there's a point to all this,' Katrina interrupted.

'Yes. I met someone you know there. Anna Probert.'

Katrina did not react. It was hardly a surprise that Anna played the gay scene, and even if she'd told people about their affair, it gave Marion little more to threaten with.

'Yes. She used to be an editorial secretary at the *Register*. And yes, we slept with each other. Satisfied?'

'I knew that. It's how I found out that matters.' She broke off as a man walked up to the table selling single roses in cellophane tubes. 'No, thanks. We're not tourists.' He went away. 'Some time ago, Anna was telling a group of us about a girl she'd met at a party. There was nothing physical, but they'd got on and Anna was starting to think it might lead somewhere until someone told her who the girl was. As she said, "It would have been almost Greek to have slept with the daughter as well as the mother".'

For a moment Katrina said nothing, stunned by such a level of determination. Was it that Teresa was the daughter Judith had never had and she would resort to anything to protect her? Even lies that could be disproved? But years before, Judith Hurst had always been totally honest, no matter who was hurt by it . . .

'Stephanie's not gay.' Why did she doubt her own denial? Why did she feel such an urgency to deny it?

'Isn't she? If you don't believe me, call Anna. I presume you understand what I'm saying here.'

'That you'd drag her in as well?'

'Yes, I would. Now do you believe I'm serious?'

They stared at each other, the image of two women lunching together, chatting about their husbands, teenage children, headaches over the au pair, diets, the curse of the menopause.

Katrina shook her head in rejection. 'I can't believe anyone could be so cruel.'

'Isn't Leonard going to be cruel to Teresa? I've told you. I won't do anything if you remain lovers. That's not a problem. Just accept that, and . . .' she smiled, and now there was genuine warmth in it 'we might be able to meet as friends again. Let's face it, this is one hell of a coincidence. I've often thought about that ghastly flat in Heaton Mersey when I've read your column or seen you on television. I don't want to hurt anyone. The only person who concerns me is Teresa.'

Had she threatened from the outset it would have been easier to defy her, but she'd been reasonable, even considerate, offering something many women would have accepted. There could be no immediate answers.

'You've got to let me think about this.'

'Of course.' She took a pen from her bag and wrote on the back of one of the photostats, 'That's the private phone in my room. If I can help, call me. I mean that. I know what it's like to love someone very much.'

Her understanding pierced as deeply as her threats.

Katrina took a taxi straight to Clapham. Anthony was out but expected back at any time. Toby didn't ask why she was there and they spent half an hour discussing his latest theatre project, the garden and drinking tea before Anthony arrived. He walked into the sitting room and gave her a penetrating look.

'Problems, I observe,' he said. He put down his briefcase, loosened his tie and sat in the Oriental wicker chair in front of her. She felt guilty about taking his time again, but Clapham had been her rest and refit centre for a long time. Normally she would have told him everything, but now left out any reference to Stephanie; she was discovering that was the worst shock of all.

'How extraordinary,' he said when she'd finished. 'I mean your meeting this Judith or Marion or whatever again. Do you think she's serious?'

'Would she have met me if she wasn't?'

'Obviously not, and . . .' He moved in the chair as if

uncomfortable. 'Let's separate the offer from the threat. She won't interfere if Leonard stays with his wife but you remain lovers on however permanent a basis. Will he accept that? Most men would.'

'I don't know, but he'll be confused if I suggest it when he comes back. What reason can I give him?'

'He's been confused for some time . . . and there's a perfectly good reason available. You could have been thinking while he's been away and have begun to worry about the effect on the daughter.'

'That sounds like advice,' she told him. 'House rule number one.'

'I'm not suggesting what you should do, I'm only pointing out a possible reason. You could say you've met someone else and fallen madly in love or are taking the veil after seeing a vision of the Virgin Mary in Bond Street. The question isn't the reason, the question is do you want to find a reason? Why didn't you just tell her to go to hell?'

'Because I'm bloody sure she means it, of course.'

'Which means you'd almost certainly lose Leonard completely. So what are you going to do?'

'I don't know what to do at the moment.'

'Then you do nothing. Negative advice is permitted. Are you going to call Leonard?'

'I do every night, but I can't talk about this on the phone.'

'Well, if he's not back for another week or so, you've got time on your side. Could you meet this woman again?'

'Yes. She's given me her private number.'

'Underlining the fact that she's prepared to be reasonable.' He watched her reaction. 'You don't like admitting that, do you? Any more than admitting she's behaving in a perversely . . . admirable way in protecting Teresa. She's putting her personal reputation on the line for a child who will never be able to appreciate what she's done.'

'I know . . . But I still love him, Anthony. I mean *really* love him.'

'Then you don't want to hurt him, do you?'

207

She reached down and crushed another cigarette stub into the conch shell ashtray on the polished pine floor beside her, taking a long time to make sure it was out.

'There are times when I wish you weren't so bloody good at pinning me down like a moth.'

'But I always let you go.'

'To get my wings burnt again?'

'You didn't come here to play metaphors. Go home and think about the rest of your life.'

Chapter Four

Stephanie suddenly mattered more than Leonard. The realization was as unexpected as it was revealing, an ironic twist of emotion; Katrina was now placing her daughter first. Her attitude towards her sex life – her private life – was of extreme ambivalence; a hypocrite if she condemned, an indifferent mother if she dismissed it as none of her business. She rationalized that what concerned her was the fact that Stephanie had been seen at Ziggy's; not all lesbians were like Marion and her friends, and a daughter who could be at risk was a justifiable worry. It was just after six-thirty when she got home from Anthony's and tried to reach her at Alison's.

'I'm sorry, she's not here. She said something about going on somewhere after work.'

'Where exactly?'

'Don't know, but she'll have left the shop by now. Can I give her a message?'

'No . . . yes. Tell her I rang and I'd like her to call me.'

'OK, but she's usually back late.'

'It doesn't matter. I'll be here. Tell her it's urgent.'

She could have been going anywhere – the cinema, a play, an innocent drink with friends. But Katrina was unable to believe that. She rang Anna because there was no one else she could think of who might be able to help. She said nothing more than that she'd met another friend who was gay who'd seen Stephanie at Ziggy's, nothing about her meeting Anna. The revelation of their affair was irrelevant.

'I'm not sure I understand this.' Anna sounded guarded. 'I've seen her at Ziggy's myself enough times. I assumed you knew.'

'Not until today. We've . . . Well, contact has become erratic. I'm worried about her now.'

'Oh. Perhaps I should have called you, but . . . look, darling, what's the problem? You wouldn't be panicking if she was straight and screwing around, would you? She's gay. All right?'

'But she's my daughter.'

She knew the protest was indefensible the moment she spoke, and Anna slapped her down. 'Oh, please! We're all somebody's daughter. Did you think about my mother when we were in bed? Or yours, come to that?'

'No, but . . . all right, I'm in no position to start getting puritanical. But what's she into? I don't know the gay scene, but I don't like the thought of some butch dyke picking her up. I like to think you'd let me know that if you heard about it.'

'I hope I would.' Anna's tone changed. 'OK, I take your point. There are some women who are always on the lookout for new kids on the block – or, of course, she might be into a good relationship. I'll ask around and call you.'

In the state of mind Katrina had driven herself into, that was not enough. 'I need to know now. Could she be at Ziggy's tonight?'

'Possibly. I've seen her there enough times.'

'Right. Where is it exactly? I know it's the Greek Street area.'

'It's in . . . hang on. You can't just turn up there on your own.'

'Watch me. If you don't give me the address, I'll find it.'

'No! Katrina, face it. Stephanie's age of consent and Ziggy's doesn't take kindly to paranoid parents making a scene. Anyway, it's members only.'

'But I need to know! That's all. If she's all right, I'll back off and come to terms with it. But if she's being . . . For Christ's sake, you know the sort of thing that can happen better than I do. Can you just see that?'

Anna sighed. 'All right, but you come with me and promise to behave. I'll introduce you as a friend – members often take straights there for a drink – and we'll *discreetly* see if we can find what's happening with Stephanie. That's my best offer, darling.

If you don't accept it I'll ring Ziggy's now and warn them about you.'

'Thank you. I'm at the flat.'

'I'll be there as soon as I can.'

Ziggy's was in a cellar, a brass plate on the wall next to an Indian restaurant the only indication, stairs lined with framed photographs, Madonna bizarrely next to the Ladies of Llangollen outside their cottage. It was bigger than Katrina had expected, the low room turning off into quiet alcoves, each glowing with wall lights; it could have been any private drinking club in London, except for the absence of men and the presence of touches of taste. There was a deep maroon fitted carpet, good original paintings on the walls, small porcelain vases of fresh flowers on the tables. Most of the members were businesswomen relaxing after work and there were three younger girls playing backgammon. As Anna signed her in and bought drinks, Katrina was aware of being glanced at, but with no more interest than that her outfit was being assessed.

'Can you see her?' Anna asked quietly.

'No, but she could be . . . I can't see into all the corners.'

'Well, don't go poking around in them.' She nodded towards a woman sitting alone reading the *Spectator*. 'Come on, I'll introduce you to Eunice.'

Eunice was nearly sixty, matronly and garrulous. Katrina forced herself to be patient until Anna was able to naturally direct the conversation.

'Quiet tonight,' she commented. 'Where is everyone?'

'It's still early.'

'Mmm. Dorothy's usually here by this time, though.' She still had to prevaricate for a few minutes, but she finally found an opening.

'Tell you who I haven't seen lately. That blond girl who works in the dress shop in Denmark Street. What's her name . . . Suzanne? No, Stephanie.'

'I've seen her.' Eunice indicated a door in the far wall. 'She's with Brenda Carr in the disco.'

211

Under the table, Anna's foot nudged Katrina's warningly. 'Oh, I thought she might have moved or something. That reminds me, I ran into Charlotte the other day. She's been offered that job in Bath . . .'

Katrina tried to analyse her reaction to the fact that her daughter was in the next room, dancing with another woman – the way she'd watched her dancing at her eighteenth birthday with a man. If Stephanie had told her later they'd ended up in bed, she would probably have been pleased and just told her to take precautions. Why should the thought of a woman kissing her be any different from the idea of a man's penis inside her? It needed an effort to accept that, but if she was honest . . . Eunice was excusing herself because friends of hers had arrived. Anna waited until she was out of earshot.

'If she's with Brenda Carr, you can relax,' she said.

'What's she like?'

'Brenda?' Anna paused as she thought. 'I don't know her all that well, but . . . Early forties, secretary to a specialist at Guy's or St Thomas's or . . . one of the big teaching hospitals, anyway. Nice woman . . . I'm almost certain she once said she used to be a volunteer with the Samaritans. Stephanie's perfectly OK with her.'

'But she's nearly my age.'

Anna drew in her breath sharply and Katrina winced as she took hold of her hand and squeezed it very hard. 'One more remark like that – just one – and I'm going to hit you. Got it? How many middle-aged men do you know who are knocking off bimbos? I don't mean Stephanie's a bimbo, but age is not on the agenda.' She relaxed her grip. 'You also seem to have forgotten that I'm a lot younger than you are. I don't recall that it troubled either of us.'

'Oh . . . shit!' Katrina rested her forehead on the heel of her free hand. 'Why do I keep making stupid comments instead of coping with this?'

'Because it's a shock,' Anna said. 'I can appreciate that. But you've got to see it as a wonderful surprise. If you can't hack it any other way, stand in front of a mirror every morning and tell yourself. "My daughter's a lesbian and I am so incredibly happy for her." You of all people should be able to manage that.'

A blast of rock music filled the bar and faded as the door leading to the disco opened and closed again; Katrina pulled back in the shadow.

'Stephanie's come into the bar?' Anna asked.

'Yes.'

'She probably won't spot you, but it might help that you can see her. Tell me what you think.'

The immediate thought was that she was holding hands with another woman; both their faces were flushed and they were laughing. They went to the bar and ordered, then sat on high stools waiting for what appeared to be spritzers. Brenda Carr was tall, with an elegance that survived physical exertion, wearing a dark, tailored skirt and fine-striped white shirt open at the neck; irrelevantly, Katrina thought that her heels were too high for dancing. In the soft orange light her hair appeared dark blonde, contrasting with the dazzle of Stephanie's, cut short but sculpted so that there was no suggestion of maleness. As she moved on the stool a gold locket glittered, and Katrina felt senselessly reassured by the fact that she wore glasses.

'So what do you think?' Anna's dark eyes emphasized the question.

'I'm not sure ... She looks ... very smart. Very ...' She smiled without meaning to. 'I want to say cultured.'

'Then say it. It's a good quality in a lover.' Anna suddenly twisted round in her chair, then turned back to her. 'Fasten your seat belt, I'm going into impulsive mode.'

'What do you mean?' When they had known each other, Anna had often abruptly done outrageous things – hammering the knocker on a door they were passing one night, then running away laughing like a mischievous child; going up to a couple of strangers in a restaurant and asking the man if his wife knew where he was. Katrina had been embarrassed, but Anna had said it was something she saw no point in controlling when it happened. She was already halfway to the bar. Half fascinated, half fearful, Katrina watched as she spoke to them, then they picked up their drinks and returned with her.

'Actually, more than just a friend I wanted you to meet,' Anna said as they reached the table. 'I decided it would be better for everyone if a few things came out in the open.' Stephanie stared, but didn't speak.

'Here we are.' Anna pulled up two more chairs. 'Katrina, this is Brenda . . . Brenda, Katrina.'

'Good evening.' She held out her hand. 'Nice to meet you.' She appeared offended when Katrina was unable to respond.

'What are you doing here?' Stephanie had not moved since she'd recognized her mother.

'I didn't mean to let you know . . . This was Anna's idea.'

'That's right.' Anna was like a cheerful hostess putting strangers at their ease. 'Now we can all talk about it and perhaps it won't be such a big deal.'

'I'm sorry.' Brenda made a gesture of uncertainty. 'What's happening here?'

'This is my mother.'

'Oh.' Brenda glanced at Anna reproachfully. 'You really enjoy mixing it, don't you?'

'I'm not mixing it.' Anna waved from Stephanie to Katrina and back again. 'These two have had a serious communication breakdown and it's time it was fixed.'

'Then I'll be at the bar.' Brenda turned to go.

'No. Stay here. Katrina doesn't have a problem with this. She only thinks she does.'

'Don't kid yourself,' Stephanie said bitterly. 'She has a problem.'

'Because you're gay? She's rather more grown-up than that. She just has to accept it.'

'Is it a problem?' Brenda asked Katrina.

'I thought it was, but . . . Well, I wasn't expecting it. I'd rather she'd told me.'

'And what would you have done if she had? She says you're not good at listening to her.'

214

'Ouch.' Katrina looked at her daughter. 'It's all right. You tell your friends things like that.'

'Same again for everyone before the bar gets packed?' Anna stood up and nodded to Brenda. 'You can help me to carry them.'

For a moment Katrina was terrified that Stephanie would walk away; when she didn't there was a sense of relief. 'Sit down. I didn't intend us to meet. Anna just went and got you.'

'But you'd come here to spy on me.'

'No. Honestly. I just wanted to make sure you were all right.'

'How did you find out?'

'That doesn't matter, but it wasn't through Anna. She used to work with me and I knew she was gay and asked her if she'd bring me.' For the first time in too many years, Katrina felt a tremendous affection for her daughter. 'Look, darling, I don't have a problem with this – all right, I'm telling myself I haven't – but . . . I think I need you to tell me that it's what you really want. I'd feel dreadful if it was defiant or something. Is it?'

'No. Perhaps it was at first, but not now.'

'At first? How long has it been going on?'

Stephanie looked unexpectedly amused. 'Remember Barbara, who was head girl? You always said how much you liked her.'

'I did . . . but I didn't realize.'

'Well, it's hardly the sort of thing you advertise.' She shrugged. 'I slept with a couple of boys later, but . . . I don't know where it comes from. It's just the way I am . . . and I was going to tell you.'

Katrina had an impulse to explain about herself, but a vivid reason for not doing so stopped her. She became anxious that Anna could be telling Brenda.

'I need the loo,' she said. 'Where is it?'

'Over there.' Stephanie pointed to a door in the corner.

'Back in a moment.' Passing the bar, she paused. 'We need those drinks.'

'On their way,' Anna said. 'We were just giving you a minute or so alone. How is it?'

'OK so far. Brenda, could you excuse us? There's something I want to say to Anna.'

215

'I'll see you back there.' She smiled. 'I'm afraid someone must have removed the chapter dealing with this sort of situation from my book of etiquette.'

'Then we'll have to vamp it. We'll be right with you.' Katrina waited until she had walked away, then asked urgently, 'Have you told Brenda about us?'

'No. I didn't feel it was my place. Haven't you told Stephanie?'

'No, and I don't want to.'

Anna frowned suspiciously. 'I hope you can justify that. She has the right to know.'

'Yes, but . . . but not yet. God, I *know* this, but it's so difficult to put it into words. If I tell Stephanie about us she'll think I'm tolerating her being gay only because I'm in no position to criticize. I want her to know I'm respecting *her* right to choose, that I'm granting her her freedom – from me! Which is what I must do. I'll tell her one day, but at the moment this needs to be . . . to be me being a mother who doesn't need to forgive because forgiveness shouldn't come into it. Am I making sense?'

'Are you making sense to yourself?'

'Perfect sense. I want Stephanie and Brenda – or whoever – to feel that it's their thing and I'm accepting it because it's marvellous, not just because I haven't got any grounds to object. And, well, I need to get there as well, but I really believe I will think it's wonderful that my daughter's very much in love. Who with isn't the point, is it?'

Anna nodded. 'You're taking big steps in a short time.'

'Hold my hand in case I fall?'

'You got it. Come on, let's get back.'

'In a minute. I really do need the loo.'

The atmosphere was distinctly less febrile when Katrina returned, and she knew Anna had done a great deal to improve it.

'We've laid out ground rules,' she announced brightly. 'Well, at least I have and everybody has to obey them. Brenda's going to tell us her life story and you and Stephanie must smile at each other three times every minute. After that I read palms.'

'I understand Anna used to work with you,' Brenda said drily. 'You have my deepest sympathy.'

After that it became a good evening. Stephanie was nervous at first, but she began to relax. Other members came in and joined them and Katrina found herself in the pleasant company of intelligent women. At one point, when everyone was laughing at a story someone had told, she leant over and whispered to Stephanie: 'It's all right. I love you.'

At about ten o'clock Brenda stood up and beckoned Stephanie to follow her. They stood a few paces away talking, then Stephanie came back and told Katrina that Brenda wanted to speak to her.

'I've told Stephanie I want her to go home so you can talk to each other alone. You need to.'

'What does she say?'

'She's agreed.' She hesitated. 'I'm very fond of your daughter, Katrina. I know this isn't your scene, but I can't believe someone like you could be so stupid as to condemn it.'

'Of course not. It was just . . . I'm still taking it on board.'

'Then if it's just the two of you for a while, it should help. Has she told you about Suffolk?'

'No.'

'We're going there on Saturday. I've rented a cottage near Lavenham for a week, so I can do some watercolours . . . and make love to your daughter.' She looked at Katrina closely. 'You can't stop her, of course, but it's very important that you mustn't want to.'

'I won't,' she promised. 'And thank you for persuading her to come home.'

'Good luck, and I hope I'll see you again.'

Katrina insisted that Anna came back with them – she felt the need of a referee – and they bought a Chinese takeaway in Edgware Road. At first it was decisions about what was what and reheating things in the microwave, then supper on their laps with a bottle of Valpolicella. Anna had an endless supply of chat to fill every silence, and was a voice of sane normality. It was turned midnight when she said she must go.

'You could sleep in the spare room,' Katrina suggested.

'Nope,' she said firmly. 'You two have private talks scheduled.'

In the hall, Katrina hugged her. 'Bless you. Can I call you if I need you?'

'Naturally, but you're the only ones who can sort this out, darling. Now where do I get a cab at this time of night?'

'Ask the porter to call one for you. Put it on my account.'

'Thanks. Oh, and ask Stephanie about those marks on her wrist.'

'What? I didn't notice them.'

'I did.' She kissed her. 'Goodnight.'

Katrina felt exhausted as she went back to the sitting room, unable to decide what to say in case she got it wrong. Stephanie was silent as well at first, then simply said: 'She's magic – Anna.'

'Yes. I like Brenda as well.'

'Good. That should make this easier.' She was playing with a crumpled paper napkin, stained with sweet and sour sauce, in her lap.

'Is there anything else I don't know about?' Katrina asked.

'What?' Stephanie saw where she was looking. 'That was ages ago.'

'But you tried to cut them?'

'Sort of. With the Yale key from the front door. You never noticed.'

'Oh, shit!' Katrina knelt in front of her, taking hold of both her hands. 'I'm sorry, sorry, sorry, sorry, sorry. Will a hundred times be enough? It won't be for me. God, I've been the bitch mother from hell!'

'Don't!' Stephanie protested. 'That's part of the trouble. You're such a bloody drama queen! Can't you just talk to me like another human being? You used to be able to.'

Katrina pressed her fingers against her lips. 'I'll try. Slap me if I get out of line. I seem to have a habit of doing that.'

'All right, and I'll start by saying something. I really appreciated that you came to Ziggy's and were so good about Brenda. Thank you.' For the first time since Stephanie had stood scarcely higher than Katrina's waist they embraced each other with real affection.

218

The following day Stephanie agreed to come home and arranged for her things to be collected from Alison's. They were hesitant at first, Katrina from nervousness, Stephanie from doubt. They needed regular agreed truces; humour helped to dilute anger. Over two days they turned over a great deal of wreckage, but with a shared desire to try and repair it. The danger – especially for Katrina – was to appear too eager, to become addicted to talking, but each of them seemed to know when it was time to back off and leave the channel open while they got on with their separate lives. The Suffolk holiday was at the right time; they needed to be apart for a period. Katrina told her to give her love to Brenda and said she must come to dinner when they returned.

And in the midst of it all, Katrina found she had come to terms with Leonard and his love for Teresa; they had ignored every feeling but those they had for each other, and marriage would be the ultimate selfishness. Speaking to him on the phone she said nothing, but she wondered what he was thinking. When he came back, she would use her new relationship with Stephanie as her own part of the reason for pulling back. Nothing else need change. It amused her to think that they might all end up like the Bloomsbury set, sharing partners, literature and liberated love; it was possible to imagine meeting Leonard's wife, one of a coterie of intelligent, sophisticated adults. On impulse she rang Marion and invited her to visit while Stephanie was away. She would tell her, and it would also be a chance for them to meet as friends again. It struck her later that it was ironic that all her motives had been the right ones.

Chapter Five

The middle classes rarely commit murder; they practise more refined and subtle forms of vengeance. That Katrina Darcy killed someone was in many ways the result of malign chance; it could even be called coincidence, in the sense that certain events had coincided. To look at it like that is to be fatalistic, but chance constantly afflicts us. Had we not gone to that party, accepted that job, bought that particular house, we would never have met the person who became our lover, friend or rival and everything would have been different. And such incidents spread further and further outwards, beyond our control and awareness, until they touch people we will never know. Two American professors, one of whom had never visited Britain, would have been horrified to think that a decision they made led to a woman's death six thousand miles away. But it could be traced back to them, or to countless other people whose lives fatally overlapped. Every time we meet a stranger, there are terrifying risks.

After Stephanie left for Suffolk on Saturday morning, Katrina felt isolated, especially when she rang Leonard. Cardiff was going well, but he missed her. She said something elliptical about them having a lot to talk about, a very small step towards what she knew she had to tell him, but it made her mind easier, that she would be able to accept and tolerate the loss. What loss? There was no reason why she should still not have a wonderful lover, and who knew what might happen in the future? The possibility that Teresa might unexpectedly die came without her seeking it, and she was stung by the imagined guilt that to want something too much might somehow bring it about. To occupy her mind, she walked almost all the way round Hyde Park, planned a dinner menu for when Brenda came, drafted ideas for her column. She felt very, very lonely.

Marion was due on Monday evening, and she wanted to make a special effort to show her appreciation. Their meeting had been a perverse blessing; if Marion had not told her about Stephanie, Katrina might have lost her for ever, and it had also enabled her to recognize that marriage to Leonard could prove a terrible mistake, a relationship that would rot on guilt. Instead she could keep him, learn to love her own daughter properly – and perhaps enjoy a new and unexpected friendship with the woman who had once meant so much to her. As she bought exotic cocktail snacks and replenished the drinks cabinet, polished the silver, changed the cushion covers, had fresh flowers delivered, Katrina began to look forward to the evening. Marion was due at seven, and vases were being critically swapped round again when the hall porter rang to say she was downstairs. As she opened the door, Katrina put her cautious look down to apprehension.

'Hello. Still very punctual, I see. Come in.' She felt an urge to kiss her cheek, but Marion had already passed her, walking down the hall and into the sitting room, instinctively taking in its space and designer elegance.

'This is rather different from Heaton Mersey . . .' She stopped as she saw a small abstract painting. 'Is that a Howard Hodgkin?'

Katrina laughed. 'I can't afford his prices. It's Gillian Ayres, but several people have thought it's him. The Rackhams on either side are originals. I like the contrast.'

'Unorthodox, but it works. And you used to be so conventional.'

'Was I? That was a long time ago.'

Shared memories were layering everything they said with private meaning. As Marion commented on other things in the apartment, Katrina found herself assessing how she had changed, looking for remains of the vibrant daring she had loved. Time and pain had shadowed the face, and remembered grace was flawed by the governed ungainliness of how she carried her left leg. Something else had vanished as well – confidence and challenge had been replaced by a sense of unease. Perhaps she feared she was going to be defied. When she had been Judith, she had never been afraid.

'I want to thank you about Stephanie,' Katrina said.

'Do I deserve thanks?'

'Very much. If you hadn't told me ... Well, I met her at Ziggy's after you did. She's with someone called Brenda Carr and it's OK. Truly. Do you know her?'

'Brenda? Yes, we met when I was working at Guy's.'

'Of course. I liked her.'

'That's good. It must be ... Well, it can't have been a complete surprise, but how are you handling her being gay?'

'I'm getting there. I've got to let her find her own happiness.'

'Yes.' Marion had crossed the room and was looking out of the window. 'I'm sorry about what I said to you last week, but in a way Teresa's my daughter, and ... You fight for them, don't you?'

Katrina nodded. 'You must love her very much – and you were right.' She paused. 'Let me get this over with, then we can just talk. Perhaps it's all tied up in my mind with Stephanie now, but I can't let Leonard hurt Teresa so much. I'll find a way of telling him and we'll settle for what we've got. I mean it. All right?'

Marion remained by the window; she didn't turn round. 'That can't have been easy for you.'

'No, it wasn't. But you were right to make me see it.' She brushed away a slipping tear, grateful that Marion was not looking at her. 'Anyway, end of speech. Now, what would you like to drink? The choice is fairly comprehensive.'

'Whisky and water?'

'You have a choice.' She crossed to the cabinet. 'Teacher's or Bell's, and I've got a Macallan somewhere if you'd prefer a malt. I'm sure there's some—'

'I'm afraid I have something very difficult to tell you.'

Caught by the tone of her voice, Katrina glanced back to where Marion had turned from the window. 'What do you mean?'

She sighed. 'I've been rehearsing how to say this all the way here. When you called me, I had the feeling you'd decided to ...' Her eyes were sympathetic. 'Judith told me yesterday she's been offered a job in Los Angeles. Deputy head of a clinic that's state of the art on skin diseases.'

Katrina began to pour the drinks. 'Go on.'

'She was approached about a year ago but turned them down because she didn't want to move to the States. Now they've written and asked her again, and she's taking it. She's sure Leonard will go with her because otherwise he'll lose contact with Teresa. I think she may be right.'

Katrina was trying to blank it out by deciding which of two glasses to offer her. 'I assume she wants you to go as well?'

'Of course.'

'How long's it for?'

'It's a five-year contract, with an option to stay permanently. That's what she'll be aiming for.'

'And when do they want her?'

'As soon as possible. Katrina, I hate to have to be telling you this.'

'Why?' she demanded bitterly. 'You've got what you want, haven't you?'

'For God's sake, it was never for me. I thought you realized that. I didn't want to hurt you.'

'Well, you made a damned good job of doing it.' She could feel anger surging out of everything that had happened. Battling to restore her relationship with Stephanie, she had leant on the promise of still being able to keep Leonard on terms she could accept. She felt betrayed. It was the wrong time to be told the wrong thing.

'Katrina, I'm so very sorry. I promise I didn't know anything about this. If I had, I would never have ... come here.'

Still staring at the drinks cabinet, Katrina stiffened as she heard Marion walk towards her, then shuddered as she put her hand on her shoulder; there were instant, vivid memories of times when she had ached for that physical contact.

'*Get off me!*'

Violently, she threw her arm backwards and felt it strike

223

Marion's face, then there was a clatter and the sound of her falling. She had stumbled against the coffee table, scattering the snacks, then the side of her head struck the arm of a padded leather chair. As Katrina turned, she was lying with her neck at a grotesque, impossible angle; a permanent weakness remained from the car crash.

'Judith!' After nearly thirty years the name of the woman she had loved leapt back, now cried in horror where once it had been called in happiness or whispered in intimacy. She dropped to her knees and held Marion's head against her the way she would have comforted an injured child. Her dress ring had cut the skin just beside the left eye and a trickle of blood ran down her cheek; Katrina gently wiped it away with her fingers, as though removing it would cure so much more.

'Come on,' she pleaded softly as she began to weep. 'This is so silly. You can't . . . I was just angry. Not with you. It's not your fault. I didn't mean to hurt you. Open your eyes . . . please.' It was a long time before she accepted.

She did not know the brain could simultaneously produce so many thoughts and still hold them all in focus. The police would want to know why Marion had been in her apartment. She had told the porter to send her up without any questions about who she was. How did she know her? What about this relationship with her employer? Had she tried to blackmail her over it? Perhaps someone would remember seeing them together on the *Queen Mary*. Somewhere in Harrow was the photograph proving they'd been lovers. Stephanie would be dragged in. People at Ziggy's would be questioned. Would the police suspect Marion had seduced Stephanie the way she'd once seduced her? That could be interpreted as a powerful motive to kill, her acceptance of Stephanie's lifestyle dismissed as pretence. So she'd invited Marion to her home, they'd argued and . . . Would anyone believe it had been an accident? It had the fantastic excess of grand opera, but it had happened in a select block of flats within the sound of commuters driving home to TV suppers in mock-Tudor, family-car suburbia.

The next thing Katrina was conscious of was passing Membury

224

Services on the M4. For a moment she panicked, unaware of why she was there, what had happened, where she was going. Then she remembered wanting to drive to the cottage. Why? It had seemed right at the time, but ... She nearly stopped at Leigh Delamere to call the police, but by then had decided she needed time to sort out ... what? Guilt? Grief? Excuses? Fabricate an explanation? Kill herself? Instead, inevitably, she wrote about it.

Late on Tuesday morning Judith Drummond was on the telephone, arguing with a sergeant at Harrow police station.

'What do you mean, you won't do anything?'

'That's not what I said, Dr Drummond. We'll make enquiries at this station, but Scotland Yard will not put Miss Blake on its missing persons list unless she doesn't return within ten days. She's over sixteen and under sixty-five with no history of mental illness, so she is not classified as being at risk.'

'Even though she's vanished without any explanation?'

'A lot of people do that, and most of them turn up.'

'But Miss Blake is my daughter's nurse! She would never just leave her. I insist you inform Scotland Yard.'

'We can do that, but I've explained what the position will be.'

'Then I'll speak to whoever I need to. This is intolerable!'

'I can let you have a telephone number, Doctor, but it's normal procedure. In the meantime ... You say that when Miss Blake went out last night she told you she was going to visit a friend. Who was it?'

'She didn't tell me. She has a private life.'

'Do you know the names of any of her friends?'

'No, I don't.'

'Have you checked if she keeps an address book?'

'I'm not happy about prying into her personal property.'

'But you are very anxious to trace her.' A silence queried Judith Drummond's social delicacy. 'If you find one, we could contact people in it.'

'No. Very well, I'll look, and if there is one I'll call them.'

'Thank you. And what about her family?'

'She has a married sister in ... I think it's Carlisle or ...

225

somewhere in the north of England, anyway. I can contact her as well – but there's absolutely no reason why she should have suddenly gone there without telling me.'

'People do unexpected things, Dr Drummond. In the meantime, we'll check hospitals and road accident reports. We'll need a description from you. How old is she?'

'Fifty-three – no, fifty-four. About five foot nine, medium build . . . white hair . . . and she has a slight limp. She was injured in an accident.'

'Any other distinguishing features? No? What was she wearing when you last saw her?'

'Brown corduroy trouser suit, green blouse . . . olive green. I can't remember her shoes. They could have been brown suede.'

'Any jewellery?'

'An oval amethyst brooch. It was a birthday present my husband and I gave her.'

'Do you have a recent photograph?'

'I'm sure there's one somewhere. I'll let you have it.'

'Thank you. And there was nothing about her behaviour to suggest there was anything wrong?'

'Nothing at all. She said she was seeing this friend, then probably going on to a club she belongs to and would be home by midnight.'

'You hadn't mentioned that. What club?'

She instinctively hesitated. Marion had long ago told her about her past and being a member of Ziggy's, but Judith Drummond had a middle-class prejudice about how the police reacted to lesbianism.

'I don't know.'

'Pity. Of course there might be something in her room that would tell you.'

'Possibly,' she agreed. 'Is there anything else?'

'I don't think so, except for the photograph. I can send an officer to your home.'

'There's no need. I'll have it couriered to you. And I want to emphasize that I'm very worried. This is completely out of character for Miss Blake. I'm appalled you're not treating it more seriously.'

'Dr Drummond, would you like to know how many people go missing in London every day?' he asked mildly.

'That's irrelevant as far as I'm concerned, Sergeant. Please contact me immediately if you find anything.'

'Of course, and let us know how you go on if you find Miss Blake's address book.'

As Judith Drummond rang off she remembered she had not asked for the Scotland Yard number so that she could ... But perhaps there was something in Marion's room that would help. Teresa had been bewildered that morning, demanding to know where her nurse – her friend – was as Judith had hastily cancelled an appointment so that she could wash, feed and dress her then run her to school. The only explanation was an accident, but a hospital would surely have found the Harrow address in her diary and been in touch ...

She felt uncomfortable going into Marion's room; she and Leonard had always treated it as her private home within their house, not to be entered unless invited. The fact that she was not only in there but considering where Marion might keep her personal things deepened the sense of apprehension. There was a small, roll-top bureau, part of the furniture she had brought with her. It was typically tidy, but there was no immediate sign of an address book. Judith cautiously probed in the wooden compartments, finding nothing more than writing paper, envelopes and a collection of postcards, before opening the top drawer. She hesitated when she saw the photograph, then recognized a much younger Marion. It was obviously not recent, but perhaps the other girl was a friend with whom she still kept in touch. She turned it over and read what was on the back, then looked at the picture again. The shape of the mouth was distinctive, and the name was not a common one ... It *was* her.

She sat on the bed and tried to comprehend. Marion and Katrina Darcy ... had once been lovers? The message clearly suggested that. But Marion had said nothing about knowing her. It seemed insane, but were all three of them somehow ... ? Judith went downstairs and rang the Cardiff number Leonard had left in case of an emergency. Mr Drummond? He might be in the common room having coffee. They'd put her through.

'Leonard? It's me. What the hell's going on?'

'Going on? In what way?'

'Marion's disappeared. She went out last night and hasn't come back.'

'What?' He sounded alarmed. 'What's happened to her?'

'You don't know?'

'Of course not. Why on earth should I?'

'Because . . . Leonard, I can stand a lot, but not being made a complete fool of.'

'What are you talking about?'

'You don't know anything about Marion and Katrina Darcy?'

'Katrina?' There was a fractional silence. 'Judith, are you all right? For God's sake, you can't have taken something.'

'Of course I haven't! I just want to know what's happening.'

'You're going to have to explain because none of this is making sense. What's Katrina got to do with Marion not coming home?'

'You really don't know?'

'No! Just believe that and tell me.'

She accepted he was telling the truth; she had never known him to lie to her. 'All right. I can't understand any of this, but I looked in Marion's room for an address book and found a photograph of them together.'

'But they don't know each other.' He momentarily remembered the brief meeting in Kensington Gardens, but it was irrelevant.

'They did once. We've known for a long time that Marion's gay. It seems that Katrina is as well. They were lovers.'

'That's ridiculous.'

'I'm not making this up, Leonard. Give me a fax number and I'll send you the picture and the message on the back. See if you can come up with another explanation. I'll believe you're not lying, so do the same for me. The fact is that Marion's missing and I'm worried sick about her.'

'You've called the police?'

228

'Yes, but they're not going to start treating it as serious for ten days. We don't know any of her friends. Or at least we didn't until now. I want you to call Katrina.'

'But . . . When was the picture taken?'

'From the clothes I'd say the sixties. Marion was teaching then, wasn't she? Where does Katrina come from?'

'Somewhere near Manchester.'

'It fits, then. That's where they must have met. Now either give me her number or call her yourself. I don't give a damn about the two of you at the moment, but Teresa was in tears this morning.'

'I still can't believe she'll know anything.'

'Possibly not, but it has to be worth trying.'

Drummond's initial reaction had been that Judith was hysterical, an emotion she could have clinically explained but never suffered. But her offer to send him the photograph proved that the incredible could be true. And if Marion had disappeared, there was the question of Teresa . . .

'All right,' he agreed. 'I'll get straight back to you.'

Judith waited by the phone, looking at the photograph again; two laughing young women from another part of their lives, one now her friend, the other her threat. There was a residual suspicion that Leonard had known something, a scientific instinct for empirical proof, but at least he'd agreed to call . . .

'Leonard?'

'There's no reply. I've tried the office, her flat and the cottage.'

'Cottage? I didn't know she had one.'

'It's in Cornwall. Near Porthcurno.'

'You've been there? That doesn't matter. Just keep trying.'

'Of course. Look, I've been thinking about coming back, but the course is sold out and they've arranged a batch of events for Martin Ross and me after he arrives from the States. I've promised David and Frances Fletcher – of course, you don't know them but . . . It doesn't matter. Anyway, Martin and I are staying with them Friday night, then there's a reception Saturday lunchtime and they're showing the film of *Black Lilies* in the evening. I'll come back if you insist, but it's going to cause problems.'

'There's no need. I can't think of anything you can do at the moment except contact Katrina. I'll call you if anything changes.'

'Right. How's Teresa?'

'Confused, but I'll take care of her. What's the fax number? You'd better see this for yourself. Right. Got it. I'll send it now.'

Over the next two days Judith's worries were amplified by Teresa's increasing distress. Where was Marion? Where was Daddy? Would Jaffer – the child's favourite stuffed toy giraffe – be going next? The school holidays meant it would have been impossible for Judith to leave the house if she had not been able to hire a nurse Teresa trusted who had covered for Marion before. And there was work she could not cancel, private consultations, a lecture at London University, an interview for a medical video. After completing that she went to Ziggy's, and became impatient when she was told the club's policy was to release no information about members.

'For God's sake, she's worked for me for five years! She's missing! Anything could have happened to her.'

'We have to respect people's privacy. Some women do not want it to become known that they're members.'

'But she's told me she is! I wouldn't be here otherwise, would I?' She glared at the secretary. 'Look, I've reported her missing to the police, but I've deliberately not told them she belongs to this club. But I'll do so if you give me no choice. All I want to know is was she in here on Monday night?'

The secretary paused. 'Can you wait a moment, please?' Judith watched as she spoke to the two women behind the bar, then came back. 'As far as I can make out, she wasn't, although she might have been in briefly and the people I've asked didn't see her. I'll ask other members and call you if I learn anything. I'm sorry, that's the best I can do.'

'Aren't you worried that one of your members has just vanished?'

230

'We worry every time it happens. Now if you can let me have your phone number . . .?'

Judith took a card from her handbag. 'Try the mobile first during the day. I always have it with me.'

When she reached home, there was a message from Leonard to say he had still been unable to contact Katrina Darcy. Judith called him.

'She's vanished as well?'

'There's still no reply anywhere and the *Register* doesn't know where she is. They're sure she'll be in on Friday. Nothing from the police?'

'No. The sergeant here keeps saying she'll probably turn up. I've complained to Scotland Yard, but they still won't put her on the missing persons list until next week. I can't make them understand she'd never do anything like this.'

'I know. Anyway, I can leave here late Sunday afternoon. Call me if you need me before then. I'll keep trying Katrina.'

In the midst of all that was wrong, it was such a little thing that he didn't finish by saying he loved her, but Judith was conscious of its sting. He hadn't even sent his love to Teresa. If Leonard had died that would have been a cruel loss; that he had changed was simply cruel, and Katrina Darcy, the woman who had slept with two of the most important people in Judith Drummond's life, was to blame for that.

231

Chapter Six

Vernon Farrant rang Kendall's direct line at the *Sunday Register* shortly after eleven o'clock on Friday night.

'Malcolm, what on earth is this about Katrina?'

'What have you heard?'

'I'm in the constituency and there's been a newsflash on the local radio. They say they've found her body in her cottage.'

'Oh, it's out already, is it? They should have said *a* body. We're not certain yet that it's her.'

'But this is appalling. What's happened?'

'We don't know. Anthony Delamere's flying down there.'

'Well, if it is the worst – and I pray it isn't – I'd want to make a tribute. This is a terrible shock. How dreadful for you all.'

'Thank you, Vernon. We're crossing a lot of fingers here at the moment, but if it's not her, I don't know who it might be.'

'I'll see if I can find anything out. I'll have a word with the Chief Constable.' He paused. 'There's no . . . scandal is there?'

Kendall had suspected from the outset that Farrant's call had political motives. 'Not as far as we know, but we don't really know anything.' He left a deliberate silence.

'Well I trust you'll contact me if anything emerges. Katrina has been one of our leading authors for a long time.'

'Of course. We're already working on a story. Katrina wouldn't expect different treatment from anyone else. If we find anything that . . . concerns you, we'll be in touch.'

'Concerns me? In what way?'

'As one of your authors – and a friend.'

'It was a purely business relationship, Malcolm. Nothing more.'

'Of course. You'll have to excuse me, Vernon. There's an urgent call on another line. We'll be in touch.'

Farrant's face flickered with outrage as the phone was put down; it had not been Kendall's place to end the conversation. And he was uneasy about 'anything that ... concerns you', the fractional pause suggesting something might already be known, or at least suspected. He dialled another number.

'Christopher? Vernon. It looks as though Katrina Darcy might be dead ... Check it on PA, I haven't time to explain! I'm going to get more details, but if it turns out there's anything suspicious, the press will start digging up the drains, so we've got to drop a word in the usual ears just in case. You know the problem. I never expected it to come up like this, but we've discussed how to handle it ... Irrational behaviour, delusions, inventing outrageous stories. Say her friends were getting worried about her mental health. You talk to the dogs and I'll call the kennel masters. If anyone mentions Italy, jump on them bloody hard. I don't want to have to resort to gagging writs. Concentrate on the Sundays, it's too late for tomorrow's papers to report anything more than the bare facts. Offer them that PPS and his rent boys if you must. It's time we used it, anyway.

'The only problem is the *Register*. I've just been speaking to Kendall and I think he suspects something. The trouble is, Charlie Taylor isn't in our court, so tell Desmond we'll need a serious rubbishing story if they run anything ... unfortunate. He knows what it'll cost him otherwise. I'll fax you a tribute to put out on the wires if it's confirmed she's dead. If TV wants anything, tell them I've got a slot at noon tomorrow after I've opened that old people's home. Drop everything else and get on with it.'

Judith Drummond was on the M4 when the news came through on the car radio. Tired and only half listening, her mind only clicked awake at the mention of Katrina Darcy's name.

'... Jennie Morrison of Radio West is in the radio car. Jennie, what's happened?'

'Details are still sketchy, Mike, but a police spokesman said

233

that the body of a woman was found in a cottage near the beauty spot of Porthcurno earlier this evening. He refused to say if it was that of Katrina Darcy, but local people say she has owned the cottage for some years, and the landlord of a nearby pub told me she has been staying there during this week.'

'Who found the body, Jennie?'

'Apparently it was a freelance journalist who'd gone to Cornwall to locate Miss Darcy on behalf of the *Sunday Register*. That's all we know at the moment.'

'Do you know why the paper sent him there?'

'According to the owner of the agency he works for they wanted to contact her urgently, but she wasn't answering her phone. Nobody seems to know why they thought she might have gone to Cornwall.'

'And are the police interviewing the journalist?'

'Yes. I believe he's been taken to Penzance police station.'

'And you still don't know exactly whose body it is?'

'Not at this stage, Mike, but the police are promising a statement as soon as possible.'

'Thank you, Jennie, we'll talk to you later. In London, a spokesman for the *Sunday Register* said the police had told them a body had been found, but they had no confirmation that it was that of their leading columnist. A representative of the newspaper is on his way to Cornwall to help with the investigation. On the line now is another top Fleet Street writer, Julia Westlake. Julia, this sounds incredible. How well do you know Katrina Darcy?'

'Very well indeed, Mike. She's one of the most respected names in journalism. I just can't believe that she might be—'

Headlights blazed through the rear window, and Judith Drummond realized she had dropped her speed to less than thirty in the outside lane. She accelerated, then pulled across the carriageway and stopped on the hard shoulder.

'. . . thank you, Julia Westlake. We'll have to stop there for a moment, but we'll be right back after the latest weather . . .'

Rain in Hampshire, Judith instinctively reflected, the first she had run into since leaving the West Country. Was this why the *Register* had been trying to contact Leonard earlier? They had

234

made no mention of Katrina Darcy, but it had clearly been urgent. So when had they known about the body? Their first call had been . . . it must have been around seven-thirty; the second one more than an hour later. But it was now half past eleven, and it seemed that the story was just breaking. She wondered if Leonard had heard anything, but it was too late to ring him. The car shook as a tourist coach rushed by, seemingly inches away; as the announcer returned with more excited questions, Judith Drummond pulled out on to the carriageway again, anxious to get home.

Delamere's plane touched down at RAF Culdrose shortly before midnight; a detective sergeant was waiting for him in the CO's office. As they drove out of Helston he called Kendall.

'I'm here. Anything happened your end?'

'Someone's leaked it because every bugger's calling us. I keep telling them we don't know it is Katrina yet, but that's the line they all want. I don't imagine the pack'll arrive until tomorrow morning, but the local radio and TV are on to it, so there may be a reception party. Oh, and you're booked in at the Land's End Hotel – used to be called the State House. They'd had a couple of late cancellations. Don't know what it's like.'

'I'm not particular.' Delamere closed his eyes as reaction and tiredness caught up with him. 'Anyway, I'll be there soon. I'll get back to you.'

He stared out of the window as the car sped along the main road towards Penzance. The moon was nearly full and the waters of Mount's Bay were splintered slate grey flecked with silver. He could just make out smudges of orange street lights on the opposite shore and a stretched shred of cloud hung like glowing muslin over the far hills. It was a night for walking on empty sands – the way that he and Toby and Katrina had done once in Cyprus, pleasantly drunk and singing 'Moonlight Becomes You'; it seemed a very long time ago. Moving out of an unlit stretch of road, the car was suddenly filled by the garish neon glare of a petrol station, the brash frontage of a tourist pub.

The driver turned on the blue flashing roof light to speed

them through Penzance, then it was darkened country roads again, the silence broken by crackling messages on the radio. Delamere could hardly make them out in the back, but he picked up the words 'Redruth', 'ambulance' and what inexplicably sounded like 'jelly'. At one point the sergeant leant forward and said, 'Three nine, confirm'. As they turned by the Miner's Hammer, Delamere saw a white glow in the gloom ahead and there was a policeman at the entrance to the lane past the farmyard, lapel radio twisted towards his mouth; Delamere noticed a man swing a television camera to follow the car. They stopped near a five-barred gate, the cottage standing about twenty yards beyond it. In the surrounding stillness the area appeared frantic with activity, searing beams of arc lights out of hooded lamps on tall metal poles catching white overalls and silver buttons on uniforms. As Delamere stepped out, he heard the sea, the bark of an unseen dog, confusion of voices, the thrum of a generator. A figure walked towards him.

'Mr Delamere? David Cheeseman. Good of you to come so quickly.' Delamere reflected that he'd reached the age where chief inspectors were starting to look young. Wearing a casual shirt and sports jacket, Cheeseman reminded him of one of the *Register* reporters, who was barely out of his twenties. The moustache was probably an effort to look older.

'Where is the body, Chief Inspector?'

'Still in the cottage, sir. Are you all right about identifying her?'

'If I can. She may not be anyone I know.' Lit by the glare of lights, his face was frozen with self-control. Cheeseman felt slightly apprehensive.

'I don't want you to raise your hopes, sir. I don't know Miss Darcy personally, but I've seen her on television, and—'

'I appreciate your consideration, Chief Inspector. Shall we just do it?'

'Very well, sir. It will assist us. If you could follow me.'

As they crossed the grass, Cheeseman indicated the Rover parked on the gravel path, doors open and a man dusting silver

236

powder on to surfaces with a brush. 'Can you confirm that this is Miss Darcy's vehicle, sir? It's registered in a company name.'

'It's her company car.'

'Is anyone else insured to drive it?'

'I'm not sure. I think they usually offer cover for wives or husbands of staff, but Miss Darcy wasn't married. I can ask someone to check.'

'It might be useful.' As they reached the cottage, a man came out carrying a cardboard box. Cheeseman let him pass, then called down the hall. 'Harry!'

A head appeared round a doorway. 'Sir?'

'This is Mr Delamere, one of Miss Darcy's colleagues. Can I bring him through?'

'Just make sure you don't touch anything, sir.'

Cheeseman stopped at the entrance to the room. A man in overalls was kneeling by the Cornish range with his back to them, half obscuring what was lying on the rug.

'If we step round this side . . .' Cheeseman took Delamere's arm and guided him. 'We can't go too close until forensic have finished, but you should be able to see.'

However much he had prepared himself, Delamere still found the moment agonizing; he had placed too much faith on the fact that the freelance had been unable to remember the ring that had been his and Toby's fortieth birthday present to her. Not that he needed to see that; he had known her too long not to recognize her.

'That's Katrina Darcy,' he said quietly. He was aware that Cheeseman was still holding his arm. 'I don't need to approach any closer.'

'Thank you, sir. We may require a more formal identification later. Would you like to sit down?'

'It's all right, but I would like to go outside.'

'Of course.'

Delamere noticed that none of the other policemen looked at him as Cheeseman guided him out. Somebody shouting for another torch as they stepped into the darkness again was an insensitive intrusion.

'I want to be alone for a few moments,' he said. 'I'll just walk to the end of the back garden.'

'I understand, sir, but please keep to the paths.' Cheeseman pointed to a caravan in the adjacent field. 'I'll be in the mobile incident room when you're ready.'

Delamere walked round the side of the cottage and down to the picket fence at the end. Beyond it the land fell slowly, then ended only yards past the coastal path. He could see nothing but cobalt sky, stars and sea – and Katrina Darcy's face, for no rational reason how she had looked, young and pretty, the first time they had met. Many years crowded his mind and he felt very angry. He stood there for several minutes, then took out his mobile phone.

'I'm afraid it's her, Malcolm.'

There was a silence. 'Oh. I was still hoping . . . You've seen her?'

'Yes.' Delamere swallowed. 'Somebody hit her on the side of the head. There was a great deal of blood.'

'OK. Thanks for letting us know. You've talked to the police?'

'Only briefly. I'm just going to see Cheeseman again.'

'What have they said?'

'Nothing so far. They're all over the cottage and I've heard a dog, but they can't start a search until it's light. I'll let you know if they tell me anything. Have you managed to contact Stephanie?'

'No, we're still trying. Nobody seems to know where she's living.'

'When you find her, tell her I'll be back tomorrow. And call Anna Probert. Her home number's on file. Look, I must talk to Cheeseman. Just make sure you say the right things in your statement, Malcolm. She was a bloody good journalist.'

'I know she was. Leave it with me.'

Cheeseman was replacing the phone as Delamere entered the caravan. 'Our press officer's chasing me. Apparently most of your colleagues have been on to him. The gentleman who found her didn't just call us.'

238

'I didn't imagine he would. I've let my office know, incidentally. They'll give them a statement. What have you said?'

'That the body has been identified as that of Miss Katrina Darcy and we're treating it as a case of murder.' Cheeseman indicated a bench seat against one wall. 'Cup of tea?'

'Thank you.'

The inspector went to the caravan door and called to someone, then returned. 'We'll need a formal statement from you, Mr Delamere, but before that I'd like the names of Miss Darcy's family and close associates as far as you know them. We've been told there's a daughter, her mother and a brother. I understand she was divorced.'

'Yes. A long time ago. They kept in touch ... because of the daughter. He has a flat in Docklands. Haven't you heard from him? He works on the *Times*, so he should have heard about this. He's called Tom Darcy.'

'We'll contact him. She never remarried?'

'No, but she told me recently she was planning to. A man called Leonard Drummond. At the moment he's visiting Cardiff University – the English department – but we were unable to reach him there earlier.'

Cheeseman nodded appreciatively. 'Thank you, Mr Delamere. That's invaluable information to me.'

'What do you mean?'

'At my request, the Metropolitan police entered Miss Darcy's London home an hour ago – and discovered another body.' He deliberately stopped; Delamere's shock was obvious, but he wanted to hear what he might say.

'Who is ... For God's sake, it can't be Stephanie!'

'Miss Darcy's daughter? Why should you think that, sir? I didn't say it was a woman's body.'

'Because we've been unable to trace her in London and ...' Delamere's eyes hardened. 'Chief Inspector, a very dear friend of mine is lying dead less than twenty yards away. I'm incapable of imagining any other horrors at the moment – which means I resent you trying to lay traps for me. Now who the hell is it?'

'I didn't intend it like that, I ...' Cheeseman hesitated. 'Well,

239

the Met will be releasing this, so your office will know. According to the contents of her handbag, she's called Blake and she lived in Harrow. The police have been to the address, but no one's there. However, the house is owned by a Mr Leonard Drummond and his wife.'

'Marion Blake?'

'I think it's Judith Marion. Do you know her?'

'No, but I've heard of her. From Miss Darcy.'

Cheeseman nodded. 'I'd like you to include that in your statement, sir. Oh, just one other thing. Does Mrs Drummond know about her husband's intention to marry Miss Darcy?'

'It's Dr Drummond. I don't know. Miss Darcy told me about the relationship, but not all the details.'

'Thank you, Mr Delamere. If you will go with Sergeant Drew, she'll take your statement in the interview room.'

Cheeseman felt the reassurance of waiting for a pattern to emerge as familiar pieces fell into place. Murder is a banal crime, motives the standard clichés, methods crude, alibis worthless if they even exist. A fraud investigation can take months, even years; killers are often arrested while the bodies are still warm. In this case, what looked like a classic triangle was complicated by having one man and three women, a wife, a mistress and, as far as the police had been able to make out, a nurse. Two dead and the others so far untraced. It was an interesting variation, but he knew the theme.

'Contact Mid-Glamorgan police,' he told another sergeant. 'I want them to locate a man called Leonard Drummond. The English department at Cardiff University should know where he is. I want him held until we can talk to him. But before that, what's happening with the Met?'

'They've entered the house, sir, and are waiting for someone to arrive. Neighbours can't help. However, the local police say that Dr Drummond reported Miss Blake missing on Tuesday morning. Said she went out the previous evening and didn't return.'

'Monday?' Cheeseman frowned. 'How long did they reckon the body had been in Darcy's flat? Several days, wasn't it? And her boss says she's been missing for the past week. So did Darcy kill her and then do a runner?'

'Possibly, but why? And what happened here?'

'God knows, unless . . .' Cheeseman picked up a pile of paper from the desk, 'this tells us something. I've only managed to read half of it so far, but I notice Mr Drummond and Mr Delamere are in it, plus a few other people we'll have to talk to. Very useful.'

Judith Drummond's car skidded on the gravel as she turned into the drive and found it blocked by a police van; there were lights on and the front door was open. As she ran up the steps a policewoman appeared.

'What the hell are you doing in my house?'

'Dr Drummond?'

'Yes. Have you broken this door?'

'One moment, please.' The policewoman turned towards the sitting room door. 'Sir! Dr Drummond's here.'

A man walked out of the room, checking his watch. 'Good evening, Dr Drummond. Inspector William Stephens, Metropolitan police. We've been waiting for you.'

'And have you forced your way in?'

'We have a warrant, Dr Drummond.'

'Issued on what grounds?'

'We're investigating a murder.'

'Murder?' She looked bewildered. 'I don't understand.'

'I'll explain in a moment. Can you tell me where you've been this evening?'

'Why do you want to know?'

'We want to know everything about your movements, Dr Drummond. Well?'

'If you're accusing me of anything, Inspector, I want to know what it is – and then I'll call my solicitor.'

'All I'm asking is where you've been this evening.'

For a moment he thought she was going to refuse to answer, then she seemed to change her mind.

'Exeter. I left this morning to take my daughter to stay with my parents. Satisfied?'

'It's a long journey in a day. Couldn't you have stayed overnight?'

'I have a business appointment in London tomorrow morning.'

'Saturday?'

'Yes. Like you, I often work at the weekend. Now I've answered your question, so you can answer mine. What murder?'

Wright touched the policewoman's arm, indicating she should stand closer to Judith Drummond.

'You reported a Miss Marion Blake as being missing earlier this week. I'm sorry to have to tell you that we've found her.'

Half an hour later Stephens was speaking to Cheeseman. 'Blake's death shook her. For a moment I thought she was going to faint.'

'What about Darcy's?'

'She'd already heard about that on the radio. Anyway, she's called her solicitor and won't say anything until he arrives. All we know is that she went to Exeter today.'

'What time?'

'Don't know. But it's ... say, three hours on the motorway. Then how long to Land's End?'

'Another two. What time did she get back to London?'

'Twelve twenty-three. Once she tells us her parents' address we can ask them what time she left. Found the husband yet?'

'No. Mid-Glamorgan have been told he's gone out with some American writer to visit friends, but nobody knows who they are. He said they were staying overnight but they're due back at the university tomorrow afternoon.'

'He may surface earlier once he hears what's happened. Unless he's got something to hide. Anyway, it's looking as though Darcy must have killed Blake.'

'You're sure it's murder?'

'Looks that way,' Stephens said. 'Her neck's broken and there's a wound on the side of her face as though she'd been hit. High-security flat and no sign of a break-in. Who else could have done it? The question is why?'

'Another rival for Drummond?' Cheeseman suggested.

'That crossed my mind. So who killed Darcy?'

'One of my sergeants has opened a book on that. He's taken forty quid in bets so far.'

'He's going for the wife?'

'Started at evens, now it's two to one on.'

'She doesn't strike me as the type.'

'Some of them don't. There was one down here a few years back done by a churchwarden with an OBE. We found his wife's body fertilizing his tomatoes in the greenhouse. He'd won prizes with them. Anyway, I'll be interested in Dr Drummond's story. We'll bring her to Penzance for questioning if necessary.'

'Right, and we'll need anything from your end that links her to Blake's death.'

'I might have some interesting stuff for you on that,' Cheeseman told him. 'What you might call a voice from the dead.'

Chapter Seven

News is not an absolute; it's what somebody wants to publish. And newspapers have their agendas and values, which means that what excites one editor bores another. On Saturday morning the *Sun* splashed an exclusive story about a stripper who said that an England footballer was the father of her child; the *Daily Telegraph* led with its opinion poll showing that a slender majority of voters mistrusted Labour's tax agenda; the *Guardian* used a report by its social affairs correspondent about a rumoured cut in government payments to single mothers. For other nationals, nothing was more important than the murder, distilled into headlines subtly crafted to their readers' tastes: 'SEX SHOCKER KATRINA FOUND BATTERED'; 'DEATH RIDDLE IN HIDEAWAY COTTAGE; 'KATE DARCY'S FINAL MYSTERY'.

David and Frances Fletcher took the *Times* ('Fleet Street stunned as leading writer is found murdered') but Drummond ignored the paper still folded on the kitchen table when he came down for breakfast. Endlessly discussing books and writers with Martin Ross, they had not watched television the previous evening and Frances never turned the radio on in the morning. Drummond refused anything more than toast and coffee and for several minutes they discussed the weather, what time he and Martin should set off back to Cardiff, the history of the ruined priory visible through the window, home-made marmalade or plum jam . . . Casually, he picked up the paper so that it opened and he saw the photograph.

'Leonard, what on earth's the matter?'

People we know – people we love – should not be murdered; that happens to strangers, unknown names that inflict no pain. We read about them, briefly dismayed or fascinated, then forget because they have only had some sort of fleeting existence in our lives. So this was insane, a personal, vivid, *real* sensitivity brutally devalued into someone else's vicarious sensation.

'I must use your phone.' Without any explanation, he ran into the hall, staring at the paper in disbelief as he punched in the number.

'Hello.' A man's voice, guarded.

'Who's that?'

'I'm a police officer. Is this Mr Drummond?'

'Yes. What are you doing at my home?'

'Can you tell me where you are, sir?'

'What? I'm in . . . a place called Ewenny. I've been . . . Is my wife there?'

'Not at the moment, sir. She's being interviewed by the CID.'

The patterned wallpaper swam crazily in his vision and he had to sit down on the chair by the telephone table.

'. . . have the precise address, and I must ask you to remain in the house until police officers arrive. Are you still there, sir?'

'What's happened?' It was as though he was listening to his own voice from a distance.

'I can't discuss that. Can I just repeat that—'

'Is my daughter all right?'

'As far as I'm aware, sir, yes.'

'Can I speak to Marion . . . Miss Blake? Her nurse.'

There was a brief hesitation. 'I'm afraid not, sir. You obviously haven't heard everything . . .'

Frances was standing opposite him, concerned and mystified. As she watched, his eyes seemed to go away as he listened, and she knelt down, holding his free hand, offering comfort for an unknown reason.

'Yes . . . I see . . . I didn't . . . Thank you . . . Pepperpot Cottage . . . Mr and Mrs Fletcher . . . Near the church. Of course . . . I'll wait here.'

As he replaced the phone his face was like a child's undergoing a torment beyond its belief, then he began to shudder uncontrollably.

'What is it . . . ? Oh, Leonard.' Frances Fletcher clasped him in

245

her arms as her husband appeared on the stairs. 'David, brandy! There's some in the pantry.' She stroked Drummond's trembling head as tears began to soak into the shoulder of her summer dress. 'Oh, my dear man. My dear, dear man. Is it Teresa? It's all right. I'm here. Come on . . . I've got you. Just cry . . . That's it.'

All the Sunday papers wanted was that nobody would be charged before they went to press; they had one day, because in a week it would be stale news, the leftovers of dailies. A total of thirty reporters and nine photographers were working on the story, Plymouth Network News was negotiating for an exclusive eye-witness report by Michael Hay, and three men who had slept with Katrina Darcy were now offering themselves for interview at the right price. Tom Darcy appeared on breakfast television saying that his former wife had been one of the best journalists in the business. The Christian League for Public Decency issued a press statement renewing its demand that Katrina Darcy's obscene novels be withdrawn from all public libraries. Every paper was tipped off about her affair with Malcolm Kendall, and a freelance agency in the Midlands was told to get a picture of his wife and ask her for a comment. Vernon Farrant expressed his sorrow, adding that it was another tragic example of violence in contemporary society when a woman could not escape to her quiet cottage in the country and be safe. A member of Ziggy's rang three papers anonymously to suggest they talked to Anna Probert . . .

At the *Sunday Register* Charlie Taylor threw down the news list dismissively. 'Everyone else'll have this, Steve. We need our own line.'

'We're trying,' Hamilton told him. 'But everything we know's common knowledge anyway, so—'

'Then find something that isn't common knowledge!' Taylor snapped. 'She was one of ours. We must know things they don't . . . What's the tie-up with this woman in her flat?'

'We know she worked for Drummond, but—'

'And she's dead! So perhaps whoever killed her killed Katrina as well . . . Are the police still holding the wife?'

'As far as we know.'

'Let's hope it stays that way. Get a pic of this Drummond woman, talk to people who know her ... neighbours, the milkman, other doctors, anybody! I do not want the fucking *Sunday Times* showing us how to do our job!' He turned as his office door opened. 'How's it going, Malcolm?'

'I've told Carol to stay in the house and keep the curtains drawn, but she's getting hysterical. They're all on to it.'

'There's better lines in this than an affair that ended years ago.'

'So do you want to use it?' Kendall asked.

'Let's see what else we get.' Taylor sounded evasive. 'But if it's going to be in the others, we won't look very clever if—'

'Don't piss me about, Charlie. Yes or no?'

'I'll give you a definite maybe at the moment.'

Kendall dropped three photographs and a hotel brochure on his desk. 'See if that changes your mind.'

Hamilton tried to see, but Taylor had picked them up. 'Where did you find these?' he asked.

'In her desk. Now I'm going to put out an absolute denial about me and Katrina and I want you to let it be known that the paper will back me all the way if I sue for libel.'

Taylor's eyes glittered with amusement. 'I'll speak to Carol as well if you want.' He handed the photographs to Hamilton. 'Page one. I'll get it past the lawyer.'

Delamere had asked for the earliest serving of breakfast and was the only person in the hotel when he went down. Land's End, which by mid-morning would be clamorous with theme-park tourists, was empty and the windows that filled one side of the room cut out the sound of breaking water and gulls gliding over the rocks. Still numb with grief that a friend had died before him and he was the one left to mourn, he stared at waves shattering into fragments round the base of the Longships lighthouse as the sun burnt residual mist off the horizon; the fact of Katrina's death was more important than the savagery of it. He had finally cried the previous night when he had rung Toby, and the deep,

247

bewildering anger that had flowed from that release was still with him. Morning television had carried interviews with people who knew her, stills of her face, her book covers, the *Sunday Register* office; images to hold the viewer's interest before a story about British holidaymakers caught up in a cholera scare, the resignation of an American politician, the critical balance of the Test match ... Someone he had loved was just another item on the schedule, to be dropped if it failed to produce some new drama. But it was hypocrisy to condemn a profession in which he had traded what ideals he might once have had for amused cynicism, accepting the rewards while insisting that somehow his own hands were clean.

He sat at one of the tables and took out his notebook, reading again the opening of the piece Malcolm Kendall had asked him to write.

Katrina Darcy and I argued more times than I can remember, and she would not expect respectful eulogies from me now. As a journalist, she was the high professional; as a person, she could be infuriating; as a friend, she was loyal. As an author – I remain honest to her – she wrote one wonderful novel, then prostituted her talents.

When I first met Katrina, she was seeking to return to journalism; later she thanked me for helping to make that happen, but it was her ...

'Your coffee, sir. The rolls will only be a few minutes.'

'Thank you.' Delamere smiled thinly at the waitress, then poured coffee and cream into his cup, dissatisfied with much of what he had written. Emotion was in constant danger of spilling into sentimentality, so that what should be honest became maudlin. He tried to visualize Katrina beside him, mocking excesses, warning him that someone would send it to Pseud's Corner in *Private Eye*, telling him to stop being ... A movement caught his eye through the window opposite. The figure had her back to him, and for a moment he thought it must be his imagination that there was a striking resemblance to ... Returning with his food, the waitress looked startled as he dashed out of the restaurant and through the hotel lobby to the entrance.

'Stephanie!' The name rang across the deserted morning with

248

an alarmed urgency. For several seconds they stared at each other, then she turned again, walking away more rapidly. He ran across the car park and reached her as she was unlocking the door.

'Don't stop me, Anthony. I must get back to London.'

'No.' He slammed the half-open door and grabbed her wrist, twisting it sharply so that she dropped the keys, then he bent down and picked them up. 'Not until I know why you're here. Well?'

'Please!' Heavy with sleep not taken, her eyes glistened with sudden, seemingly desperate tears. 'I've got to see ... You don't understand!'

'Then tell me.' His fist closed as she tried to grab the keys from his hand. 'I'm sorry, darling, but you're not leaving here until you explain.'

'It doesn't matter now. Why are you here, anyway?'

'Because of what's happened to Katrina.' Delamere felt his grief tip into a deeper, unthinkable blackness as she gave a whimper and made a gesture of protest, a dismissal of something that must not be spoken of. 'In God's name, what happened?'

Stephanie jumped as a squawking herring gull landed close by her, beak greedily snatching a fragment of stale junk food that had been thrown away by a visitor then flapping away. She made no resistance as Delamere put his arm around her and led her to a low stone wall beyond which boulders dotted the slope that ended in granite precipices breaking the incoming sea. They sat side by side and looked across sun-silvered pale aquamarine water in silence for a few moments.

'I flew down last night after we heard,' he said finally. 'The police called the paper. We'd been trying to find you ... to let you know.'

Stephanie opened her handbag and lit a cigarette, cupping her hand to protect the lighter flame, expelling smoke that instantly vanished. She swallowed, but remained silent; Delamere found it difficult to look at her.

'When did you get here?' he asked.

'Yesterday afternoon.'

'Did you go to the cottage?'

'Yes.' She pulled on the cigarette as though the action would prevent her saying more.

His shoe stirred a small pebble at his feet. 'Why did you come?'

'It's a long story.'

'I've got all the time you need, darling.'

She turned to him. 'If I tell you, you must let me go to London.'

'What for?'

'Because I have to tell somebody else . . . Promise.'

'All right.' He could see no alternative but to lie. 'But I want to know something first. Did you see Katrina at the cottage?'

'Yes.'

'And was she . . . all right when you left her?'

Very, very briefly she smiled at him sympathetically, then bit her lip fiercely. 'You really want me to tell you she was, don't you? I've never seen you look so unhappy. I'm sorry.'

Delamere leant his elbows on his knees and put his face in his hands, rubbing it as if he was very tired. Somewhere out to sea two fishing boats blew their sirens in greeting across the murmuring water. An instinctive professional realization that this was a major front page sensation nauseated him.

'You said it was a long story,' he said quietly.

She dropped the cigarette and ground it out. 'There's so much you don't know. Had Mummy told you I'm lesbian?'

'No, she hadn't.'

'Well, you at least shouldn't have any problems with it.'

'Did she?' he asked.

'I thought she'd realized, but . . .' She began to pick chipped varnish off her fingernails. 'Somebody told her – I don't know who – a couple of weeks ago. Then she turned up at Ziggy's. I was with my partner, Brenda, and I thought there was going to be a scene. But Mummy appeared to be . . . OK. Anna Probert was with her. Do you know that she's—?'

'Yes,' he interrupted. 'Go on.'

'Mummy seemed to accept it, she even seemed to like Brenda.'

She sighed. 'That meant more to me than anyone can understand. I agreed to go back home and we spent the best couple of days together we've had for years. When I went away last Saturday with Brenda, she told me to have a marvellous time. I thought she meant it.'

'Didn't she?'

'No.' A fragment of blue-green enamel was flicked away. 'She was lying. Brenda and I had to leave Suffolk yesterday because there was some panic at work and they asked her to go in. We set off early in the morning, and I got to the flat at . . . It must have been about eleven o'clock. The porter hadn't seen Mummy all week and asked if she'd gone on holiday as well. There was a pile of post and I was going through it as I walked into the sitting room. I almost fell over the body.'

Delamere didn't look at her. 'Marion Blake.'

Stephanie moved away, suddenly suspicious. 'You're tricking me! You know about—'

'No! All I know is what the police told me last night. They went into the flat after . . . How do you know her?'

'She was a friend of Brenda's. I met them together at Ziggy's.'

He was attempting to adjust to how Stephanie could have seen the situation. 'So what did you think when you found her?'

'Isn't it obvious? Only Mummy could have let her in. She must have found out about her through Anna and invited her.'

'Why would she have done that?' Delamere asked cautiously.

'To tell her to make Brenda end it with me. What other explanation is there?'

'That's a big conclusion to jump to.'

'Have you got another one? Anyway, why did she kill her?'

'What makes you sure she did?'

'Her neck was broken – at least that's what it looked like. And the coffee table was overturned and there were bits of food all over the carpet.' Stephanie wrapped her arms across her stomach. 'She was cold and starting to smell. The porter hadn't seen Mummy since late Monday afternoon. Come on, Anthony, anyone can work it out. She must have had an argument with

251

Marion and killed her, then run away instead of calling the police and admitting it.'

Delamere began to see a perverse, terrible logic in what she was telling him.

'But how did you know Katrina was here?'

'I assumed she must have left London, and I found her passport where she always keeps it. When I rang the cottage I got the answerphone, but she leaves it on to stop people pestering her.'

'So you came down?'

'Yes. It was a pig of a drive. The traffic was awful, and it was stinking hot, and I was shaking with rage, and ...' She gulped back a sob. 'And I hated her so much.'

The remainder was academic now. 'What time did you arrive?'

'Five o'clock? Five-thirty? Around then. I saw her car and just raced in, screaming at her.'

'What did she do?'

'She looked ... frightened. Asked me what I was doing there ... and I told her she bloody well must have known. That I'd found Marion.' She went silent.

'And then?' Delamere prompted gently.

She lowered her head. 'I'm not sure. I accused her of lying to me, of not wanting me to have my own life, of even being prepared to kill to stop me.'

'Just a minute ... Katrina wasn't the sort of person who kills people.'

'Then who else could have done it? Nothing else makes sense. You give me another explanation.'

'I think there has to be one, because there are obviously things you don't know. Tell me the rest.'

'There's a lot I can't remember,' Stephanie said. 'She began screaming at me, something about her life being pointless, or ruined, or ... I wasn't interested, anyway. Then she slapped me, not hard, but it stung.' She turned to him pleadingly. 'I didn't mean it.'

'But you hit her back?'

'There was no one else there who could have done it. All I can really remember is that suddenly I was holding one of the serpentine ornaments off the mantelpiece and wondering where she was. Then I looked down and saw her.' Unstoppable tears began.

Delamere took hold of her hand. 'Why did you come here?'

'I wanted to go back to London, but I was too tired.' She gestured at the hotel. 'We used to come here for dinner ... I tried it on the off-chance they'd have a room. If they'd been full I was going to find a bed and breakfast place. I've still got my luggage from Suffolk, so they'd just think I was on holiday.'

'And where were you planning to run next, Stephanie?'

'I have to talk to Brenda. After that I'll go to the police. I'm not going to—'

'I'm sorry, but you can't. Not now.' Delamere stood up. 'I'm going to call them.'

'But you promised!' she protested.

'I know. I lied. I'm sorry ... No!' He stepped back as she made another grab for his hand. 'Don't try fighting me. Even if you got away, I'd give the police a description of your car and they'd stop you.'

'You've never been cruel to me before.' Her eyes held a childish resentment.

'And I'm not being now,' he replied. 'You can phone Brenda while we're waiting for the police, and I'll go and see her when I get back to London if you want. I'm sure you'll be able to see each other soon.'

She seemed to shrink in defeat. 'Do you hate me very much, Anthony?'

He shook his head sadly. 'I've loved you too many years for that. And you know how much I loved Katrina as well. I'd never—'

He stopped as he heard someone walk up behind them; it was the waitress. 'Would you like your breakfast outside on the terrace, sir? It's such a lovely morning. Is the lady joining you?'

Perhaps the clock had been stopped deliberately, so that suspects would not know how long they had been in the interview room. Cheeseman had apologized that there was not a free office at

Penzance police station for them to discuss Delamere's statement. He was reading it again, occasionally turning back a page as if to refresh his memory of some detail. Heat and the chatter of voices seeped through the partly open window; unrestricted by anyone having been charged, the media were besieging Devon and Cornwall Police for the new angle, the dramatic snatched pictures, bewildered answers to shouted, confusing questions.

Cheeseman put the statement down and picked up a silver propelling pencil, sliding it between finger and thumb against the table top. 'So Miss Darcy told you Miss Blake had threatened to blackmail her, and—'

'Read it again,' Delamere said sharply. 'She'd only said she would take certain actions if Katrina didn't agree to just continue as Mr Drummond's lover, not marry him.'

'And did Miss Darcy agree?'

'I don't know. She didn't speak to me about it again.'

'But it seems she must have invited Miss Blake to her apartment.' Cheeseman indicated a fax among his papers. 'According to my colleagues in the Met, the porter remembers her arriving and Miss Darcy telling him to send her up. That was late on Monday afternoon, after which he saw neither of them again, but we've been told that Miss Darcy was seen here the following day.'

'But there's no proof of what happened,' Delamere insisted.

'I think there may be,' Cheeseman corrected. 'Miss Blake had sustained a wound to her face and her neck was broken. No one else had access to the apartment, so the only explanation we can see is that Miss Darcy must have struck her . . . and we may find evidence to support that.'

'What evidence?' Delamere demanded.

'The ring Miss Darcy wore on her right hand has a large stone set in a claw with four metal points gripping the surface. One of my officers is on his way to London with it. Forensic want to check it against the wound on Miss Blake's face. If it matches, there won't be any arguments about who hit her.'

Delamere's face twitched as a spasm of physical pain flickered across his lower back. He was too tired to argue.

'You'll forgive me if I still don't believe it,' he said.

'As you wish, Mr Delamere.'

'And what's happening with Stephanie?'

'We'll be questioning her as soon as your newspaper lawyer arrives.' Cheeseman looked at his watch. 'Should be any time.'

'So she hasn't been charged?'

'Not yet. But she will be if she tells us the same story she told you.'

'With murder? Of her own mother?'

'That remains to be seen.'

Delamere took a bottle of pills from his jacket pocket. 'May I have a glass of water?'

Cheeseman nodded to the policeman standing by the door. 'He'll find you some. Thank you, Mr Delamere. If you want to leave by the side entrance to avoid your colleagues we can arrange that. I need hardly say that I don't want you to tell them anything about what happened this morning.'

'No, you don't need to say . . . and I want to see Stephanie again.'

'I can't promise that, but if it's possible . . . Leave it with me. Where can I contact you?'

'In the nearest pub, Chief Inspector . . . not talking to my colleagues.'

'Try the Turk's Head in Chapel Street. It's only a few minutes' walk and they serve good food. I'll phone you there if anything can be arranged.'

As Delamere left, Cheeseman was met in the corridor by his sergeant. 'The newspaper lawyer's just arrived, sir.'

'Good. Do the Met know what's happened?'

'Only that we've arrested the daughter.'

'Tell them we should be charging her soon . . . and tell Peter in the press office that I'll release a statement. No conference. And have a magistrate on standby in case this lawyer starts demanding bail.' He turned to go, then paused. 'Finished Darcy's manuscript?'

'Nearly . . . Interesting bit where she admits killing someone and talks about a body in her flat.'

255

'Yes ... Pity she doesn't tell us exactly what happened. But Delamere says Blake was threatening her.'

'What about?'

'I'll fill you in later. Tell you one thing, though. She's given her colleagues a bloody good story. Love, money, famous names, lesbians and a girl who murdered her own mother. Hold the front page.'

Before her trial began, an agent claiming to represent Stephanie Darcy opened negotiations with two newspapers for her story; he received advances totalling ten thousand pounds before he was exposed. She was jailed for five years after the prosecution accepted a plea of manslaughter. Leonard Drummond is living in California with his wife and daughter and, because of the often ironic consequences that can result from meeting certain people, Brenda Carr and Anna Probert became lovers. Toby Lawrence died, very suddenly, of a heart attack, and Anthony Delamere now lives alone. His cancer has returned.

Vernon Farrant's influence produced stories insisting that the photographs of him with Katrina in Italy were an innocent chance encounter while he had been on holiday with his wife and family; Mary Farrant supported him in several interviews. He said it was despicable of the *Sunday Register* to suggest impropriety at such a tragic time, but he would not stoop to suing them. People who read responsible newspapers could draw their own conclusions.

In any event, within a few weeks Katrina Darcy had lost her news value.